A Touch

menacing

LEAH CLIFFORD

Greenwillow Books
An Imprint of HarperCollins*Publishers*

A Touch Menacing
Text copyright © 2013 by Leah Clifford

The text of this book is set in 11-point Ehrhardt MT.
Book design by Paul Zakris

Library of Congress Cataloging-in-Publication Data
Clifford, Leah.
A touch menacing / by Leah Clifford.
p. cm.
"Greenwillow Books."
Sequel to: A touch morbid.
Summary: "Eden is a Sider, a being caught between life and death, with unspeakable powers. And she's in love with Az, a tortured soul—a fallen angel. To save each other, to save their friends and life on earth itself, Eden and Az may have to sacrifice themselves"—Provided by publisher.
ISBN 978-0-06-200505-2 (trade ed.)
[1. Future life—Fiction. 2. Angels—Fiction. 3. Demonology—Fiction.
4. Dead—Fiction.] I. Title.
PZ7.C622148Tm 2013 [Fic]—dc23   2012046047
13 14 15 16 17 LP/RRDH 10 9 8 7 6 5 4 3 2 1
First Edition

 Greenwillow Books

To my Darklings, who make me feel feared. I adore you all.

*He stood between the living and
the dead, and the plague stopped.*

—NUMBERS 16:48

CHAPTER 1

*E*verything hurt.

Eden clenched her teeth as the ache in her gut sharpened to a knifepoint. *One more minute,* she promised herself as the pains worsened. She grabbed the edge of her closet door and used it to keep herself standing.

A week ago, Az had found out the reason she was sick was that she wasn't taking out Siders. That without using her strange ability to kill the Siders and absorb their Touch, she would turn to ash. *And now Az is gone,* she thought. *And you're still crumbling from the inside out.*

A stubborn tear dripped down her cheek and hung from her chin. When it dropped and soaked into her sleeve, the ring of gray residue left behind proved to her how badly she needed to take out a Sider.

Her whole body seized with pain. "It'll stop," she croaked, knowing the worst part was coming. She wrung the bottom of her shirt, fighting not to cry out. The ache spread. *A few seconds and it'll be—*

Gone. Eden let loose a sigh so full of relief it trailed off into a whimper. Exhaustion and fading adrenaline buzzed through her brain.

After a few moments, she figured this bout was over. On wobbling legs, she moved around the nightstand and parted the thick curtains hanging in front of her window. From what she could see, the alley to Milton's was nearly impassable with drifts of ice and snow. They hadn't been going out to the coffee shop anyway, since Jarrod had quit his job there. With both the Bound and the Fallen angels after them now, a job was too dangerous. Yet every day they stayed in their apartment, the danger still grew. The Bound would find them. Slaughter them, if they could. They had to move—she, Jarrod, and Sullivan had to run.

"Soon. Today," Eden promised, just as she had yesterday. Her exhale clouded the glass.

She smeared the fog as she spun away. *Things will seem better after coffee,* she thought, heading out of her room toward the kitchen. At least coffee would warm her bones, help her think. Halfway across the living room, she heard a soft tap from the apartment door.

Eden stopped dead.

They're already here, she thought. *It's too late.* She stared at the door.

The hallway stayed silent. *Great, now I'm hearing*

things. Even as she moved again toward the kitchen, three gentle taps sounded from the door. Eden changed direction, creeping closer. Obviously, whoever was knocking had gotten in the building's security door. The weak chain lock and dead bolt on their own door were enough to keep out a mortal looking for Touch, or a Sider searching for Eden, but if it was an angel. . . . She thought about yelling for Jarrod, but then whoever was outside would hear her.

As she took a step toward Jarrod's room, a voice called. "Eden. It's Gabriel."

Eden sagged. The last time she'd seen Gabriel, he'd shown up cradling a blood-soaked and blue-lipped Sullivan, set her down on the couch, and left without a word. A week ago. His appearance had been how she'd known that Az was really gone. Since that night, there hadn't been a word from him. And Az would never be allowed to come back to her.

It took a few seconds before she collected herself enough to click the dead bolt. She undid the chain and swung open the door. Beyond it, Gabriel shifted uncomfortably, staring at his shoes. Part of her was surprised to find it really was him out there. Snow had melted into a puddle around him, enough that she wondered how long he'd been out there before he knocked. Had he been waiting to sense her thoughts leaving her bedroom?

His hazel eyes, dead and dull, skirted over her face

before dropping again to the floor. With his head dipped forward, the hood of his jacket obscured his blond curls and his high cheekbones. There was no easy smile to set her at ease. She missed the old Gabe.

Gabriel teased the edge of the puddle with his shoe, spreading it across the worn concrete floor. His gaze lifted and slipped slowly over her shoulder to the living room beyond. "Is Jarrod here?" he asked.

Eden blinked in surprise. "Is Jarrod here? That's all you can think of to say?"

"I—" His voice broke.

Eden hesitated, for the first time wondering if it was guilt that had kept him away, and what had brought him now. It was Gabe who'd taken her life. Gabe who now stood before her, Bound again. And the Bound were her enemies. Her palms grew slick. *It's Gabe,* her brain insisted. Still, she couldn't help the urge to back away from him.

His irises darkened from hazel to blood red. "Not all of us *want* to be your enemy, Eden," he said, his voice cold. "I am *begging* you not to make this harder on me than it needs to be."

A flush—embarrassment more than anger—burned her cheeks. Whether he meant to or not, he'd read her mind and heard the truth.

Shame wrenched his voice into something hollow and haunted. "I'm sorry," he said. "I try to stay out, but you can't help what you feel and I can't help hearing the broadcast."

She couldn't stop concentrating on his hands. The same hands that had held her under the waves. She had no memory of her actual death, though it wasn't easy to shake away the gruesome imaginings. "It's . . . okay," she offered.

"No, it's not." Gabriel subtly moved his hands behind his back. "Pathless or not, I took your life. I made a terrible error in judgment."

She stared at him. His words sounded like a recording, something memorized and spat back.

"Can I come in?" he asked. Only when she nodded did Gabriel slink past her into the apartment, as if it was holy ground and he didn't belong. He stopped in the middle of the room, his back to her. "I'm so sorry about Az."

The words hit her like a sucker punch. "Some of your things are still here," she said instead of responding. "I'm holding on to his until—well—if you want yours . . ." She knew how silly it sounded, like Az would come back from Upstairs to claim a few pairs of jeans and some shirts.

As long as Gabriel had been Fallen, and she tied to him, the Siders Eden took out would have ended up Downstairs. Thinking that meant Luke would gain followers, she'd stopped sending Siders on. That's when she got sick. To save her, Az had done what he'd once considered unthinkable—used his wings to go back Upstairs, become Bound again to clear Gabriel's name. Now they knew more. The Siders Eden sent on weren't harmless. They were a poison, killing souls, and now saving herself meant unleashing a plague Upstairs. Everything Az sacrificed had been for nothing. All she had left were his things. His sweatshirt smelled like him, crisp and clean and a little like the air when snow's about to fall.

Gabriel's shoulders slumped. "Eden."

"It's worse, you know," she said quietly as she shut the door. "Than when I thought he was dead." She stared at the back of Gabriel's puffy parka. The hood dropped from his head. "We were supposed to be together, and now he's just *missing*. And there's this hole, and I can't seem to . . . I don't . . . " She trailed off, locking her arms around herself. "I need him." She didn't care how stupid it sounded. "Tell me where to find him. How to get to him."

"I can't."

"You *have* seen him, though?" She steeled herself. Now that he was Bound again, Gabe couldn't lie. There'd be no sugarcoating. "Is he okay?"

Gabe flexed his fingers and then unzipped his jacket, glancing back at her before he sat on the couch. His cautiousness set her even further on edge.

"I'll tell you what I can. It won't be much." Once she'd sat down in the armchair, he began. "Michael convinced the council of angels that time was of the essence, that they needed to hear Az's testimony immediately because I was in danger of becoming unredeemable." His tone didn't change, stayed monotone and dead. Eden had met Michael only once. The terrifying Bound angel had treated her like she was repulsive. He hadn't treated Az any better. "Az told them that you didn't have a path, so you weren't on record. That you weren't mortal when I took your life. He told them I had been investigating the Siders and planned on reporting everything I knew." Gabe fell silent, running his hands through his curls. "It was enough," he said.

"I'm proud of him," Eden said, surprised by the lack of bitterness in her voice. "He did the right thing. You shouldn't have Fallen because of me. I was going to die anyway."

Gabe shrugged a shoulder. "Once they accepted his testimony, they brought me back Upstairs. When it was time for him to become one of us again, he . . . He's not Bound."

"What does that mean? He Fell?" *Az wouldn't stay away,* she thought. *Not by choice.* The words stole her breath; her hands started to tremble. "Where is he now?"

He's gone, she thought, *and I didn't know.* "Did they—" she got out before everything inside her broke. *Did they kill him?* She couldn't get the words past her lips, but with Gabriel, there was no need.

Gabe looked stricken. "No! Oh, sweetheart, it's not that."

She slumped, her sigh choking off in a cough. Concern filled Gabriel's eyes.

Swiping the tears on her face, she snuck a look at her palm as she dropped it to her lap. The center was gray-black with ashes, her fingers inky. "Keep going," she said. "Please."

"He came Upstairs willingly," Gabriel continued, "so they know he had true intent. They're sure it's only a matter of time before he gives in and agrees to become Bound again. They *will* wait." His irises burned in turbulent swirls of color. "He's in a cell."

"You're not just going to leave him there," she said in disbelief. "Can you get to him?"

"I can't, Eden." His voice shook.

Gabe wanted her to know. Why? Why had he come to tell her this when he hadn't shown his face until now?

You can't help Az, she thought, *but I can. Is that what you want, Gabe?*

He winced as if tasting something terrible, and she knew he'd wanted to lie. Gabriel had grown used to being Fallen.

She got to her feet and strode across the room to the door, the idea of how she could get Az back beginning to take shape. She had to get down to the alley.

"Why the alley?" Gabriel asked as she yanked on one of her boots and zipped it up her calf. "What are you going to do? Your thoughts are scattered."

"Oh, come on, Gabe," she snapped, pulling on the other boot. When she glanced up, Gabe was off the couch, circling around her. "If I *can* help Az, I'm doing it alone. There's not a chance I'm bringing you down with me. Leave."

At the demand, the air in the living room almost seemed to thicken. Gabriel's shoulders pulled back, stiff with tension. "Look, you shouldn't interfere with this," he said. "It's suicide!"

Eden smirked. "Not for me."

I have the upper hand against the Bound, she realized. Siders she sent on *stayed* Siders, passing Touch Upstairs. It worked differently up there. Here, mortals were passed Touch and it only amped up what they were feeling, for good or bad. Upstairs—or Downstairs, for that matter— the Touch killed the souls. Permanently.

Fine. If the Bound thought they could take Az, could hunt her and her friends, Eden would declare war. "They want to see what infecting their realms really looks like? I'll show them." She grabbed her coat as she opened the door, refusing to let her terror shake her resolve the way it shook her hands. "Tell them I'll stop when they let Az go."

"Eden, they already want you most of all. You can't act

against them," Gabe said. "I can't allow it."

Clenching her jaw, she forced away the fear she knew must be so obvious to him before she turned back. "Luckily, I'm not asking your permission."

"I'll hurt you if I have to," Gabriel said as he grabbed her arm. She looked down at his hand in surprise, pain radiating from the already forming bruise. "Step away from the door. Back toward the couch," he commanded. Any resemblance to the gentle Gabe she remembered dissolved. "Now where the hell," he said quietly, "is Jarrod?"

CHAPTER 2

$\mathcal{S}$tretched out beside Sullivan, Jarrod couldn't help the way his stomach flip-flopped as she sighed softly in her sleep and leaned into him. There was something different about having a girl fall asleep on his chest, head tucked against his shoulder, an arm draped across his stomach. Maybe it was just something about Sullivan.

He hadn't planned on liking her as much as he did, uncertain what was happening between them. The newness of it made it feel like it could crumble apart at any moment.

Two weeks ago, she'd shown up at Milton's while he was working. She'd been mortal then and addicted to Touch. His stomach churned at the memory of the night Luke took her life, of her blood soaking Jarrod's legs, the gush and gurgle of her last breaths and his disbelief when, hours later, she took another.

As if on cue, Sullivan's eyelashes fluttered. "Hey," she

murmured, stretching against him. Jarrod felt the brush of skin in every nerve, his body humming for her.

He tangled his fingers in her hair, moved slowly to give her warning. She held her breath as his mouth hit hers. A pulse of Touch surged through him, slid back into her. Another, stronger one raised the hair on the back of his neck. Each drove a spike of need deeper into him. Sullivan grabbed his shoulder, squeezing. Lungs bursting, he tore himself away with a delayed gasp. "Sorry," he said as he leaned back, biting his lip.

"You okay?" she asked, searching for any sign that he wasn't.

He wanted to keep going, knew they had to be careful. Because Luke had killed Sullivan, she was tied to him, the same way Eden was tied to Gabriel. If they slipped up, and Sullivan exhaled at the same time Jarrod inhaled, he would wind up Downstairs in a cage. It had put a serious damper on their make-outs.

When he didn't answer, she touched his shoulder. He leaned closer, his tongue pressed to the top of his mouth, blocking his airway just in case. Sullivan's kiss was barely a peck. When she pulled away, he saw the fear in her eyes.

"We'll figure this all out," he promised.

Sullivan nodded, then seemed to reconsider. "Everything's so different. I mean, between two weeks ago and now. . . ." she said.

"It gets easier. Passing Touch, dosing. All of it," he said, trying not to let her see he was distracted.

Outside his closed door, he heard movement. For a second, he was almost sure he heard voices as Sullivan rolled away from him. "I meant you and me," she said.

"Hey." He took her face in his hands. "We'll figure that out, too," he said before his attention turned back to the sounds coming from the living room.

A cry from Eden. *It's the Bound. They found us.* Jarrod vaulted up, over Sullivan. *I knew I heard something!* He chastised himself. *I let my guard down. She's in trouble.*

The springs of the mattress creaked as Sullivan sat up. Jarrod turned to her, one finger over his lips for silence, the other pointing to the clothes she'd discarded last night. She moved to get dressed without questioning. He put his ear close to the keyhole. It took every ounce of resistance not to bolt through the door. He concentrated on any clues about how many were out there, if it was really the Bound, and then he recognized the voice yelling over Eden's.

"What the hell?" Jarrod said as he swung the door open. Gabriel.

Gabriel, who'd found him and Sullivan in the park the night she'd been killed. Gabriel, who had gotten them back to the apartment. Who'd spied on Downstairs so that Madeline had known how to save Eden.

Gabriel, who now had Eden by the wrist.

"Bullshit I can't leave!" she seethed. "If they won't give him back to me, I'll infect Upstairs with every Sider I can find!"

"Let her go right now!" Jarrod yelled as he motioned for Sullivan to stay back. *What the hell's happening?*

Eden stopped fighting at the sound of his voice and took a step toward him. Gabriel released her, relief flooding his face.

Two black tears rolled down Eden's cheeks. As soon as she was within reach, Jarrod grabbed for her hand and rolled it over. Ashes tumbled from her palms. *Shit.* A deep bruise circled one of her wrists. He kept his attention on Gabriel, backing Eden slowly toward Sullivan and his room. "What did you do to her?" he demanded.

Gabriel shook his head. "Nothing. You got here in time. She's not hurt."

Eden tried to speak, but coughing broke up her words, and Jarrod couldn't make out what she was saying.

She sucked in with a wet, crackling noise. Her lungs sounded full of cellophane. "Slow breaths," he commanded.

Without enough Touch to heal, her body was shutting down. He watched her throat convulse as she tried to swallow. An injury as simple as that bruise on her wrist was enough to tip the scales. "Sullivan, grab a glass of water. Hurry."

Sullivan ducked into the bathroom, going for the

plastic cup they kept on the back of the sink. He heard the water turn on.

Suddenly, Eden's full weight dropped against him. This was going to get bad. Very bad. "Hey!" he said. Easing one arm around her waist, he tilted her head back into the crook of the other. "Focus on me."

Her fingers clawed at her throat, her nail beds going pale and then blue. This wasn't a mere tickle in her throat that water would fix. What Eden *needed* was a Sider, to take in their Touch, which would mean four flights down to the front stairs, where they tended to gather. She wasn't going to make it that far.

He thought of the extra Touch Sullivan had passed him when they'd kissed. "I'm passing to you, okay?"

The little air Eden had left cut short. He heard footsteps beside him, could feel Sullivan's stare. Did she understand? Did she know that he wasn't getting off on this, only felt worry? Touch transferred from him to Eden with a tingle, and he pulled away.

"Water?" he said, holding an arm out behind him. He couldn't bring himself to look at Sullivan as she slipped the cup into his hand. He held it for Eden, watching as she took desperate gulps. Suddenly she knocked the cup aside and wheezed in a lungful of air as his Touch healed her lungs enough to stop more ashes from forming. It was a temporary solution, but it would tide her over until he could convince her to head to the stairs. He helped her down to the floor.

"Why isn't she better?" Gabriel asked, something frantic in his voice. "I didn't think she'd be so weak. She should have gotten better when she started sending on the Siders again."

"Because," Jarrod spat at Gabriel as he stood. "She *didn't* start taking them out again. She didn't want to get *you* in trouble!" He moved forward, putting himself in front of Eden and Sullivan. Gabriel was a Bound angel, and the Bound were trying to kill them. It didn't matter if he had been Eden's friend once. "You should leave," Jarrod said.

"No," Eden croaked from the floor. "The Bound—Az. Holding—he's not—" A cough racked her as she got to her hands and knees. Black flecked the carpet.

Jarrod looked to Gabriel.

"He resisted becoming Bound once he knew I was cleared. But he's locked up," he said. "She thinks she's going to kill enough Siders to strong-arm them into letting him go."

Jarrod crossed his arms. "Well, if it gets her taking out the Siders again, I'm all for it."

"If they're not stupid, they'll hand him over," Sullivan added, slinking into the space beside him. "Hell hath no fury like a woman scorned."

"It's not Hell she needs to worry about," Gabriel said. "The Bound aren't playing games anymore."

"So where does that leave you?" Jarrod asked.

When he looked at Jarrod, Gabriel's irises were ringed in yellow, the rest bright purple. Eden had told him once about each color giving away how an angel felt. All Jarrod could remember was that yellow meant fear. *Purple. What does purple mean?* he thought.

Gabriel gave a subtle shake of his head, held his hands low, as if he wanted Jarrod to know he wasn't a threat. "You've got to keep her safe. They haven't figured out how to kill normal Siders yet, only those like Eden and Sullivan. They are *close*, though, Jarrod."

Loyalty, Jarrod thought suddenly. *Purple means loyalty.* On the floor, Eden wiped at lips smeared with charcoal.

"You better?" Gabe asked her.

Jarrod glanced down at Eden. "She's sick as hell," he answered for her. But sick didn't really cover it. If Eden didn't start taking out the Siders again, she wasn't going to make it. "Her Touch levels are so low anything sets her off."

"Not an issue anymore," Eden said with a rasp. "Get me downstairs. If the Bound have a problem with it, I'll—"

"You'll what, Eden?" Gabriel snarled, startling them all. "Kill them? *Do* you know how to kill an angel? Because every one of us knows how to kill you! It's not going to be a challenge." For just a moment, Jarrod saw Eden's anger crack as Gabriel moved methodically closer. "You'll be so easy to kill. You can't even fight back. You don't have the right weapons."

So there is a weapon that can take out an angel. Was that a slip, or something Gabriel meant to say? *Could I kill him if I had to?* A quick vision hit him, his hand ripping Gabriel's head back, a knife digging in, Eden screaming. He shook the image away. He'd do what needed to be done to get them through alive. No matter what.

Sullivan's hands gripped his shoulder, pulling him back. "Jarrod, look at him."

Gabriel's glare hit him full strength, crimson burning.

"Do not threaten me," he growled. "I don't want to hurt you." The veins in his neck stood out, throbbing just under the skin. His arm muscles corded.

"Easy," Jarrod said. A sheen of sweat broke over his skin as he realized what had set Gabriel off. "It was just a stupid thought. Let's not get out of control."

Sullivan pushed past him, heading toward Gabriel. She didn't look back. *What the hell is she doing?* Jarrod grabbed for her, missed.

"Gabriel, you remember me, right?" Sullivan's voice was soothing. He jerked his head in a nod. "Sullivan," she said anyway. "And *I* think, if you planned on hurting any of us, you would have done it already. Right?"

"I . . ." Gabriel winced. "I can't answer."

Eden whispered his name, sounding shaken. Gabriel's nonanswer explained his agitation, the careful wording he'd used—"I don't want to hurt you" instead of "I'm not going to hurt you." Had the Bound *sent* him? Was he fighting against orders he'd been given?

Sullivan went on. "You're not gonna hurt us in the next *five minutes* then, right?"

His red irises slowly dulled to amber. He nodded. "Right," he managed.

With the murder Jarrod had seen in Gabe's eyes, it was hard to believe.

"Okay," she said. "So we have a guaranteed five minutes. If you need to say something, now's the time." She grabbed Eden's hand and helped her up. "I'm guessing you didn't just come to catch up?"

"No," Gabe said, and he looked at Jarrod, speaking to him alone. "I need your help. I want you to track down the territory leaders. Kristen, Madeline, Erin"–his eyes flicked to Sullivan–"Vaughn. I know they were the original Siders. There has to be something that links them."

"Like a patient zero," Sullivan said.

"What good is that going to do?" Jarrod asked.

Gabe shrugged, at a loss. "You're in the bodies you had as mortals. You're not alive, though blood is still pumping. Your hair grows and you heal, which means your cells regenerate. You're not dead and you're not alive. It's almost like without paths you're just . . ." He hesitated, his brow wrinkled in concentration. "Paused."

Jarrod raised an eyebrow. "So what happens when we get unpaused?"

Gabe didn't answer. "Do you remember anything strange from your last days as a mortal? Times you would have been on Touch and not known it then?"

"Um," Jarrod said, hesitating. Memories crept through him from the last month or so of his mortal days. Screaming matches with his foster parents. Taking off in the middle of the night. A trickle of sweat dripped down his neck as Sullivan and Eden shifted to look at him. Sullivan's hand slid across his shoulder, easing down his arm until she could lock their fingers together.

He bit the inside of his cheek, not wanting to answer. "I don't know," he said finally. "I mean, the state came and took me away from my mom's. The place they put me was worse, so after a few months I bolted. I was afraid the cops would find me and take me back." He faltered, embarrassed and unsure of whether to go on. "I did things. Stole. I had to survive. I never hurt anyone," he added, vehemently. "I'd never done anything like that before. I was crashing with guys I didn't know well. There could have been a Sider in there, I guess. We were all messed up a lot of the time." He couldn't be certain. "It might have been Touch."

Gabe's gaze was still on him. "So none of the Siders you know of now were there? None of the territory leaders? Kristen, Madeline, Vaughn?" Gabe asked. "Think *hard*."

Kristen and Madeline wouldn't have lasted more than a few minutes around the group he'd taken up with those last few weeks. Vaughn would have stuck out. Jarrod shook his head. "No, I would have remembered."

"How long were you with these guys?"

"Little over a month?" Jarrod guessed.

"Eden? What about you? Times you could have been on Touch," Gabriel asked, though his eyes never left Jarrod. *Why's he looking at me like that?* Jarrod wondered.

"Before I met you and Az?" she stammered, and Jarrod knew she felt the same strange disconnect he did. Their mortal days were gone. Forgotten.

The same way their mortal days had forgotten them.

Eden coughed weakly. "The first month or so of summer, there were a bunch of parties. I went to all of them. I didn't really know everyone there, but it was the same crowd. Then I stopped getting invited. My friends stopped calling." Her last words were almost inaudible before she rallied. "They were forgetting about me, because I was losing my path, weren't they?"

Gabriel seemed to ignore her distress. "Do you remember seeing any Siders?"

Jarrod shot a glance her way to catch her shaking her

head. "No," he answered for her. Gabe's agitation worsened, the angel's irises darkening to rust-colored rings. "Sullivan became a Sider because Vaughn's group passed her too much Touch and her path got eroded. I think you were all exposed that way." His voice lowered to a mumble of concentration. "A month of parties, a month for Jarrod. And then death. But Sullivan was with Vaughn much longer."

"No!" Sullivan piped up, and then stepped back against Jarrod. "I mean, I was with him for six months, but he kept me alive. He kept me from killing myself."

Gabe blinked quickly. "The Siders started in New York, but someone was spreading enough Touch in New Jersey that Eden was exposed to it a significant amount." He stepped back toward the door like an animal afraid to be caged. No one made an attempt to stop him. He sucked in hard, clenching his hands. "Question Madeline, Kristen, Vaughn . . . Erin if you can find her. If you can trace it back—"

"No." Jarrod cut in before Gabe could go on. He didn't bother to hide his anger. "We're staying here. Inside. We can't go wandering around with *your kind* out there. Look at Eden," he said, tipping his chin toward where she leaned against the wall, swaying a bit.

"I can't," Gabe whispered. "Jarrod, please. If you can find out how the Siders started, maybe I can find a way to fix things."

Jarrod tensed when Gabriel dug into a pocket, but rather than a weapon, the angel pulled out a folded piece of paper. "The Bound are coming. Some are already here, searching for Siders, trying to figure out how to kill them. When they ask me where you are . . ." Jarrod heard the heartbreak in Gabriel's voice. "Please don't be here."

"Can't they just materialize anywhere we go?" Jarrod said.

"Not if they don't know where that is. They won't be able to appear *inside* this apartment because they haven't been in here, but your security door isn't exactly going to hold them out." As he palmed the paper to Jarrod, Gabe pulled him close. "I've already been inside," he whispered in his ear, too low for the girls to hear. "Get out. Now."

Then, as if to prove his point, Gabriel was gone. Jarrod still held the note. A moment passed in silence before Sullivan engaged the useless dead bolt.

"What'd he say, Jarrod?" Eden said. Her voice cracked, weak, as she spoke.

Jarrod slid the note through his fingers. The creases were damp and deep, as if Gabe had been worrying it in his pocket for hours. Slowly, he unfolded it.

In nearly illegible scrawl, was a single sentence.

Do not leave Eden alone with me.

CHAPTER 3

Once, Eden had asked Az what Upstairs was like. He'd told her it was a figment of the imagination, filled in with the fantastical thoughts of those mortals whose paths led Upstairs. The Bound themselves didn't dream, incapable of contributing to the beauty around them.

You're not one of them, Az reminded himself. Still, despite his efforts, everything around him—the walls, the bed, the locked door—was white as blank canvas.

Not for long.

Az pushed all his energy into remembering the exact shade of Eden's eyes, deep cerulean like the undercurl of waves. Imagined that same color washing across the pillowcases, dripping onto the white tiled floor, puddling.

You can do this.

"Blue," he whispered. "Turn blue." Gripping the sheets in his fists, he prayed for even a single thread to change. If he could imagine the color into reality, he could create a key, envision a portal, create an escape. He could find a way back to her. So far, his efforts had yielded only a headache. His eyes burned, watered. *Please.*

Nothing happened.

He pushed off the bed and started pacing the floor again, his shoulders heaving. An angry growl burst out of him, building to a scream. He'd ripped off fingernails clawing at the bars on the window, though they'd healed. He'd spent the first two days attacking anyone who entered the cell, fighting to get past them and out. He never made it.

Every fiber in his body ached for Eden. For the scent of her shampoo when she curled up with him on the couch and the way she pushed her sleeves up when she was frustrated, and her eyes, those eyes so blue he wanted to drown in them forever. And yet . . .

Through the bars of his window, he could hear water babbling in a nearby stream. Birds chirping as the warm glow of the sun once again lit the realm. Others souls' dreams painted the scenery with glorious mountains dotted with columbines. Air free of exhaust. Beauty. It called to parts of him he'd secreted away deep inside, tortured him with its siren song.

Home. He curled his hands around the bars. The thought was there before he could stop it, his heart catching in his throat.

No.

He ripped his hands away, ashamed, and dropped back onto the bed. *Don't give in,* he commanded himself. *Don't forget her. You have to get back to Eden.*

The click of the door unlocking sounded. Az slid back across the bed until his shoulders hit the wall as he recognized the angel entering his room. Raphael.

When he'd been Bound, Az had been one of the few trusted to stay in the mortal realm. Then he'd fallen in love, been spotted with her by Michael, and brought before the council. The angel standing before him now was the one who'd handed down the punishment. Az hadn't seen him since.

The memory of that day coursed through him, ripping open old wounds. Az remembered the laugh he hadn't been able to hide when Raphael told him he was to be cast out. He hadn't cared, would have sacrificed himself a thousand times. His sentence only meant nothing kept him from the girl he loved, the one he'd chosen to give up heaven for anyway. But while he'd been Upstairs in front of the council, the Fallen had made their move. By the time he got back, they'd captured her.

The Fallen, angels he'd once known as friends, had held him back as they passed her around, each of them tearing out bits of her skin. Even now, after so much time, the memory of her screams made his bones ache. When the life had finally drained out of her, they'd tossed her aside like a broken plaything. Under the weight of his new wings, Az had stumbled away, broken with loss. Only Gabriel's constant vigilance in the years afterward had kept him from Falling.

A wave of fresh resolve filled Az at the memory. He finally met Raphael's pale eyes. The irises were almost white, barely distinguishable from the rest. Light shimmered across his dark skin, seemed to leak from within, a holy radiance.

"Still not a word?" the Bound angel said, each syllable echoing like a musical note. The corner of Raphael's mouth turned up. "I'd forgotten how much I admire your tenacity, misguided though it may be at times."

Az pressed his lips together, straightening. Upstairs, words could be dangerous. Speaking to any of them was a risk he wasn't willing to take. Plus, his silence irritated them, making it all the more appealing.

"It's good to see you again, frien—"

Never will I be one of them. Bound or *Fallen,* he promised himself.

Raphael recoiled. "Oh, your hate is so strong," he murmured. The cadence of his words altered, a melody of sadness. "Not for us, though. You *despise* yourself."

Caught unprepared, Az tightened his jaw. Raphael's head tilted in concentration.

"You flicker, Azazel. The light is inside you." He held a hand out as if to trace Az's cheek. "It aches to flare bright again! Why do you fight?"

Az jerked away. He couldn't bear the need inside him to be complete. One of them. Whole again.

"How sorely you ache for this to end," Raphael said. "Forgive yourself as we've forgiven you. Release yourself of this guilt, Azazel. Let go."

The words, *the name*, wormed into his mind, clogging his thoughts until they didn't make sense. Tension spooled loose from his limbs, left him docile. His eyes slipped shut as he tried to call up an image of Eden, something to make him strong. But her face wouldn't come.

"You want this, Azazel. We've missed you so." Raphael gave his shoulder a tender squeeze.

Az cupped his hands over his ears. In his palms, he heard the rush of his blood, pounding like waves against the shore. He latched onto the image. *You met her on the beach. You couldn't bear the thought of not knowing her. You fought to be with her.* A dozen memories of Eden surfaced, suddenly crystal clear. *She loves you as much as you love her. Be strong.* He could almost hear her voice, encouraging him.

"Stubborn," Raphael tsked. "Even before your return, we beckoned you home. Does the honor not please you? To be so needed?"

There's no honor in this, Az thought, but didn't give him the satisfaction of saying it aloud.

When there was no response, Raphael looked dismayed. "I won't deny that they're fascinating, these Pathless creatures you're so taken with," he said lightly. "It's almost as if they believe they're still mortal. They don't seem to understand why they can't be allowed to survive."

Az looked up. Had the Bound already begun wiping out the Siders?

"Surely *you* understand why we must end them. This could be your glory, Azazel. Ridding us of this plague." Raphael leaned closer, his pale eyes persuasive. "Their ends are swift. The pain lasts but a moment."

"You stay away from them!" Az yelled, and leaped forward. He swung his fist, but Raphael flashed away before it could connect, reappearing behind him.

Az spun to see Raphael's grin stretched wide with victory. "Come now," Raphael said gently. "Was it truly so hard to speak?"

A thousand curses died unuttered. Raphael had wanted him angry, wanted to prove that his silence was breakable. And he'd done just that. The fire inside Az scorched red-hot, but he ground his teeth and swallowed the heat down.

"You're returning to us in the smallest ways," Raphael said. "But you *are* returning."

Never, Az thought with all his might. He shook his

head, but without saying the word aloud, it did nothing except make him feel weaker, beaten.

"You had the will to use your wings. The longer you remain, the more you'll see the light." He scrutinized Az's face, studying him. "Gabriel, too, struggles with his emotions. At first, some suggested to trust him would be a mistake. Fortunately, he erased our doubts." Raphael strolled toward the door, his fingers clasped behind his back. "Perhaps your own temptation will ease once Gabriel fulfills his promise," he mused.

A cold current passed through Az, electric fear. Spoken aloud, promises were binding, the compulsion to complete them even stronger than the desire to confess sins. "What temptation?" The words were out before he could stop himself. "What promise?"

Raphael looked as if he'd been offered a gift. "He pledged to end the Sider who'd caused his Fall."

"Eden?" Az whispered in shock. "Gabe promised to kill Eden?"

Raphael's cheer dimmed, his face forlorn. "Your heart is so heavy, Azazel. When her suffering ends," he said quietly, "I pray yours will, too."

CHAPTER 4

Gabriel's sudden presence startled a group of pigeons when he appeared in the abandoned building the Bound had chosen as their gathering place. He dropped to his knees, exhausted from the effort, not of traveling, but of resisting what he'd promised to do, every muscle in his body stretched tight from holding back.

The room he'd materialized in was far from the other Bound angels. He knew it seemed suspicious that he didn't freely seek out their company, but he couldn't quite bring himself to care. So they watched him with sidelong glances, untrusting. They were right to do so.

After a moment, he got to his feet.

He came out of the room into the core of the building. Natural light streamed in from the glass atrium of the ceiling. Beautiful railings lined an open center; balconies on each side led off to rooms on the nine floors rising above him. Aside from peeling paint and a few broken panes of glass, upon first glance, the place seemed entirely livable. *How could anything so beautiful be forgotten,* he wondered.

Gabe heard movement. He pictured himself several stories up. A second later, he felt the balcony beneath his feet.

Four days ago, one of the more derelict rooms on this level had received a strange renovation. Most of the floor had collapsed through. The door to the room below it had been nailed shut, and barbed wire fencing secured over the windows, effectively making it a pit accessible only from above. The next day, a waiflike boy had been inside, dirty and shivering. A Sider. *Please,* he'd called up when Gabe had come to the threshold. *Please help me.*

The boy's pleas haunted him. Gabe had done nothing, left without a word. He couldn't save all the Siders, not if he wanted freedom enough to help his friends. Besides a quick phone call to Kristen and another to Madeline, he hadn't dared communicate with any of the Siders since the night he'd gotten back. Today, being near Eden and warning Jarrod had been an enormous risk. If he'd been seen by the Bound or if he hadn't been able to resist the vow he'd made . . . Any other Sider could be hurt, tortured even, but Eden and Sullivan could be killed. *Please listen, Jarrod,* he thought. *Make her leave the apartment.* Eden could be stubborn, but he knew she was sick and scared.

Now, it was Gabe who felt scared. Earlier this morning, Michael had requested he be present at a council meeting for the first time since he'd become Bound again. The invitation had spurred him on to warn Eden, tell her what she needed to know about Az. Gabe didn't know if he'd be able to get back to her. The meeting could end with him punished. Or worse.

Other Bound wandered through the building, looking lost and uncertain. For some, it had been centuries since they'd felt earth under their feet. Taxi horns unnerved them. Their noses wrinkled in disgust at the heavy scent of bus exhaust. To his left was the council room, reserved for higher-ranking Bound, the place where decisions were made. As he drew closer, he cleared his mind. Carefully practiced in the art of hiding his thoughts, he meted out only what he wanted the others to hear.

Gabe held his head high as he swung open the door. An argument stuttered to silence as they all turned to him. At the head of the table, Michael's normally gray eyes caught Gabe's, happiness lightening them to pale blue. "May I voice my pleasure at your acceptance of our invitation."

The others didn't look quite so happy to see him. Gabe looked at each in turn. "The invitation is an honor," he said. His answer skirted a line; being invited to a council meeting *was* considered an honor; it just wasn't one he wanted.

"Sit," Michael said, gesturing as he turned to an angel beside him.

Gabe felt himself flush, the confidence he'd worn like armor dented. Every chair was occupied. A purposeful slight.

No one moved.

"Take mine." Raphael said, and pushed back from the table. He waited until Gabe took his place before laying a hand on his shoulder. "You've been scarce these past days, Gabriel."

"Yes," Gabe answered. There was no point in attempting to fashion a cloaked truth when there were so many real reasons. He chose one. "I thought perhaps it would be best to give everyone time to adjust to my return."

Raphael shot him an annoyed glance. "May we speak of the Siders, please?" Raphael asked. A creak broke the silence as Michael leaned back in his chair, his fingers forming a tepee.

"Of course," Gabe said uncomfortably.

"We've learned how to kill them," Raphael continued. The ten angels sitting around the table turned expectantly between him and Gabriel, following the exchange as it bounced back and forth. "We'll be moving forward with the extermination."

Gabe licked his lips. "I don't believe that's necessary." He stood, his words desperate but careful. "There may be options we haven't considered. The Siders were mortal once. I think they can be cured if . . ."

He trailed off as their faces changed.

"Cured?" one said, wearing a look of condemnation.

Dropping his head, he wanted to give them an image of Madeline helping him when he'd been Fallen, of Eden and how much her friendship meant to him. Kristen, and the bond they shared. But the other Bound wouldn't look beyond the unnaturalness of the Siders. "Make them mortal again," he said quietly. "So that there's no reason to kill them."

Slowly over the years, he'd learned the Siders spread Touch, which made the mortals become either manic or depressive. Touch was addictive and ate away at the path of a mortal each time it was passed until there was nothing left. "Their bodies *act* as if they're still alive. Without a path, they can't move forward. I think the Touch is the key. We need to figure out what it is and then . . ."

Raphael walked to stand beside Michael, clearly disappointed. "These are not things you should be investigating, Gabriel. Our only task is to eliminate the threat."

"But—" Gabe started, and Michael slammed an open palm against the table.

"Gabriel, this ceases immediately." Michael suddenly appeared next to him, catching him in an embrace. "Do you not realize how we fear for you? You *Fell* for these

LEAH CLIFFORD

creatures. No Bound has ever come back from that, save you. And yet you seem so eager to dispose of this glorious turn." Michael kissed his cheek softly.

Having Michael this close triggered memories of why he'd left Michael decades ago.

It'd been slow and subtle, the way Michael had isolated him from the others. First, simply extra assignments around the mortals. Then the official position as Messenger. As one of the only Bound allowed to travel back and forth between the realms, Gabriel had been lonely, ached for Michael and the moments they were able to steal together. He'd met Az when Az was a Watcher, one of the Grigori. They'd both been on assignment. It'd been so nice to have a friend, someone to team up with and pass the time. When some of the angels—Az included— had started mixing with the mortals, Gabriel had turned a blind eye, even though it was forbidden.

But Michael hadn't. He'd accosted Gabriel for letting it go on and made sure Az's indiscretions came into light. When he'd made an example of Az, Michael had finally lost Gabriel once and for all.

Now Gabe felt Michael tense. Had he picked up a bitter thought Gabriel hadn't meant to send out? "If you cannot bear the strain, you can tender a resignation as Messenger."

"No!" If he was kept Upstairs, Gabe wouldn't have a

36

chance at helping the Siders. They'd be slaughtered. "I'm strong in my beliefs," he said. "I can do what needs to be done."

"Prove it," Raphael said, standing up. "We know you have the location of the death breather. Why have you not ended her? Her destruction would benefit many."

"I will go, but it's possible she and her crew have already gone into hiding." Gabe bit the inside of his cheek.

Michael sent a thought screaming through his mind. *You're in such danger, Gabriel. You must satisfy them with a Sider.*

"I . . ."

Give them what they want! Michael insisted.

Gabe racked his brain, frantic. He had to give them something. "There's a coffee shop," he said, shame burning through him even as the words blurted out. He couldn't stop. "She goes there sometimes. It'd be a good place to check." And then, casual enough to sound like an afterthought, he added, "A Sider works behind the counter. He's high-ranking and might have information."

But Gabe hoped Zach wouldn't. And that Zach would forgive him.

CHAPTER 5

Madeline squeezed her ungloved hands, trying to coax warmth into her fingers. This close to Christmas, the sidewalks were thick with mortals grabbing gifts for friends and family. The best of her Queens crew were out in pairs, making friends with perfect candidates for new Siders—guys built strong for fighting, girls lithe and clever—and then luring them back home.

Once Gabe had told her what he'd learned, that creating a Sider was as easy as super-loading the mortals with enough Touch to erode their paths, she'd gotten to work. Only survival mattered. She wasn't about to face the Bound without the biggest army she could muster.

The war was coming.

Of course, Gabe knew nothing of what she'd set out to do. *I helped him,* she reminded herself. In truth, she'd risked more than she should have to help Gabe when he'd Fallen. Kept him from committing the worst of sins, aided him when he'd spied Downstairs. *Using what he told me isn't wrong. It's payment.*

Honestly, only time would tell how flawlessly her plan came together, if making Siders actually worked. So far, none of the few mortals they had captured seemed close to going suicidal. Time ran shorter than her patience.

A dark thought needled its way in, not for the first time. A way to speed things up. Before she could pursue it, an arm curled around her waist, a voice smooth as honey in her ear. "Now where are you rushing off to?"

Her heart skipped a beat, but her feet didn't falter. She called up a well-practiced smile as she turned. "Hello, Gorgeous."

"Only as gorgeous as the company I keep." Luke's arm lifted from her hip. "Goddamn, I must be stunning just now," he said, and gave his disarming grin. "What have you been up to?"

She shrugged, the initial nerves Luke always brought out slowly calming. "Oh, the usual. Waiting for the so-called good guys to wipe out me and everyone I know. Bringing about the apocalypse. Shopping."

"Nice to see we have our priorities straight, at least. Shouldn't you be storing Touch?" Without warning, he brushed his hand down her arm and into her pocket, then pulled out her bare hand and held it up. Luke's friendly farce disappeared, his eyes piercing, black as pitch. "You really should have gloves on, Madeline. You'll catch your death."

She laughed. Any other reaction would be a dead giveaway that something was up. Siders couldn't *get* sick, not from mortal diseases, and her death had come years ago when she'd become one. She watched for traffic before crossing the street, not bothering to check to see if Luke's eyes had lightened, if the danger had passed. Innocent people didn't check to see if they were being believed. He fell into step beside her.

Madeline stopped them at the window display of a jewelry store, concentrating on slowing her heart under the guise of admiring a pair of emerald earrings. *Keep him talking.* "So, my wicked arm candy," she said, putting her arm through his casually. "Were you just lonely? Out and about?"

Luke chuckled. "Not exactly." He held a finger to the glass, pointing. His shadow darkened the pair of beautiful green stones. He tapped the window once. "I need a favor. I'd be truly grateful."

Suddenly skittish, she realized what he was implying; the jewels were a payment. Luke didn't *ask* for help. She gave her head the slightest shake, the idea refusing to settle. "I don't understand."

He sighed. *Fake*, she thought instantly. *Practiced. He's acting.* Madeline took an unconscious step back, but he reached for her. "Now, now. None of that," he growled as he yanked her in front of him, against his chest. He leaned his chin on her shoulder. "Didn't Gabriel tell you the Bound are gearing up for an extermination of the Siders?" he asked.

She swallowed hard. Her days as a double agent had apparently come to an end. "Yes. A few days ago."

"So you know Upstairs has openly declared war and you're *shopping*?" Luke demanded as he loosened his grip.

Madeline smirked. "I'm multitasking. Give me some credit."

"Right now, all credit's going to Kristen. I've been told she's organizing the Siders. That she's having a ball. Bringing the territories together."

"Yes," she answered carefully, surprised that he knew. She and Kristen had decided having one big group meeting would be the best way to earn the other Siders' trust. Everyone who attended would be on the same page, everything out in the open. Of course, Kristen had immediately wanted to make it into one of her gothic eyesores. Though, even Madeline had to admit, there would be a better turnout for a ball than a strategy meeting.

"Will Gabriel be there?"

"Of course not," Madeline said. It was a Sider event, Sider business. At least that's what Kristen's excuse had been. Madeline herself didn't trust him, now that he was Bound again. *So who told you, Luke?* she wondered. *Kristen?* When Gabriel had Fallen and Kristen had gone missing, Luke had been scarce. Madeline knew they'd been together. The very night Gabe became Bound again, though, Kristen had come out of hiding, sane and in control of herself. Despite her best efforts, Madeline hadn't learned what game Kristen had been playing with Luke, where her loyalties truly lay.

"My favor . . ." Luke drawled, making her muscles clench. *Relax,* she commanded herself. The key to dealing with the Fallen was to stay calm. Never run when they see you as prey. Never show fear if it could be helped. "Convince Kristen to make it a masked ball. I'm attending, but I don't want to cause a stir. Quite the opposite, actually. I want no attention drawn to us."

In the reflection off the window, she couldn't make out Luke's face. A slow nausea started in her stomach. "Us?"

"I'm bringing along friends from Downstairs."

Her jaw dropped in disbelief. Spying for Luke, giving him information, was one thing. Sneaking him in crossed a line she would have trouble justifying even to herself, let alone Kristen. What he *asked* was impossible, not to mention ludicrous. The Fallen. Demons. Luke wanted to bring them to the ball.

"Why?" she asked before she could stop herself.

42

"Multitasking," he shot back. "Kristen broke a promise to me. I need to collect."

Madeline cocked her head, studying his reflection, the strange challenge in his tone. *What on Earth did Kristen get herself into with you?* "I need her, Luke. Kristen and I are the strongest. Together, we can lead the Siders against the Bound. If you want me to pass along a message to her, I will, but I can't do what you're asking. Even you alone . . . It's not right. If you're going to hurt her . . ." The arm around her waist cinched tight. She swallowed her gasp of pain. Gabe had told her tales of Luke's wrath, what he was capable of when denied. She couldn't set Kristen up to be a victim. Even if it meant facing his anger herself. "Luke, I can't—"

"Shhh," he whispered in her ear. She heard amusement in his tone. "You're overreacting. Kristen will not be harmed at the ball. You have my word. I just need you to ease our entry."

Knowing he never bothered with outright lies did nothing to quell her unease. She shook her head. "Crash it if you have to. I can't stop you. I want no part in whatever you're plotting."

"That is disappointing." He released her. She winced away, but he only opened the door to the jewelry store. Holding it ajar, he gave her an expectant look. When she didn't move, he rested his hand on the small of her back.

"Give me a chance to change your mind."

The slight pressure of his fingers pushed her through the door, across the store, and to the counter.

"Can I trouble you?"

The salesgirl glanced up at Luke's voice, then did a double take. She rushed toward them, practically tripping over herself. "Is there something I can get for you and your . . ." Her gaze flitted over Madeline, then slipped to Luke's arm around her. "Sister?"

Madeline snorted. The girl blushed fiercely. When Luke wasn't busy with devilish plots, he channeled his charisma and swoon worthy vocal skills into fronting his band. A band this girl clearly knew.

"There's a beautiful display of emeralds in your window there," Luke said, pointing with his free hand. "If you'd be so kind as to bring the earrings?"

As soon as the girl scurried off to retrieve them, Luke leaned in close to Madeline. "The Bound see the Siders as pathless, uncontrollable. Not only out of Upstairs influence, but through Touch, able to loosen any hold the Bound have on mortal souls. You're their worst fear come to pass. To the Fallen, though, that chaos is very attractive. And every day, there are more Siders." He leaned an elbow against the glass counter. "Can you imagine a world comprised only of the Pathless? Immortal and gone wild with no fear of punishment? To me, it sounds delightful."

When the salesclerk returned, he held out his hand for the earrings before waving the disappointed girl away. "You're smart, Madeline. More clever than you let the others see. You must know the Siders can't face the Bound on their own. At this ball, not only will the Siders be together, they'll be willing to listen. I'll have a chance to explain that the Fallen are not to be feared by your kind. Our goal is the same. The Siders' survival. A new world." His grin widened. "A devil's playground."

"And all your protection will cost us is Kristen?" she snapped sarcastically.

Instead of arguing, he went for her hand, gently working open her fingers. "Kristen will come to no harm," he repeated. "I just need her in a position of surprise. If she's given time to, she'll argue." He dropped the emerald studs into Madeline's palm. After a moment, he raised an eyebrow and gestured to her ear. "Let's see how they look."

Madeline fingered the emeralds. Finally, she put them on. "Well?"

Luke took her chin in his fingers, tipping her head first one way, then the other. "They were meant for you," he said as he handed over a card to pay.

"If it goes bad, I can't have this traced back to me," she said quietly as she stared into the mirror on the counter. "Despite your bribery."

"Merely a gift," Luke said as she regarded him in

the reflection. "To remind you how kind I can be to my friends."

She tapped a finger against the counter, not missing his threat. If she turned him down, chances were he'd approach the other leaders. She'd be left alone against both the Bound and the Fallen. Or worse.

"I get Kristen to have a masked ball," she said. "That's it?"

He nodded.

She tried to picture the world he no doubt imagined, damned and out of control. A world built for Luke and his kind. One that could save herself and her friends.

She rotated a fraction and the emeralds caught the light. Their sparkle was brilliant. "I think I can do that."

At her words, Luke's snapped his fingers to bring the attendant back. "I've changed my mind," he told her apologetically. "Bring her the necklace, too."

Madeline turned to him in surprise.

A corner of his mouth cocked up. "My clever friend needs something around her neck to remind her of me while I'm away."

CHAPTER 6

The hem of Kristen's black dress tickled against her calves in the breeze. At the head of the grave, a preacher quoted a passage from the Bible while the crowd sobbed softly into handkerchiefs. Gears creaked against the cold as the coffin lowered. "Ashes to ashes," the preacher went on, "and dust to dust."

"May God rest his soul," Kristen said, and tossed a handful of dirt into the hole.

Her house had been chaos. Decorations and rearranging furniture and finalizing the preparations and it wouldn't stop until the conclusion of tomorrow's ball. She'd needed space. She'd needed air. She found herself in the cemetery, standing in quiet repose at a stranger's funeral. From the turnout, the man had led a good life, died old and loved.

All the things you'll never be, her brain spat. *You were happy with Luke. Safe and sane. And now the Bound are coming for you. Gabe will abandon you again. What then?*

Kristen cut off the thought. *No regrets,* she reminded herself. She'd made a promise. No longer would she blame herself for giving in to Luke's lies, for believing him capable of caring about her. She would bear no guilt over choosing him when her Second, Sebastian, had come for her. No guilt over abandoning her Siders. No guilt over mistakes.

She concentrated, picturing the inside of the coffin, mentally locking her lingering feelings for Luke inside. Soon they'd be buried, gone. Another woman stepped forward. Another scattered handful of dirt.

You miss him. The wind whisked through Kristen's hair, tangled the strands into snarls. *You were stronger with him.*

A small boy crept to the edge and dropped in a rose.

On the antennas of the cars in the funeral procession, flags snapped in the wind. The crowd thinned.

A man gave her arm a gentle squeeze. "I'm so sorry for your loss," he said.

She nodded gratefully. "It's better this way," she said. It wasn't until his confused frown that she realized what she'd said. "With no more suffering," she added.

Her voice was embarrassingly loud, but she liked how strong it came out.

You were hardly suffering. Luke gave you everything you

could ever want. He considered you an equal.

"Then why did he betray me?" she whispered as the man walked to his car, leaving her alone.

Kristen kept her eyes open until the air dried them. She hadn't shed a single tear for Luke, for what they'd had, for what could have been.

Still could be, a stubborn voice persisted. It wasn't a delusion, as much as she wished it were. The thoughts were hers.

Somehow that made everything worse.

A handful of dirt flew over her shoulder, hit the coffin, and skittered off the lid.

Kristen whipped around to see Madeline brushing off her palms. "Friend of yours?" she asked.

"How did you find me here?" Kristen demanded. She'd told no one, not even Sebastian, where she was going. "Did you have me followed?"

Madeline gave her a Cheshire cat grin and batted her lashes innocently. "You think I'd know by now to call before popping up unannounced! You never were one for surprises."

In Kristen's early days as a Sider, when Gabriel had found her ravaged by her schizophrenia and squatting in a funerary chapel, Kristen had thought she was mad with her need to touch others. After healing her as best he could, Gabriel, who'd been observing Madeline from a distance, had brought them together. The years since had seen herself and Madeline somewhere between friends and adversaries but never outright enemies. Despite their differing loyalties to Upstairs and Down, she respected Madeline. She'd *thought* Madeline did the same. *She's been watching me,* Kristen realized. The idea of Madeline's spies catching a glimpse of her when she'd been weak sickened her.

Madeline fiddled with a garish earring, the stone an impressive fake, but far too large to be real. The green only intensified her eyes—deep, wet forest colors. "Can we take a walk?" she asked. "We have a problem."

They strolled away from the open grave, threading through the tombstones and crypts. "This is far enough," Kristen said, stopping between two crypts, out of sight of any stragglers left in the cemetery.

Madeline gradually slowed. "So I told my Siders about the angels. I held this big dramatic thing," she said with a flourish of her hand. "Called everyone in and told them about the Fallen and the Bound."

"They took it badly?" Kristen guessed. Her own Siders had reacted with stunned surprise, though honestly they'd handled it better than she expected. All things considered, she wasn't sure why it should be such a stretch for a room full of immortals to believe angels existed. Of course, telling them those angels wanted them exterminated was a different story.

"Not exactly," Madeline said. "They did pretty well with the whole holy war issue. The problem is . . ." She trailed off for a moment before she rocked uncomfortably, snow crunching under her high-heeled boots. "Look, I don't want to piss you off, but here's the deal. They aren't happy about being"—Madeline raised her hands in air quotes—"paraded around in front of the enemy."

"That's ridiculous. You know I didn't invite Gabriel. He wouldn't harm them anyway!"

"You can't guarantee that. But they weren't talking about Gabriel." Madeline mirrored her frown. "They were talking about you."

"Me?" Kristen scoffed. A cloud of breath hovered in the air between them as the words sunk in, her anger slowly replaced with confusion.

"They started asking questions—how I knew about the Bound and how I knew we were being targeted—so I tried to explain that you were close with Gabriel, but all they seemed to hear was you're on the side of those that want to kill us." She stared off into space for a moment, her brow wrinkled in thought. Finally, she shrugged. "They're scared, Kristen. Can you blame them?"

This is how it starts, Kristen thought. She twirled a ring around her middle finger, her nail clicking against the stones. *She'll draw the others away, turn them against me.* When Kristen spoke, her voice didn't have the bite she'd wanted. "You threw me under the bus."

"I told them what I thought they could handle. They need time."

Her head snapped up. "You could have mentioned I'm not the only one close to Gabriel. And we don't *have* time," she said, fighting to keep her emotions in check. "Everything is already in place. Erin's coming from Staten Island. She agreed to a truce with Vaughn, if we can find him."

Erin had left her territory in Manhattan when she heard Vaughn was selling Touch to mortals and had torn down the whole operation. If Vaughn and Erin were able to set aside their differences, they understood the direness of the situation. And yet here Madeline stood, calm and collected, prattling on about how her Siders weren't coming.

"I made sure Vaughn knows about the ball," Madeline said. Kristen shot her a look, but Madeline didn't clarify how she knew where to find him. She didn't need to. Her spies had apparently been busy as of late. "None of us are enemies now, right?" Madeline's grin didn't exactly set Kristen at ease. "Stop being paranoid."

Kristen glared. "Stop being paranoid? Tell that to your crew!" Her face flushed in anger. "You're in charge of them. Demand they come!" She twirled away just long enough to regain her composure. When she turned back, she made sure her voice was steady before she spoke. "Madeline, if we can't get everyone to work together, the Bound are going to trounce us." At her waist, she laced and unlaced her fingers. The vulnerability she felt sickened her. Even worse, she knew Madeline picked up on it.

"Kristen, my God, you're a wreck!" she said, her voice brimming with sympathy. "Relax! I got them to compromise."

"What?" she managed.

"You didn't think we were going to pull out?" Madeline smiled reassuringly.

"What else was I supposed to think?" Kristen said through gritted teeth.

Madeline's eyes sparkled nearly as brightly as her earrings. "Someone had the rather brilliant idea of asking you to make it a masked ball. That way, everyone's anonymous. My Siders will be satisfied, and I'm sure Vaughn's group wouldn't be opposed to concealing their identities." She dug a heel into the graveled walk. "Thoughts?"

Kristen tried to keep her relief from showing. "Masks? That's it?" Madeline nodded. "Well," she said carefully. "Can you pass along word to Vaughn? I'll tell Erin."

For just a split second, Madeline glanced away.

"Is there something else?" Kristen asked.

"Kristen, I talked to . . ." She pressed her mouth into a hard line, then gave her head a shake as if talking herself out of whatever she'd been about to say. "Vaughn and Erin are covered. What about Eden?"

"No," Kristen said instantly, and started back toward the entrance of the cemetery. "Absolutely not."

"Can you please for once not act like a child?" Madeline said, throwing her hands into the air. "Look, Eden didn't exactly beg Gabe to kill her. She didn't ask for this any more than we did."

Kristen kept her voice low, a quiet threat. "Listen to me very carefully. Without that girl, Gabe never would have Fallen in the first place. The Bound wouldn't be after us. And I—" *would never have gone to Luke,* she thought, part of her wondering if it would have been better that way, another not wanting to know. "I won't have Eden and her pathetic minion dragging us down. That's final."

Madeline sighed. "Without us, she's on her own. And she's already lost Az, Kristen. We could use her—"

"What about what I lost?" Kristen shouted. A flock of blackbirds flapped out of a nearby tree, cawing their displeasure.

Madeline's gaze followed the birds as they flew over a frozen pond and settled again on the peaked roof of a small mausoleum.

"Let it go." Kristen's voice was flat. "She ruins everything she touches."

"We all do," Madeline said quietly. "Kristen, she called

me. Just before I got here. She's sick, and on the run."
Madeline tucked her hands into the pockets of her coat.
"Her apartment wasn't safe. She needs Touch to survive,
and now she has no way to find Siders."

"If she's that weak, she's a liability anyway." Kristen
felt her dress snag on the rough edge of a gravestone.

Madeline grabbed her shoulder. "Would you stop pun-
ishing the girl just because you're not Gabriel's special
little princess anymore! Get. Over. It."

"So I'm supposed to what?" Kristen spat, her cheeks
burning. "Have her kill Sebastian so she feels better? Or
maybe you can offer up Jackson?"

At the mention of her own Second, Madeline's glare
grew cold.

"And when she needs another Sider in a day? And then
another? We're searching out everyone we can to fight
the Bound, and all the while Eden's killing them off one
by one. That makes her an enemy." Kristen softened her
voice, leaning against the stone crypt. "It's not that I hate
her, Madeline; I just don't want her close again. Because
eventually?" she said. "Something unpleasant is going to
have to be done about Eden."

CHAPTER 7

When Eden licked her lips, she tasted ash. The outburst with Gabe earlier had cost her, and she'd already burned through the little Touch Jarrod had passed her. Each inhale of cold air only made her lungs worse.

"This is stupid," Jarrod mumbled, but it was half-hearted. They'd been out of the apartment since just after Gabriel bolted, unwilling to risk the Bound showing up. When they'd left, there'd been no Siders on the stairs, no time to wait. She, Jarrod, and Sullivan had kept on the move, loitering in shops only long enough to get warm. Eventually, Eden had needed Sullivan's help to walk.

Now, grit caked Eden's palms and nail beds. She could smell the cinders on her cheeks, the ashes flaking from her hair. Slowly, she removed her scarf. "How bad?"

Sullivan winced, swiping at Eden's cheek before she licked her thumb and wiped harder. The skin there felt tight, fragile and falling apart. "God, you look like death warmed over," Sullivan whispered.

A well-timed shiver shook through Eden. She managed a weak chuckle. "Not so warm."

Jarrod studied her face, concerned. "Just a few more minutes, Eden."

"I'm hanging in there," she wheezed. A cough tickled her windpipe, but she swallowed it down despite the taste in the back of her throat.

Jarrod took her elbow, Sullivan on the other side. "I really don't like this, though," he said.

"I don't like it either," Eden said. Earlier, Madeline had agreed to help them, to meet her. Half an hour ago, Eden had gotten a text from her abruptly retracting the offer. When Eden asked for a reason, there'd been no response. Kristen hadn't answered her calls. She had no number for Erin, or Vaughn, though she couldn't imagine calling him.

Eden scanned the pedestrians walking on either side of the street, the rooftops above them. Coming back to the apartment after Gabe's warning was foolish, stupid, but she had no choice. Without a Sider, she'd crumble to ash. "If there's anyone on the stairs," she said, trying to reassure Jarrod and Sullivan, "I'll take them quick and we'll head to Milton's. Maybe there's a chance Zach can help us. We at least need to warn him."

"And he should know how to find some other Siders in the area," Jarrod said.

Eden squeezed Jarrod's shoulder hard as a sharp knife of pain stabbed through her. Just as they reached the alley, her legs wobbled. She fought to stay on her feet. Jarrod hitched her up. "You've gotta walk, Eden."

"It hurts so bad," she panted. Agony blurred her vision. The stairs were so close. If she could just rest for a bit, she knew she could make it. "Stop. Just for a second."

Before she knew what was happening, Jarrod had set her down and taken off. Sullivan called his name and he twisted around as he ran. "Stay with her," he demanded.

Eden curled up, not caring about the dirty slush she lay in. "If I don't . . . Take care of Jarrod, okay?" she begged Sullivan.

"Jesus, Academy Award, he's already on his way back." The sarcasm nearly hid the fear in Sullivan's voice. "You're not gonna die in the next ten seconds."

Eden swiped the gathering ashes from her eyes, didn't believe it until she saw four blurred shapes hurrying toward her. Jarrod dropped down beside her, lifted her until she was sitting. "Ready?" he asked, panting.

The first Sider, a girl, came forward, close. Eden let out a strangled exhale and the girl disintegrated into ash, settling on the dirty drifts of snow.

A tingle spread over Eden's cheekbones and tickled down her windpipe as her body used the Touch to heal. She laid her head back against Jarrod's shoulder in relief.

Her skin buzzed, electric. She didn't have to look at her hands to know the gray on her fingers would be gone, if only for a little while.

Sullivan stared at her in wonder. "You look *much* better," she said.

"We cut it a little too close that time," Jarrod said as he moved out from behind Eden.

Eden dragged the sleeve of her coat over her face. When she looked up, her vision had cleared, though her eyes were still irritated. "I need another," she said.

There were two guys left. One stepped forward. The closer he got, the more she could see the heaviness of the Touch he carried. How much he wanted to be free of it. More importantly, he hadn't been passing.

"Wait. You," she said to the other Sider as she struggled to her feet. "Have a phone?" He nodded uncertainly. She took it from him and programmed her number in. Instead of a name, she hit the asterisk and handed it back. "Tell everyone you know to spread the word that the Siders are under attack. For protection, they should head to one of the territory leaders. Anyone who needs me, you give my number. I'll be on the move so they won't find me here. Have them call and I'll meet them." She pointed to the head of the alley, hoping her urgency would be enough for him to take her seriously. "Spread the word today and you can call me tomorrow."

He gaped at her, holding the phone. "Under attack by *who*?"

"Get your ass out of my alley," she snapped. She watched him walk away before she turned back to the Sider left behind.

"Hurry, Eden," Jarrod said from a few yards away. Tension stiffened his stance, as he surveyed from one end of the alley to the other. Sullivan moved from her side to join him.

The Sider in front of her watched in a mixture of reverence and respect. He held out a crumpled fifty-dollar bill. She shoved it into her pocket without thinking.

"So, here's the deal," Eden started, her voice low enough not to carry beyond the two of them. She slid closer to him, her feet moving almost on their own. When she took in his Touch, it would make everything so much better. "You're gonna keep spreading your Touch Upstairs, okay?" She didn't know if he'd heard about the angels, if he'd remember any of this. "And when they catch you," Eden went on, squeezing his cheeks, "you tell them to send me Az. Got it? Send me Az or I won't stop." She probably looked like a raving lunatic, but didn't care. The boy breathed faster. She grabbed the collar of his coat. Pure need coursed through her veins.

"Wait. I don't think I want to—" His mouth pressed into a tight line, his head jerking. Eden exhaled in a steady stream. "Wait!" he cried, and then gasped.

His last frightened cry echoed through the alley as his ashes scattered.

"Send me Az back," she said, her collarbones thrumming as his Touch settled into her.

"Eden!" Jarrod called sharply. "What the hell?"

She stared down at the freshly trampled snow at her feet. "He panicked at the last second."

"That was one long 'last second.'"

"I had to take him." Eden snapped her neck to the side until it gave a satisfying pop. "I don't need the guilt trip."

"When do I need to start doing this?" Sullivan asked.

Eden walked them toward Milton's. "I'd guess you've got another week or so before things get bad. The problem is, with the first Siders you send Downstairs, Luke's gonna know you exist."

Jarrod kicked at a chunk of ice. "I don't think we should wait until she's sick, Eden."

Like me, she thought. *Weak. A burden.* He didn't say it, but it was written all over his face.

It was a miracle Luke didn't seem to know about Sullivan already. It would only be a matter of time before he tracked her down once he did. He'd let Eden live because he'd thought her useful, and now because her Siders infected Upstairs. Because Luke had been the one to put an end to Sullivan's mortal life, she was tied to him.

Something he wasn't going to be thrilled to find out. For now, their best bet was keeping Sullivan's identity hidden, which meant she shouldn't be taking Siders out until they had no other choice.

"Jarrod, don't push this," Eden said when they got to the street. Her nerves ratcheted up. The Bound could be anywhere. Watching.

Waiting.

Had they seen Jarrod at the stairs? Were there angels waiting this moment for the three of them to come out onto the street? A surge of adrenaline quickened her steps.

"Faster," Eden said. The Bound wouldn't attack them in front of mortals. If she could get to Milton's, they'd be safe. She burst onto the sidewalk, jogging across the street. When she got to the door, she dove for it. The bell clanked against the metal handle as Jarrod and Sullivan barreled in behind her. The mortals in line turned to stare.

Behind the counter, Zach stood frozen, a cup in his hand, halfway through making a coffee. "You finish this," he said slowly to the other barista standing beside him. "I'll be right back."

Zach waved them around the side of the counter, holding open a swinging door to the kitchen. He gave Sullivan a quizzical look as she passed by him. "So she is a Sider, after all?" he asked Jarrod when they were through.

The only time Zach had seen Sullivan was when she'd

come into Milton's looking for Jarrod. Before Luke had killed her. Eden coughed hard, and Zach let it go. "What's wrong?" he asked.

She couldn't get the words to come. Didn't know where to start. Instead, she looked around helplessly. Rows of shelving units took up the right half of the room. To her left, heat waves rolled off a commercial-sized oven. She could smell pastries baking. Her stomach turned.

"We need help," Jarrod said finally. "Someplace to hide out. Maybe crash for a day or two?"

"You're that freaked out?" Zach asked, confused. A week ago, she'd sent Jarrod to warn him about the Bound, but Zach had seemed nonchalant. "They can't kill us," he'd argued. "What are they gonna do, kick my ass and force me to make their lattes with extra whipped cream?" She had to make him see that the threat was real and the Bound were dangerous.

Zach went for a corduroy jacket hanging from the edge of a tiered shelving unit. Digging into a pocket, he took out a set of keys.

"My apartment's small, but there's plenty of floor. *Mi casa es su casa*," he said, handing them over to Eden. His expression was solemn as he took out a pen and an order pad from his apron. He scribbled down an address and handed her the page. "No one knows where I live, Sider or mortal. I don't get off until seven, so you guys can either hang out here or head there. Up to you."

"Thank you," she said. She folded the address in half, then again. "We wouldn't ask if—"

He shook his head. "Happy to help. Just tell me what happened."

"We were warned," she said quietly. "The Bound are closing in on our place. Listen, I don't think it's a good idea for you to stay either." When Zach gave her a sardonic smile, she grabbed for his arm. "This is serious."

"I can handle myself," he said, heading over to the oven. He peeked in through the window to check on whatever baked inside. "If it gets too crazy, I'll bolt, okay?"

"Erin!" she said suddenly, looking up at him. He'd been at Milton's when Eden took over Manhattan. Maybe he would have a lead on where to find Erin. At the name, Zach tensed.

"Who told you about me and Erin?" he demanded. "Was it Kristen? Madeline?"

Eden shook her head, baffled at his reaction. "Gabe wanted us to help figure out how the Siders started. Did you know her? We have to reach her."

He let his head drop back with a sigh of self-loathing. "That is *not* where I thought you were going with that," he whispered.

"I was supposed to talk to Madeline, but she blew me off. Kristen's not answering. I'd rather not deal with

Vaughn. Erin's my last hope." She leaned in, studying him to gauge how far she should push. "What do you know about Erin?"

He leaned forward to bounce on his toes. "Look, I don't think this—" He gave Eden a pitying look. "Don't be pissed, okay? This isn't how I wanted to tell you."

"Tell me what?" she said. Distrust moved her toward Jarrod.

Zach gave the door a weak shove and checked the line out front. Satisfied, he turned back to her again, grim. "When Erin was in charge, she was cool with some of us being on our own as long as we stayed in contact. I didn't just live here, Eden. I was part of her crew."

"Her crew?" Eden repeated, stunned. She'd always thought Zach had stayed under the radar. She'd admired the rebel in him.

"I kept track of the Siders who didn't live with her. We all helped each other out and were there for Erin when she needed us. It was a pretty good system."

"What happened, though?" Sullivan asked. "Why'd Erin leave Manhattan?"

Beside Eden, Jarrod tensed, knowing what was coming. He squeezed Sullivan's hand, the only warning he could give her.

Zach leaned back onto a metal counter, oblivious, balancing himself on his arm. "Erin picked the short straw and had to go deal with the huge douche that was running Staten Island." He turned back to Eden. "You *know* all this, though, right? Why Erin went? That Vaughn was selling Touch there?"

Eden hesitated, unsure what to tell about Sullivan. The girl had somehow managed a flawless poker face.

"We knew," Jarrod said. Before Eden could take up the conversation again, he hit Zach with a level look. "If you were part of Erin's crew, why are you still here? I thought she took all her Siders with her."

Zach stared at him for a long moment before he answered. His words came slow, careful. "The day Erin left," Zach said, "Kristen came over and told her about this new Sider, different from the rest of us." He fiddled with the edge of a bag of sugar on the counter.

"Me," Eden said quietly.

He nodded, not looking at her. "Kristen said you were going to take over Erin's territory while Erin was gone, that everyone needed to act like it was yours permanently. There wasn't time to argue. Erin asked that I stay behind. Keep an eye on you. We didn't know what to expect, because you had some sort of ties to the Bound."

Eden went still. "You couldn't have known about the Bound then, though. Jarrod just told you last week."

"Erin told me what I needed to know about them a long time ago." Zach's brow furrowed. "I'm her Second, Eden."

She jerked away from the counter, away from him. "No. That's impossible," she said in disbelief.

Eden stared at Zach, everything she knew about him warping, distorting. The simple guy she exchanged wise-cracks with every morning faded away. Conversations they'd had ran through her brain. She liked Zach because he didn't ask questions about her past. Didn't ask about Az and Gabe. Never pressed. Now she knew it was only because he already knew the answers.

Jarrod looked positively dumbfounded. "Is that why you gave me the job here? You just wanted me to tell you more about us?" he demanded, his tone sharpening as shock turned to anger.

"It's not like that," Zach swore. "Not anymore. I know you guys needed help." He offered her an apologetic shrug. "Helping out the Siders in Erin's territory is kind of what I do."

"Erin's territory?" she asked.

Zach threw his hands up, clearly hoping to set her at ease. "That's between you and her," he said. "I don't do politics."

The door swung open, and the kid from the front counter popped his head through. From the sound of the chatter, the postwork rush had started. "We've got a line," he said. "Can you come back out?"

"Sorry. Five seconds, Clay." When he was gone, Zach

heaved a sigh of relief. "Wow, this is a load off," he said, his grin reappearing. "I had no idea how I was going to explain if you ran into me and Erin at Kristen's together."

"Kristen's?" Jarrod asked.

"Her ball," he said. Eden shook her head. "Tomorrow. You mean you're not going?"

Jarrod scoffed. "Apparently we weren't invited."

"No, *everyone's* going," Zach insisted. "We're going to figure out what to do about the Bound and the Fallen. See if we can come up with a way to fight them."

They're leaving us out, Eden realized. She'd expect Kristen's wrath, but this was different. Madeline and Kristen were planning, scheming. Being abandoned while the others worked together left them isolated. Vulnerable.

Knuckles knocked against the window. "Help!" Clay mouthed from the other side.

Zach squeezed her shoulder before he took a step toward the front of the shop. "They're not doing this to you guys," he said, his gaze jumping between the three of them. "Even Vaughn and his crew will be there. We're in this together now. All of us. I'll talk to Erin for you."

The look of determination Zach wore was sincere. He wanted to help them. "Thank you," she whispered.

He put a hand up on the door. "Jarrod, take them out the back way. I'll meet you guys at my place in, like, two hours, okay?"

He didn't wait for an answer before heading through. Eden jangled the set of keys before tucking them into her pocket.

"Unbelievable," Jarrod said.

"Which part?" Eden mumbled.

"If the others don't want us to help, screw them. When shit hits the fan, they can battle Upstairs and Down without us, too." His voice fell quiet. "But they'll beat the angels, Eden. I know they will. And when it's over," he said, looking up, "we'll still be here. We've done this on our own so far. And we're all okay."

She saw in Jarrod's face the moment he realized what he'd said. They'd lost Az. Gabe was as good as an enemy. Not to mention the others they'd lost since everything had started. Adam. James. Things weren't even close to okay.

"Look," he said carefully. "We've never once given up in this whole thing, and we're not gonna start now."

She dropped her chin to her chest, not bothering with the truth. She'd given up so many times she'd lost count. "What about Kristen's? Do you even think it'd be worth—"

Sullivan grabbed her wrist, cutting her off. She pointed to a shelving unit ten feet from them. At the end of it, behind the large cans, was a scrawny girl. Eden froze, instantly wary. A second ago, there had been no one else in the storage room.

"Who's there?" Jarrod asked. He crouched and slid sideways in one smooth movement, easing open a drawer and plucking out a knife. "Come out. Now."

The girl moved into the open, taking him in with a lazy ogle. Her greasy hair was tied back under a hood, her cheeks blushed an unnatural pink. To Eden's surprise, a small boy joined her.

At the sight of them, the hair on the back of Eden's neck stood up, though she couldn't figure out why. Angels were easy to spot with the too-perfect, carved-from-marble look they all had. These two, though, dirty and disheveled, looked more likely to show up on the stairs. The rational part of her thought perhaps they'd broken in through the back exit Zach had mentioned. And yet deep inside her, a primal terror blazed.

"No one's allowed back here," Jarrod said. Eden turned toward him. With the kids in her peripheral vision, their skin wriggled as if something slithered just underneath the surface. She whipped back to them. Staring at them dead on revealed nothing like what she'd just seen.

As Jarrod stepped forward, Eden grabbed his shoulder. "Don't," she whispered. "They're not human. They're . . . something else."

At the words, the girl's lips split with a grin, revealing teeth black and rotten. What hadn't broken off was filed to points. A forked tongue snapped like a miniature whip, chattering like a rattlesnake's warning. "Something . . . else," she repeated. Her voice tinkled and crackled like bells broken underfoot. "Something wicked. And yet something other to you."

Eden jumped when Jarrod moved in front of her and Sullivan. "What the fuck are you?" he demanded.

Staring in horror, Eden watched as the girl pointed at her with a sharpened fingernail. "Is she the Sider who poisons the Upstairs realm?"

The boy's leer glimmered with a mixture of malice and excitement, and then his head wrenched sideways violently. He hissed, baring his teeth at Sullivan, but the girl with him nipped his cheek hard enough to draw blood. He cowered as the blood dripped, black, to his chin.

The girl focused again on Jarrod. "The Enslaved Ones seek your leader bathed in burn and bone," she snarled, teeth glistening with spittle and tar-colored blood from the boy's wound. "The Morning Star, however, wishes for her continued survival. The pretty poison she spreads pleases him."

"The what?" Eden managed.

The demons whispered to each other as Jarrod answered Eden. "Luke," he said. "They're demons, Eden. They're his demons." He sounded broken and hopeless, though she didn't know why. If the two were demons, they looked like they wouldn't put up much of a fight. Eden had just taken out two Siders. *It's not me,* Eden realized. Luke's demons weren't looking at *her* at all.

"Oh no," Sullivan said.

The boy demon's spindly fingers were curled around his partner's ear. Her eyes widened, so much white showing that it yellowed and then reddened around the outside. "Clever catch," she said to the boy, and then cocked her head in Sullivan's direction. "You've been hidden well, death breather." The demon lifted a hand, and Sullivan jerked against Jarrod. "Flinching flower," the girl pouted. "You would seek to destroy us, and *I* only want to pluck a single petal from your face."

The boy came forward. "When you're slaughtered," he promised Sullivan with an icy glower, "I'll make this broken boy eat your heart." His long fingers fluttered in front of Jarrod like he was playing piano. "Does she know how you hate that you love her? How it destroys you? Weakness oozes where once was a warrior." The demon licked his teeth, crept closer to Sullivan as Eden watched Jarrod's face harden.

"That's not true," Jarrod said.

Fury radiated off Sullivan as she stepped around him. "You must know the Bound can't find all the Siders Eden sends Upstairs," she said. "Do you really think Luke can find all of *mine*? And every Sider I send down below destroys more of you. In fact," she said, moving closer to them, "are you so sure I couldn't end you myself? Right here? Right now? Threaten the three of us again."

Eden had no doubt that Sullivan itched to carry through on the threat.

The girl demon's grin only widened. "Our flinching flower has thorns," she said appreciatively.

The demons circled like crows around carrion.

"What are you waiting for?" Jarrod said. "Get them! They can't tell Luke about you!"

Without warning the demons dropped, their knees cracking against the tile hard enough that Eden cringed. Fear flashed in their eyes at a noise beyond the door, a shouting match at the counter. *What the hell are demons afraid of?* she thought as she whirled toward the sound. Writhing in agony, the girl demon grabbed for Eden's leg. "You've no time to kill us. Lucifer sent us to warn you only if the Bound come close. We can't be in their light. They break our shadows." True pain shattered her words apart. "They are *here.*"

Eden spun for the door, then back to the girl hanging off her calf. "Here? Now?"

Zach. She had to get Zach. Eden went for the door, but the girl held her back, gripped onto her ankle.

"Run," the demons said before they swirled away in a viscous smoke. The blackness floated near the ceiling and then shot off through the shelves.

"Out the back!" Jarrod said, grabbing her arm. Sullivan ran in the direction he pointed, the same way the smoke had gone.

"But Zach." Eden strained in his grip.

The door swung on its hinges, a blood-smeared hand clutching wildly before it was hauled out again. The door shut, but it didn't blot out the screams.

Jarrod's eyes darted to the small window. "We have to leave him," he said. "Come on. Now."

They didn't look back.

CHAPTER 8

Madeline crossed her legs on the tattered sofa. Near her knee, foam peeked through, the threadbare fabric unraveling. She'd had Eden and her two tagalongs followed to Milton's. The girl who'd been tracking them now stood in front of Madeline. Tears streaked her face, her arms wrapped around her stomach as she shook violently.

"Calm down, Allison," Madeline said. She heard the heavy footsteps from the hallway beyond the living room. Jackson, her Second, finally joined them. "Okay," Madeline said to the traumatized girl. "Tell us, slowly, what happened."

"I was right there," the girl babbled. Fumbling, she undid the band that held her ponytail in place. "I have glass in my hair!"

"Easy, easy," Jackson murmured as he took Allison into his arms. He stroked her back gently, and she melted against him, hiccuping. "You're safe now."

He caught Madeline's glance, and she gave him a subtle thumbs-up of approval. "You were following Eden," he prodded.

Allison nodded, pulling away from him. "She went into a coffee shop. I stayed outside by the front window, but I couldn't see her in there," the girl said as she stripped off her gloves and let them fall to the floor beside Jackson's sneaker. "I was about to go in and then this guy, he just jumped up on the counter and perched there like a freaking bird!"

"Damn it," Madeline whispered. It could only be the Bound. If they'd gotten Eden, unlike the rest of the Siders, all they had to do was keep her from getting Touch to kill her off.

Madeline wasn't prepared for the disappointment she felt. She'd spent time with Eden while Gabriel had been Fallen, looked out for her and her Siders, though Eden had never known the extent. Whether out of respect or pity, she'd felt a kinship with her. Already Madeline regretted letting Kristen talk her out of helping Eden.

Madeline couldn't quite place the emotion in Jackson's eyes. Not fear. He was calm, steady. "The Bound got her?"

"I didn't see. Once they got Zach, I ran."

Madeline jerked in surprise. "They got Zach?"

The girl nodded, and Jackson sunk down beside Madeline on the couch.

They listened in numb silence as the girl told them how the window had shattered when Zach had been thrown through it. One of the broken shards sliced his arm on the way out, the wound jagged and gushing. As he'd struggled to his hands and knees, Allison said he'd looked up at her.

"Only for a split second," she said. "He didn't ask me for help. I don't think he wanted them to know I was like him. One of the Bound threw Zach over his shoulder and ran. The ones inside just disappeared." She ran her fingers through her hair. Bits of glass fell to the floor. "I should have done something."

"No," Jackson said, unfocused and distracted. He cleared his throat. "No, you were right to escape."

"Allison, you couldn't have done anything for him. Go rest. Take a shower." Madeline turned to Jackson. "I need to speak to you upstairs."

Jackson's attention didn't waver from Allison. "The best thing you could have done was get out of there."

Madeline padded up the stairs to the second floor, down the hall. Past Jackson's bedroom, and her own, was a door to what everyone else thought was an empty room. Leaning against it, she waited for Jackson to catch up before she pulled the key from her back pocket. He made a quick sweep to be sure the hall was empty, that no one hovered near.

Satisfied, she opened the door.

They slipped quickly inside. On the floor, an unconscious slip of a girl laid with her arms folded across her chest. The girl almost looked like she was sleeping, but Madeline knew otherwise. "She's out? For sure?"

Jackson bit his thumbnail. "I injected them all about two hours ago."

Madeline nodded distractedly. In a room downstairs there were six other mortals, all on Touch but drugged to unconsciousness. Early on, Madeline had made the decision to clue her Siders in on what she and Jackson were attempting, making others like themselves, an army to fight the Bound. She'd left out a few details, namely her plans for this specific girl. Yesterday, Jackson had carried her upstairs, separating her from the others.

"She's been passed to how many times again?" Madeline whispered.

Beside her, Jackson paced a tight circle. He stopped, staring down. "Thirty over the past three days," he answered. Every one of the Queens Siders had given her Touch, most multiple times. "But only you and I have passed to her since yesterday."

"Jesus," she whispered. She couldn't take her eyes off the girl. "Okay, we need to do this."

"You're *sure* you don't want to give it another day? Wait until after the ball?" Jackson scratched absently at his arm. "I thought we were going to run this by Kristen first," he said.

She shook her head. "I'll tell her about the attack, but earlier she basically told me something was going to have to be done about Eden before she took out any more Siders. How do you think Kristen would react if she knew what we're going to do?"

Madeline couldn't risk being stopped when their plan had the potential to help them all so much. *They're going to torture Zach until they figure out how to destroy us,* she thought.

She pictured what Allison had described, Zach's flying body shattering the front window of Milton's. His blood seeping into the sidewalk. "I should call Erin. I have to tell her. About Zach."

Jackson stroked her face. "Then let's do that instead."

On the floor, the girl shuddered.

Madeline brushed away his hand and picked up a railroad spike of a syringe. "No. It's time."

"I don't like this." Jackson sighed, and rubbed his palm over his shaved head.

"Gabe said the paths were eroding because the mortals were getting too much Touch. Ergo, when she dies, she'll be a Sider." Madeline flicked the oversized syringe.

"Yeah, but she's not killing *herself.* This is murder, Mad. If it even works, and she does go Sider," he said, "won't she be like Eden? A death breather?"

"I'm *making* her, the way Gabe made Eden," she whispered, watching the bubbles rise up the tube. "When he was Bound, the Siders Eden killed went Upstairs. When he was Fallen, they went Down." She trailed off as she crouched beside the girl and took her limp elbow. She felt Touch pass. *Once more for good luck*, she thought. "I'm going to do this and find out where hers go," Madeline said as the needle popped through into the girl's vein.

She pushed the plunger.

"Has anyone ever done this before?" His hand pressed against the small of her back as he helped her up. The touch reminded her of Luke at the jewelry store.

She rolled her shoulder, pulling away. "Not that I know of," she said.

The girl bucked suddenly, startling them both. The whites of her eyes were visible through the thin crack between her eyelids. Her fingers clawed the floor in rigid swipes.

"God, I can't watch this," Jackson said. Madeline heard him cross the room and close the door behind him.

Madeline couldn't look away. Some part of her wanted to drop down, tell the poor thing she would be all right. It was a very small part. A thin line of foamy spittle drooled from the girl onto the floor.

"You're going to save us," Madeline promised, not sure

if the words were meant for herself or the thrashing girl. *This will work.* A terrible thrill crackled through her as the girl stilled. *This has to work.* After a full minute, Madeline snapped up the limp wrist. There was no pulse. "Done and done," she said as she stood.

Her phone trilled in her pocket.

She pulled it out as she backed away from the body, expecting any name but the one that showed up on her screen. "Eden? You're alive!" She couldn't help the shock in her voice. "How did you get out?"

Eden's voice was sharp. "Were you told before or after the Bound came to kill me? Took Zach?"

Shit. Stupid mistake. "That's not fair," Madeline said. "If I'd known, I would have warned you. My sources told me a few minutes ago, no more." She kept her tone even. "I would never cross you like that. Or Zach. He seems nice," she added, covering.

Eden let out a laugh full of disbelief. *Does she know who Zach is?* Madeline wondered.

"So when's the ball, Madeline?" Eden demanded. "You're not leaving us on our own now that the Bound are attacking Siders in the open."

Madeline switched the phone to her other ear. *Great,* she thought. "Eden, you cannot show up there, do you understand me? You need to stay the hell away from Kristen."

"Why?" Eden asked.

"Because she wants you dead," Madeline said. "And right now, she thinks you are. The purpose of the ball is to gather as many Siders to her as possible. You *kill* Siders. I'd say the conflict's pretty clear."

On the floor, the dead girl's eyes were still open a slit. Crouching down, Madeline closed them. "I've got plans in motion. All I need is a little more time, and Kristen's issues with you will be obsolete." *By morning,* she thought. Then they would know for sure. For now, though, she had to be sure Eden was somewhere safe. "Where are you planning on staying?"

"Hidden," Eden answered instantly, and Madeline couldn't help feeling a bit of hope for her.

"Good girl," she said. "Trust no one. Stay out of sight. The ball's tomorrow night. I'll call you when it's over."

She hung up without waiting for a response. Now, all she had to do was wait. In a few hours, she and Jackson would know whether the first part of her plan had worked. If not, Madeline would be Googling the hell out of how to dispose of a body.

CHAPTER 9

Kristen strode down the hall, shoulders back, head high. She had told no one about the attack on Milton's after Madeline's call. Now, more than ever, the ball had to go on as planned.

She halted at the top of the stairs and leaned against the railing. At her heels was a young Sider.

With a flick of her hand, Kristen gestured to the room below. "Furniture will need to be moved to the outskirts, and I'd like speakers and refreshments set up to the right of the stairs. Lights strung across there," she said, pointing up to the exposed beams of the ceiling. "Like stars. Don't skimp."

She whipped around to find the Sider scribbling on a small pad of paper.

"And what sort of music?" the girl asked.

Music. Kristen's brain lodged in a memory of fingers coursing over frets, gentle strumming. *No.* Lips against

her skin. Luke's fingers in her hair. *Do not think about him.*
Her grip tightened on the banister. The timbre of Luke's
voice flooded her brain, dragged her under, and stole her
breath. *He's not here.*

"Kristen?"

"Let Sebastian choose the music." Her voice came out
weaker than she would have liked.

"You don't want to?" the girl asked.

Kristen's dress billowed around her as she closed the
distance between them. "Did you in any way *not* understand," she challenged, "or are you second-guessing my
decisions?"

"I wasn't. I would never," the girl stammered.

"You would never second-guess?" An angry heat filled
her chest, scorched away the last thoughts of Luke. "So
I'm to gather you're stupid?"

"Kristen. Stop." She startled at Sebastian's sudden
presence. The sharp sound of his voice unleashed her temper even before she heard the next word. He had been at
her side since before she'd become the leader of the Bronx
two years ago. He knew better than to speak against her.

"I won't tolerate stupidity. Put her in the east wing." She
mocked the girl's sharp intake. The east wing was where
the Screamers were kept, locked in, and made to store their
Touch until they went mad with it. "I want her suffering."

Sebastian looped his muscled arm for the girl to take,

but instead of leading her away, he stood stock-still. "Perhaps that's a bit rash?" When Kristen didn't immediately answer, he turned, spinning the girl with him. "Go, Shanyn," he said to her. "Stay out of sight today."

The girl was down the stairs before Kristen's jaw even had a chance to drop. She shook her head in disbelief. "Who do you think you are?"

"Your Second," he said softly. "Though you're treating me like your enemy." Sebastian met her glare with sad brown eyes. "What are you so angry about?" he asked.

"I'm not. I'm fi—"

He held out his hand to cut her off. "You're not fine," he said loudly.

She swiveled to survey the preparations below. The Siders down there were setting up decorations and candles along the mantel. They hadn't looked up at Sebastian's words.

"My room," she commanded. "Now."

When they were beyond prying ears in her bedroom, she closed her door. She kept her hand on the wood, trying to collect herself as he paced behind her back.

She swallowed hard, unsure how to tell him about the attack at Milton's. Eden and her Second were gone, along with Zach. "Sebastian, I . . ."

"I shouldn't have undermined your authority," he said. "Especially after your absence."

The floorboards creaked as he shifted, giving away how

uncomfortable the confrontation made him.

"You can't hurt our Siders, Kristen. To beat the Bound, we need strength and we need numbers. Losing either is unacceptable." As she turned to face him, Sebastian took a deep breath and began again. "Is it your illness that has you acting this way?"

Being in charge, he'd grown bold.

She felt her face flush. "Cruelty isn't a *symptom*."

Nothing would wipe away how she'd felt seeing Sebastian at Aerie, where he and Eden had come looking and found her with Luke. Eden had gone for insults and personal drama, but Sebastian . . . he had only wanted her safe, wanted her home. If he'd come alone, she just might have listened to him.

She wondered if Luke would have let her go.

Sebastian led the others to believe her absence was a planned event. As always, he seemed to know exactly when to give her space and when to push. They needed to trust each other. Secrets now could get them killed.

"You're afraid?" He raised an eyebrow, waiting a moment for her to contradict him, then plowed on. "Don't be. Tomorrow, we have the ball. The others will come and—"

"Gabriel said last week the other angels were close to figuring out a way to kill us. They may already have found one." She licked her lips as she broke eye contact. "There was an attack today in Manhattan."

"Today? In broad daylight?" Sebastian balked. "On Eden's crew?"

Kristen nodded. "Eden, Jarrod, possibly another girl with them. And one other." She wanted to be strong for him. "Zach."

His face fell. She barely heard his whispered curse.

"No one is to leave the house," she commanded. "Not together, not alone. Not at all. We need everyone here and ready to fight if necessary." *I need you safe. By my side,* she thought but didn't say. He had to know how important he was. How she leaned on him. "Are you all ri—"

"Numbers don't matter if we can't kill our enemy. Why haven't you asked Gabriel?" The coldness in his voice cut through her like ice.

"What, how to kill the Bound?" She ran her fingers through the wild mess of her brown hair until she hit a snarl. "He would never tell me. What would the Siders do to me if I told the Bound some way to kill *us?*" she asked, exasperated.

The rationalization didn't give him pause. His brown eyes burned with anger. "Manipulate him. Guilt him into it."

She blinked at him in surprise. "He's my friend!"

"No. He's one of *them,* Kristen, and from what you told me, he's pretty desperate to remain so. You'd do well to remember he's an enemy."

She shook her head, but it did nothing to stop her

thoughts. Gabriel's face on the train when he was Fallen, how he'd hurt her, his grip bruising her wrist. The black and blue marks had been nothing; remembering how he'd cast her aside cut deeper. *Will he do it again, for the Bound this time?* "Gabriel's done more for me than—"

"Past tense. *Done*," Sebastian said before she could finish, stabbing a victorious finger in her face.

"This conversation is over." She turned away, couldn't look at him, couldn't bear to acknowledge the truth in his words. "Are we clear?"

"Fine." Sebastian crossed his arms. "What about Luke?"

Heat rose slowly up her neck to her cheeks. "You just don't stop, do you? I told you that was done."

"And I believe you. But would *he* tell you how to kill angels?"

The idea took hold even as her anger slid away.

"Kristen?" Sebastian prodded. "Would Luke tell you how to kill angels?"

She shook her head, rattling the thought away. It didn't matter. "Not anymore." She'd denied Luke in front of Gabriel. He'd laced her up in his delicate puppet strings, left her feeling foolish and unraveled. It was over. "Lucifer isn't exactly one to trust in an alliance anyway," she said.

Sebastian took a step toward her. "Are you sure? Our lives depend on it." She glanced up at him.

"I'll do what I can." Her voice was barely audible. After

closing the door behind Sebastian, she stood lost in her thoughts.

Luke's dangerous. He used you. The voice in her head belonged to Gabriel. She wanted to listen. And yet, she'd seen the rage on Luke's face when he realized she was leaving him. Angry *after* Gabriel had been Bound, when any Siders Eden killed off were back to infecting Upstairs, not Down. Why had Luke been so livid at her leaving if he'd already won his game?

Her eyes slipped shut, the memory of the last night at Aerie replaying. Eden suffering, Gabriel Bound again, sanity. And Luke, beside her, the whisper in her ear. *This is everything you wanted,* he had said.

But what had *he* wanted?

She rolled a gaudy sapphire ring around her thumb, pondering. What would happen if she listened to Sebastian? She pictured herself showing up at Luke's apartment unannounced. Even in her imagination, the smug smile that she knew he'd wear irked her. He'd cock his hip against the doorframe, maybe surprised to see her there, but maybe not. She wondered if he'd force her to say the things that her presence would tell him anyway: that she'd made a mistake, should have stayed. Missed him.

Kristen sighed. There was only one reason she couldn't go through with it.

Luke would know it wasn't a lie.

CHAPTER 10

Hunkered down inside Zach's tiny efficiency apartment, Eden couldn't focus. She and Sullivan had pulled a futon in front of the door. The only other furniture in the place—a broken dresser with a small television balanced precariously on top—Jarrod had moved in front of the window.

They went through the apartment, meticulously searching for anything that would lead them to Erin. Torn and dog-eared paperbacks were piled up in a corner waist high. Clothes hung haphazardly in a half-open closet. While Eden and Jarrod had brainstormed about how the Siders originated, Sullivan stayed in the kitchen going through the few papers Zach had lying around, looking for a number for Erin, an address, anything. Eden knew she wouldn't find it. What reason would Zach have to write it down?

Eden sat cross-legged on the futon, adding names to

the pad of paper on the cushion beside her. They *had* to figure out where the Siders came from. "Madeline won't talk to us until tomorrow night, Vaughn's pretty much out of the question, and Kristen apparently wants to kill us." She tapped the pen against her cheek. "We have no way to get a hold of Erin."

"Someone has to know *something*!" Jarrod said, pinching the bridge of his nose. Eden gave him a sympathetic look. In truth, she was worried about him. His focus clung to her and Sullivan like they'd disappear any second, tracked them, kept them locked in a haunted gaze she'd never seen from him before. Even now, he leaned back just enough to see Sullivan, though they both could hear her rummaging. "Seriously, Eden. It wasn't magic. The four of them didn't just pop out of thin air."

"Wait." She balanced her elbow on her knee, leaning forward on her palm. "Not four," she said. "Five. When I first became a Sider, Kristen told me there were five originals. When they started to find more Siders, they split into the territories. Madeline's in Queens, Kristen got the Bronx, Erin was Manhattan, Vaughn had Staten Island," she said, pointing to each name. She drew a quick map, filling in the names. She tapped the hole between Staten Island and the others. "Why does no one ever talk about Brooklyn?"

"You're right," he said slowly.

She leaned back, puzzled. It couldn't be that easy. Could it? "Someone's gotta be there. Otherwise they wouldn't have given me Erin's territory. Plus, if it was empty, someone should have claimed it by now, right?"

"Have Kristen or Madeline *ever* mentioned who's in Brooklyn?" he asked. She shook her head as he closed the distance between them. "Sullivan!" he called out.

She came around the corner from the kitchen. "Yeah?"

"Vaughn." Sullivan startled at the name, and Jarrod laid his hands on her shoulders. He brushed back her long black hair, kissing her gently on the forehead. "When you were with him, did he ever mention any Siders from Brooklyn?"

An ache bloomed inside of Eden, but she didn't bother to look for ashes on her palms. This pain had nothing to do with lack of Touch. *At least not that kind,* she thought. Watching the tenderness between Jarrod and Sullivan, she could almost feel the sensation of Az's fingertips on her skin, his lips soft on her collarbones. *I'll get him back,* she promised herself. *I will. But I can't think about him.*

She couldn't lose herself down that spiral. Not now. "Sullivan," she said. "We need you to remember this."

Rather than answering immediately, Sullivan took a second to think it over. She'd been out of her mind on Touch for most of the time she'd been with Vaughn. "Well, *I'm* from Brooklyn," she started slowly. "But I don't think he ever mentioned it."

Jarrod's hand tightened on her shoulder. "How long did you live there?" he asked, a desperate tone in his voice that Eden didn't understand. "Sullivan, did you live there when you were fourteen?"

Her face wrinkled in confusion. "Yeah, until about a year and a half ago."

Jarrod whipped around to Eden. "Then Vaughn's from Brooklyn. That's where he was when he went Sider. When I fought him in the alley, he was saying Sullivan was his girl, that she'd been his girl since they were both fourteen."

"What?" Sullivan said. "No, I just met him, like, six months ago."

Jarrod softened. He took her hand. "He said you were with him for three years, Sullivan," he said. She backed away, shaking her head. Jarrod stayed with her, step for step. "He'd stayed away from you for over a year, and then you came into a club where he was selling Touch. You'd forgotten him, because he turned Sider and you were still a mortal."

"That's not true," she said, the last word lilting up at the end in her uncertainty. She looked at Eden as if she'd have the answers. "I would remember him." Sullivan's face clouded over. "I wouldn't have stayed with him for three years. He was *mean*. He did things . . . things I can't even . . ."

Jarrod took her into his arms and met Eden's eyes over

her shoulder. "Do you think it started with Vaughn?" he asked.

"Stop," Eden said. She concentrated, trying to remember her first week with Kristen. There'd been so much information, so much to learn. Still, something wasn't right. "Sullivan, how long were you with him?"

"We dated, like, three months? But I met him at the beginning of summer, so I've known him around six."

"Six months," Eden whispered, jotting down the information in the notebook. "And a year before that when he said he left you alone . . ." She trailed off. *It doesn't match up*, she realized. "When I stayed with Kristen, she said the five of them split into territories two years ago. That would be before he was a Sider!" Eden crossed Vaughn's name off the list and looked up at Jarrod. "He moved to Staten Island because Sullivan moved there. Which means Vaughn wasn't the original territory leader. He wasn't even a Sider when the others decided on boroughs."

"Which means there are two Siders we have to find," Sullivan said. "Whoever's in charge in Brooklyn and whoever *was* in charge before Vaughn got to Staten Island."

Why didn't anyone tell me? Eden thought. Kristen and Madeline had played it off like Vaughn had been there from the start. *What are they hiding?*

CHAPTER 11

$\mathcal{S}$quinting, Jarrod rubbed the strained muscles in his neck. He'd spent all night in the same position, on watch, propped up against the wall. Sullivan had passed out on the futon, and Eden had curled up in a pile of blankets on the floor. Now, Jarrod blinked slowly. The girls weren't there.

Staggering to his feet, he grabbed for the blankets as if they'd hold some clue. *They're gone.* He laced his hands over his head. *You fell asleep and they're gone.* "No. Fuck, please," he whispered.

A laugh sounded from the kitchen, smothered instantly. "Hello?" he yelled.

"In here!" Sullivan's voice rang out, the most glorious thing he'd ever heard. He stumbled forward in disbelief. She sat on the kitchen floor, leaning back against the cabinets with an open box of Cap'n Crunch.

Eden tossed a handful of cereal into her mouth. "Sleep good?"

When he didn't answer, Sullivan looked up. "Jarrod?"
The smile dropped away. "What's wrong?"

"I thought you were gone. I thought you were both . . ."
He leaned against the wall and slid down it.

"No!" Sullivan said. "We just didn't want to wake you
up. You were out cold."

"Snoring and everything," Eden added, like it was
a joke. Like he was supposed to laugh when he'd fallen
asleep and his mistake could have cost both Eden and
Sullivan their lives.

"How long was I out?" Vague memories surfaced of
the sun coming up, the light weak behind the dresser he'd
pushed in front the window. Dawn was the last thing he
could remember.

"I woke up around ten and you'd already crashed."
Eden chewed and then swallowed her cereal. "It's four
now," she said.

"*Six* hours?"

"You needed the sleep," she insisted.

Instead of arguing, he rubbed his eyes with the heels of
his palms. "Okay. What are we doing? What did you guys
come up with?"

Eden answered. "If we want to talk to Madeline,
Kristen, and Erin, at least we know where they're all going
to be tonight."

He glanced up to find her dead serious. "We are not

going to that ball, Eden," he said instantly.

Both girls immediately responded.

"Jarrod, just listen to her—"

"Zach said everyone would be there! Maybe this Sider from Brooklyn will be, too!"

"You've got to be shitting me," he said. "Kristen wants to kill you, not to mention what Vaughn would to do to us. Madeline's not gonna have your back if you make her choose in front of them. You know that, right?"

Eden huffed and set the cereal aside. When she spoke, her voice grated on him, calm enough to be condescending. "We *are* going to Kristen's tonight. I'm not sitting here waiting for the Bound or the Fallen to find us. I'm not waiting for them to take *us* like they did Zach."

"That wasn't my fault!" he yelled at her as he stood.

"*Your* fault?" Confusion furrowed Eden's forehead, the defiant attitude gone from her as quick as it'd come. "Of course it wasn't," she said softly.

How could I just leave him? Even as he thought it, Jarrod knew there'd been no other choice. Zach would understand; he would have done the same for Erin.

"Jarrod?" Eden said.

His attention flicked between the two of them. Minutes had separated them from capture and escape. Minutes and demons. He had a vision—Sullivan's screams as the Bound snatched her from his arms. Eden being dragged across the back of a booth and out the window. Both of them gone. Nothing he could do. A hard knot of terror and rage tightened in his stomach.

Jarrod spun suddenly toward the wall and slammed it with a punch. The drywall caved around his knuckles. He grimaced, cupping his fist to his chest. For almost a full minute, he stood there, dizzy with pain, endorphins, and embarrassment.

"What the hell was that about?" Sullivan said, standing up and reaching to check his hand.

Everything inside him built. He couldn't lose it in front of the girls any worse than he already had. He staggered toward the bathroom, the only private place in the apartment. "Sorry," he called out over his shoulder. "I'm sorry."

Sullivan followed him and wedged her foot in the door as he tried to close it. "Would you wait a second?" she said. "Talk to me!"

She stood, stubborn and unmoving, until he finally moved aside. He was acting like a complete ass, but he didn't know what else to do, how to make things better. He leaned, his hands braced on the wall above his head as she closed the door and slid past him. Already his knuckles were blue and bruising. Now, his body would be wasting Touch he could be passing to Eden on healing himself.

Sullivan sat on the edge of the tub. "Come here," she said, waving him down.

Adrenaline fading, he sunk to the floor in front of her and rested his forehead on her knees. His arms curled around her legs.

A drop of sweat ran down his nose and splashed on the tan tile. "I'm sorry I scared you," he said.

"You didn't." Her tentative fingertips touched his neck, traced slowly from his hairline. He kept his head down, lost in the sensation of her touch, his lungs still heaving. "Your hand okay?" she asked softly as he rose onto his knees.

He nodded, his eyes burning and blurry. "I keep thinking about how it was almost us. If they got—" His voice cracked, and he leaned into the space where her neck and shoulder met. He kissed her there, brought his uninjured hand up and buried it in her hair. He prayed she wouldn't pull away. He'd break. Lose it. *If they got you, I couldn't handle it.*

Everything inside him felt on fire, searing. *What if they come and I can't stop them?* "Please. I just . . . I need . . ."

His mouth crested over her jaw. He cupped the back of her head, his lips rough on her skin. His teeth grazed her earlobe, and the fingers that had been so gentle on his neck tightened.

They're going to find us. His hands clasped her waist, the bare skin where her shirt lifted. *I can't let them.* His palm slid across the fragile bones of her spine. Breakable. *I don't want her to die.*

"Jarrod?"

A sound escaped him as his name left her, something wild and animalistic. The part of him that clung to control recoiled. He trembled, unable to catch his breath, one hand keeping her from falling into the tub.

"Hey," she whispered, concern in her voice. She touched the side of his jaw gently. "Stop."

He stared into her uncertain eyes. His face burned as he pulled away. "I'm sorry, I just can't . . ."

"What can I do to help?" she asked before she slid off the tub to join him on the floor, moving to sit beside him. Her chin settled onto his shoulder. "Tell me what you need."

This, he thought suddenly. *I need this. I need you.* Frustrated, he dropped his forehead against hers. Why couldn't he just say it? "I just want all of us to come out of this okay," he finally got out.

For a long moment, there was only silence.

"Jesus, Sullivan," he whispered. "I used to want to die so bad, I'd *pray* for car accidents. Even after, when I was a Sider. I just wanted it over." He dropped his elbows onto his knees, leaning over. He couldn't look at her. Didn't want to see her face when he spoke the next words. "It's how I met Eden."

With her sharp gasp, he knew she'd caught his meaning. "You wanted her to *kill* you?"

He nodded, not quite sure he wanted to tell the story until it started spilling out.

"When I became a Sider, I felt so trapped," he whispered. "I heard rumors about what Eden could do, so I tracked her down." He remembered the first time he'd seen her, the steely look she'd given him, the way she'd sauntered past like he was nothing. In his mad scramble to follow her, he'd dropped the fifty she charged and almost lost the money to the wind. It'd taken him a few seconds to chase it and catch up.

"This guy who was waiting with me went first. Only I guess he didn't have the money. So she said no—" Jarrod broke off, started again. "By the time I came around the corner . . ."

"Take your time," Sullivan said quietly.

"He thought he could make her do it anyway." Jarrod swallowed, making himself go on. "He hit her. Hard. I lost it, Sullivan. I just lost it on him."

"Oh my God," she whispered.

"When it was over Eden was leaning against the wall and she looked up at me. Blood was just pouring out of her nose, but she didn't even care. She *smiled* at me. And she said . . ." He glanced up at Sullivan. "'You must really want to die.'"

He couldn't help the disbelief in his voice, hadn't even really believed Eden's reaction then, with the red smeared over her teeth, dripping from her chin to soak her sweater. It had been that moment—his adrenaline pumping and his hand throbbing, standing in the alley with the girl who was supposed to end him—when something changed.

"I got a second chance, and I took it. And now it's going to be taken away from me." He flexed the fingers of his swelling hand and winced, only partially from the pain. How stupid to give himself an injury and lose some of his Touch in healing it. His words came out slow and quiet. "They're going to win."

"Jarrod, no." Her fingers slid between his. "That's not going to happen."

"It's already starting. Eden's one of the strongest people I know, and I'm watching her fall apart. Az is gone. Zach is . . . God knows what they're doing to him."

"But Eden will get better and she'll get Az back." He heard her swallow. "Maybe we can find Zach?" she tried.

"They'll use him to figure out how to kill us. He's not coming back. I have to protect you and Eden." He dropped his gaze in misery.

She gave him a small laugh, but it didn't sound genuine. "Sorry to burst your bubble, Prince Charming, but Eden and I are self-rescuing princesses."

Irritated, he yanked his hand from hers. "Did you see Eden in the alley yesterday? She couldn't stand, she couldn't fight. If the Bound get you, Sullivan, they'll hurt you until you can't heal. When you're turning to ash, how are you going to rescue yourself?"

"So how can you possibly be strong enough for *all* of us? You're passing her all your Touch, we're running from the Bound and probably now the Fallen," she said. "You're doing your best, Jarrod. Eden knows that. I know that. But you can't take this all on yourself."

When he finally met her eyes, he saw the terror she'd kept from her voice, watched as her false bravado began to chip away. She leaned suddenly, her arms coming around his neck. He wanted to tell her it was going to be okay, but the words lodged in his throat, wouldn't come.

"I'm scared," she whispered.

He held his breath and kissed her. Not like before, to distract himself, and not like she'd kissed him in the hotel when they'd met, a last hurrah. A real kiss. Soft and slow and full of all the things he felt but couldn't say.

"Me too," he said.

CHAPTER 12

Since Raphael's visit, Az had watched the sun dip behind the mountains in a blaze of orange and red too stunning to be real. He'd tracked the slow arc of the false moon. The sky was not the same sky Eden looked up to see. He had no way of knowing how long he'd been gone.

She'd been safe yesterday. He'd been terrified enough the Bound had already found her that Raphael's promises of her future demise gave him a sick relief.

Az stared down at the white sheets. She would be expecting an enemy. She would open the door to Gabe without hesitating. How could Gabe throw away everything the three of them had been through together? *He would never do that to me,* Az thought, but no matter how much he wanted to believe it, the kernel of fear inside him only grew. Promises were binding. Driven by compulsion.

If Gabriel hadn't been able to resist Falling, how could he fight this? *What if he doesn't want to fight it?* Gabriel had made the vow; Raphael couldn't lie.

Everything inside Az became focused fury. Gabe intended to kill her.

"No." Az's voice rang out, loud and true.

Sudden color.

He sucked in, almost choking in surprise, and reached for the sheet. Deep navy gathered around his fingers like fresh bruises, spread through the threads. But it didn't stop there. Blue bled onto the floor, snaked up the walls and across the ceiling. Az watched in awe.

"It worked," he whispered. The color he'd imagined into existence proved there was a chance he could imagine a key or an unlocked door. But to Az it meant more. *I'm not one of them. They can't break me. I'm getting out.*

He dropped the fabric and spun to the door. *Okay, time to bring out the big guns.* "Open."

The syllables left him over and over, a low hum. He didn't dare blink. In his mind, the inner workings of the lock spun, the tumblers falling into place as it disengaged. He heard a faint click, and hope flared inside him. "Come on," he whispered.

With a creak, the door opened. Leaping off the cot, Az let out a triumphant bark of a laugh.

Until Michael stepped through.

He refused to feel disappointed. *It doesn't matter how the door opened,* Az thought as he glared at Michael in silence. *It's not closing again with me in here.*

Unlike Raphael, he'd seen Michael recently and not Upstairs. The angel had been searching out information on Gabe, and accosted Az when he'd been dancing with Eden at the Rockefeller Center Christmas tree. In New York, Michael's movements had been jerky, unnatural, but Upstairs, he glided into the room.

"Raphael brought words from you. You may as well speak again. Have such inane barriers not been broken down?" He paced the floor. It was only then that Az really looked at him.

Nervous. The thought struck him an instant before Michael's yellowed eyes met his. "What's going on?" Az asked.

Michael kept pacing. "Your knowledge is *necessary*, Azazel. The council persists in the belief you shall return to us fully, but I believe they've made a grave error."

Az shook his head slowly. "I don't know what you're talking about. Knowledge about what?" *He's right, though. I'm not taking the vows. I'm not giving up.* The thought was there before he could stop it.

"The Suiciders." Michael stalked across the room until he was uncomfortably close.

Az bent his face away. "Gabriel told you everything we know."

"You lie." A mournful wail burst from him. "Are you so lost to us? Some say you've broken. Has the light seeped from the cracks inside you, Azazel? I fear for you!"

Despite everything, Az couldn't help the trickle of shame inside himself. "I'm not lost," he said quietly. "I'm just different now."

"Azazel, you must tell me if you know how they started and what they're for. The Siders sent Upstairs are infecting the souls here, destroying them utterly. Our sources speak of the same infection Downstairs. Is it true?"

He shrugged, made his eyes wide and baffled. "Gosh, I just don't know." A second later, he dropped the sarcastic act. "I'm not telling you *anything*."

Az recoiled when Michael dropped gently to his knees in front of him. This didn't seem like the same angel he'd seen at the Christmas tree with Eden, all uncoordinated anger. Az wondered now how much of that rage had been fear for Gabe.

"Please," Michael murmured. "You would stand by and do nothing while the world falls to ruin?" A single tear slipped down his cheek. "Have you become so selfish?"

Az gave his head a slight shake. Guilt turned his stomach, ripped away the last of the sarcasm he clung to. "You don't understand. The Siders aren't these terrible creatures you all are imagining. They're not a plague, Michael; they're souls!"

"They're a handful of souls. We must protect the souls here and on Earth. Months with them have convinced you to undermine entire worlds?"

"You don't know them like I do," Az said. He thought of Eden, memories spilling through him. Michael's face soured.

"What happened between yourself and that Sider was not love, Azazel. She used you to learn our secrets. They aim only to spread the plague of their kind!"

Az blew out a breath in contempt.

"She lured Gabriel with her helplessness, did she not?" Michael's tone gentled. "Called out to him like a siren."

"No," he said, but his mind hung on Eden the night they'd met on the beach. Gabriel had told him later that she'd seemed to be desperate for help. "Eden couldn't have planned it. She was *mortal* when we met."

Michael straightened, leaning toward him. "You told the council she had no path, even then. You swore."

Az opened his mouth to answer, to defend her, but there was nothing he could say that didn't feel like entrapment.

Michael caught Az's glare, held it. "Your time with her has been but a flash. How can you call it love, as if love were so simple."

The cadence of his words wormed into Az's head, pumped through his veins like a drug. He couldn't shake his thoughts free, part of him wanting Michael to see them, to know what he knew in his heart. "It's love," Az insisted.

"She lied to you, didn't she," Michael said, staring

straight into his eyes. "She tricked you, Azazel."

Az's head dipped slightly. "That's not . . . You don't . . . Don't do this to . . ." The thought spun away before he could grasp it. He flinched at the pressure of Michael's finger under his chin, the black pupils fixed on his.

"Azazel, tell me her secrets."

Something stirred deep inside him. The words seeped out slow and slurred. "She puts herself in danger. She'll die for her friends before she lets you touch them." Distress bloomed in his chest. "She hates when things are complicated, and so she should hate me, but she doesn't." Az tasted a metallic tang of terror but couldn't remember why he should be afraid. His brain ached, itchy and hot.

"More," Michael whispered. "Where did she come from?"

He fought for the answer through his confusion. "Jersey?"

"Where did the *Siders* come from?" Michael asked, his voice a melody. "Who made them?"

Az blinked slowly, his limbs heavy. An infectious heat invaded his mind even as Michael's cool fingers wrapped around his head. A trickle of sweat slipped down his temple. "Tell me what you know," Michael pleaded.

The door opened. "Michael!"

At the sound of his name, Michael pivoted, broke eye contact. Az doubled over in agony. Everything inside his head screamed, ripped loose and bruised. He squeezed his temples, barely noticing the angel that had entered his room.

"What suffers him so?" Raphael's voice.

"I came to find answers," Michael replied, his tone cutting. "You interrupted."

Az rolled off the mattress, dropping gracelessly onto the floor. He made it to his knees barely in time to brace himself for the first retch. His throat burned, each exhale scalding. He tried to crawl away, but Michael seized him, pulling him back even as the retching started again. Thin strands of blood-streaked spit dripped from his gaping jaw.

Raphael touched his back gently before pressing his hands against Az's neck. Instantly, the heat dulled. "Better methods weren't considered? Were it not for him, Gabriel would be Fallen still. Have you so swiftly forgotten?"

"There are more pressing matters than comfort, Raphael."

Their angry voices pounded in time with the pulse in Az's head, tripled the pain. His vision blurred.

"You would rip his mind apart like spider's webs to find what you seek?" Raphael chided Michael. "Look at him!"

"Necessary measures. He desired to assist us, or it wouldn't have worked."

Neither the Bound nor the Fallen could work their tricks without permission, but Az had been vulnerable.

Michael had lured him in with the challenge against Eden. The need in him to prove Eden loved him, to prove she was good, had allowed the connection to take. *I let him in,* he thought. *I let it happen.* He could still feel the fiery heat Michael left behind.

"What was learned?" Raphael asked.

Az cradled his head against his knees, shivering, feeling violated and exposed. *Oh no. What did I say?* He couldn't remember, didn't know how badly he'd betrayed her. He waited, terrified.

"Worthless bits of nothing," Michael said. "Pathetic laments to her loyalties and love. He's bespelled over her."

Az's throat was ravaged, but he managed to get his voice. "I love her," he said. "She's not evil. Especially not compared to you."

Michael shook his head sadly. "Look what you've become. Selfish and misguided. Singing the praises of a damned girl, Azazel? Again?"

Az flinched.

"Michael," Raphael chided. "Frustration is blinding you to his pain. Can you not see how he suffers? Perhaps you should leave."

"You'd do well to remember he's not an innocent in all this," Michael said, and then slammed the iron door shut behind him.

Az waited almost a full minute before he sent out

thoughts to Raphael, words he didn't dare voice Upstairs. *If Gabriel is really supposed to destroy Eden, he should have done it already. He's failing, isn't he?*

The intensity in Raphael's stare sent a chill through Az. "You should know I'm not vulnerable to your manipulations, Azazel. I am aware of a lack of progress. Soon, other arrangements will have to be made."

"No," Az said, shaking his head. "You can't do that!" He swallowed hard and shut his mouth. *You'll damn him. It's different if Gabriel can't get to her, but you know full well if Eden ends at anyone else's hand, his promise* can't *be fulfilled.*

Even as the thoughts formed, Az froze. The reason behind Gabriel's seeming betrayal suddenly slipped into perfect clarity. Once the promise had been made to end her, none of the Bound could do it *but* Gabriel. He was protecting her the only way he knew how. A small smile flickered across Az's lips.

Well played, Gabe, he thought before he could help himself.

Raphael's face purpled with rage. "Misguided wretch," he snapped. As the angel stalked out into the hall, he snatched the blue sheet and took it with him. "If Gabriel chooses not to fulfill his promise to destroy the death breather, to sacrifice himself, I cannot stop him. I *can* assure you it will be in vain," he said over his shoulder. "If necessary, I'll end her myself."

CHAPTER 13

The ceiling twinkled with thousands of tiny lights. Kristen admired them as she slowly dropped down each step, drawing out her entrance. Her instructions on decorations had been executed flawlessly. The white gown she'd chosen to wear swirled around her, ethereal and flowing. Below, the room was frenetic. Sebastian's musical tastes veered toward bass-heavy dubstep, techno mixes of what she assumed were popular songs chopped up and spit back almost unrecognizable.

And the masks made a difference. With faces obscured by everything from simple cardboard to intricate works of beads, feathers, and ribbons, the Siders' hesitations were lost. They danced, chatted, and laughed, introduced one another to friends. The ball was everything Kristen could have hoped.

Only Erin sat alone in a corner. They had agreed not to tell anyone beside the leaders what had happened to

Zach until later, when the true planning began. As much as Kristen despised the idea, Zach's disappearance would draw them all together, solidify them in their fear of the Bound. Soon, the music would be stopped, and she'd read the speech she'd prepared.

They would fight. They would win. Together.

Madeline met her at the base of the stairs, matching her pace as Kristen wound her way toward Sebastian's post at the makeshift DJ booth. "Look at them and take a cue," she said, shoulder bumping against Kristen's. She kept her voice low enough that only Kristen would hear as she pointed to the Siders on the dance floor. "They're having fun. Go dance before we have to get all businesslike!"

Kristen snorted in contempt. For the first time, she took in the green velvet dress Madeline wore. The sleeves draped her wrists in wide bells of fabric. Gloves hid her hands. Even the mask she wore wasn't the simple eye style, but covered the upper two-thirds of her face. The only bare skin was her neckline. From it, a strand of emeralds sparkled so brightly they seemed to suck the glow from the stars on the ceiling. Kristen reached to admire it.

Madeline skittered back a step, her eyes suddenly wide. "I . . . I'd rather you didn't touch it." She laughed as she shook her head. "Sorry. It's new. Overreaction."

"I'd say." Kristen grabbed Madeline by her covered upper arm. The way the other girl winced didn't go unnoticed. *Why is she so worried about dropping her glamour?* Kristen wore gloves, and it no longer mattered who was more powerful, now that they were on the same team. Kristen narrowed her eyes. "Were I you, I'd start speaking. Now. What are you hiding?"

Madeline didn't struggle. "I was going to wait until after the ball. But—" She jerked her arm away. Her attention strayed from Kristen to the Siders milling around them. "Okay, at least agree this isn't the best place for me to be spilling secrets."

Kristen stared at her for a long second. "We'll go upstairs," she said.

Madeline's whole body was practically vibrating. "Jesus, Kristen, it's gonna change *everything*. It's just . . ." She laughed and clamped her hands over her mask to smother it. *She's telling me because she can't keep it a secret any longer.* The music swelled but couldn't drown out Madeline's excitement.

Kristen startled at a tap on her shoulder and spun around to find a guy there. His mask covered the entire left half of his face, but the visible eye was sightless and pale. *He must be wearing a special-effects contact,* she thought. Not one of her Siders. He raised a hand to the others swirling around them, then raised an eyebrow in question.

"No, thank you," she said, but he grabbed her around

the waist and spun her off into the crowd. In the shock of the moment, she caught only a blur of Madeline heading up the stairs, holding her gown so she didn't trip over it. When she passed by another Sider, she skirted closer to the banister and left a wide wake between them. At the top, she leaned over and found Kristen, then pointed toward the back stairs. She nodded to Madeline.

A new song began, this one a step down from the throbbing cacophony. Her partner wouldn't let her go.

One dance, Kristen thought angrily. She'd use it to make her way through the revelers, to the front door. Sneak around to the back entrance and put an end to the ridiculous theatrics.

Kristen let the guy guide her deeper into the crowd. At the center of the floor, he twirled her in a pirouette. He'd clearly had lessons at some point in his past. Despite herself, a smile broke across Kristen's face as her hand found his shoulder.

"You're good," she said, her feet slowly working them toward the door.

He pressured her backward, taking away the ground she'd gained with a quick flurry of steps. She gripped his arm to keep from stumbling. He winked over her shoulder and then released her.

An arm curled around her waist. With a spin she was off, captured, twirled from one partner to the next in a spiral of white fabric, faces passing in blurs of sequins and painted fleurs-de-lis until the song ended. Everything slowed, bass deepening to a steady heartbeat.

Her last partner's grip tightened instead of letting go. His mask had a long beak nose, decorated with black sequins and elaborate patterns of filigree, more macabre than celebratory. Appreciating the touch, she lifted her gaze.

Kristen faltered and he leaned in.

"You'd recognize me anywhere," Luke whispered. The beaked mask scraped across her cheek as he pulled away. His hand tightened on hers, the other falling to her hip, guiding her movements. "Keep dancing."

She swallowed, swaying stiffly to the music. Luke. A cascade of emotions roiled through her. "You shouldn't be here. Gabriel. Gabriel is coming, and he'll be here any moment." Her voice shook with the lie.

A teasing sort of pleasure danced in Luke's eyes. "You're concerned about me?" he asked as he rocked her to the beat.

Seeing him was worse than she'd ever imagined. Not because she was afraid of him, but because with Luke in front of her, the questions that plagued her rose up her throat. *Was it* all *a game? Every moment?* She hated herself for needing to know. As if it mattered what he felt as he'd manipulated her.

She scanned the crowd for help. Sebastian's DJ booth

was surrounded by a group of Siders, their faces full of laughter. *Look at me*, she begged silently. *Please, look up.* Luke's shoulder blocked her view as he turned her, moving them closer to the edge of the crowd. "I'd really rather you didn't make this . . . difficult."

The other Siders around her laughed and gossiped, parting to let them through. Not one noticed her distress. "What do you want?"

"You look troubled." Luke raised the hand he held, twirling her. "Enjoy this with me. And then," he said, ripping her roughly back into his arms, "we have unfinished business, you and I."

She let out a failed attempt at a haughty laugh. "Oh, trust me. Everything about us is quite finished."

He dropped her back in a deep swoop, bringing a gasp from her before he snapped her back against his chest. As the music swelled, she found her hand in his again.

"I thought so, too," he said. "Imagine my surprise at your invitation."

"I didn't invite you." She jerked away, but he had her around the waist. "Why on *Earth* would I want you here?"

"You mean to tell me you made it *this* easy for me to walk right through your front door with no intention of doing so?" He tsked his disappointment. "Admit it. You wanted me to show, in your heart of hearts. You were waiting for me. Searching."

"The masks weren't even my idea. Madeline wanted her Siders to . . ." Kristen fell silent before a bitter laugh burst from her. "Well played," she said. "But you called in a favor from Madeline, which would mean *you* wanted to see *me*, no?"

Luke's eyes sparkled behind their rim of black plaster. "Details."

He wanted to see me. Her breath hitched, but she covered it with a scoff. So what if Luke wanted to see her? He'd used her as a pawn. *And I never saw it coming,* she thought angrily. The flutter inside her from their banter fell away. Left behind was the same hollow ache she'd felt that night at Aerie. "I made my choice, Luke."

"Yes. But you chose wrong." As the song ended, he stopped their dance. "You also made a deal. With me."

She flashed back to her room upstairs, Luke on her bed. Gabriel's location in exchange for a favor from her. A simple promise Luke had cashed in for one week with her. A deal she'd broken when she left the club with Gabe.

The sure smile evaporated from her face.

Luke's soft chuckle sent a chill down her spine. "Now you remember."

She could beg for mercy, throw herself at his feet, but an outburst didn't suit either of their styles. That, and she wouldn't give him the satisfaction. "What happens now?" she asked.

"Two choices, just like before." He held up his fingers held up. "You leave with me, or you don't."

She licked her lips.

"Decide."

There had to be more to it than what he revealed. Luke was a poison, but she could draw him out before he did any damage. Perhaps, if she played her cards right, she could even do what Sebastian had suggested, get Luke to tell her how to kill angels. "I'll go," she whispered, her tone hesitant yet strong, already starting her game. "I'll go with you."

Instantly, he dropped a hand to the small of her back and bore her ahead of him to the front door.

"Luke, wait, it's freezing out," she said, even as he opened the door. The icy air stole her breath. "Why do we have to leave now? At least let me get my coat!"

But he rushed her down the walk. Halfway to the street, he grabbed her upper arm and hauled her off the stones and into the untouched lawn, where her dress draped across the growing snowdrifts.

"Damn it, what the hell is wrong with you?" she yelled, trying to high step. "You're hurting me!" Her heels sank, and she stumbled in the deep snow. Luke only caught her enough to ease her fall into the bushes lining the boundary of her yard. A cascade of snow powdered her dress. Only the deep ruts of their footprints marred the pristine snowscape. As she watched, the holes their feet had left quickly started to fill in until any trace of her and Luke's route had vanished. No slide marks from her stumbles, no wide stance where Luke had braced her. "What the hell?"

"Now no one will find us." He laughed, pressing her further into the scratching evergreens. "Are you ready for your punishment?"

The words brought a hard gasp from her, clouding in the frigid air between them and mixing with his breath. As it drifted away, she was left staring into his pitch-dark eyes.

And then he was behind her, one hand cupped suddenly over her mouth, the other arm squeezed around her. She fought, but his hold was viselike, tight enough to bruise.

"You have to be quiet," he demanded in a harsh whisper, turning her toward the house. Her nostrils flared as she struggled to get oxygen.

A figure appeared on her porch, popping into existence midstride.

At a barely audible thunk, her gaze flew upward. Luke's hand dropped, but she didn't make a sound. Three more figures alighted along the peak of her roof.

"Someone tipped off the Bound to your ball," Luke breathed into her ear. "And they've learned how to destroy Siders. They've come to exterminate."

"No!" She yanked against his hold, gaining a few inches before he pulled her back into the camouflage of the bushes and covered her mouth again.

His voice hissed in her ear. "Shut up before they find you, too."

The front door opened as an angel entered. A shadow slipped down the chimney.

The music stopped just as the screams started. Piercing. A loud wail and then the sound of shattering glass. After that she couldn't tell the screams apart. Sebastian was inside, Madeline, Erin, Vaughn. All the others. They were there because of her.

"Shhh," Luke cooed, stroking her hair as he held her up and against him. "Watch. Don't you dare look away."

Shadows passed behind the lace curtains of the windows. Someone stumbled out of the house, onto the porch, and one of the shapes on the roof flicked out of existence. A second later, it was only a step behind a Sider running full tilt for the street. The angel shoved the boy's shoulder, sent him off the path on the opposite side of where she and Luke stood against the bushes. Snow flew as the Sider went into a frantic crawl. He didn't get far before he was flipped over onto his back. His pleas echoed in the still night.

A mechanical chitter filled the yard. At first she thought it was only noise until the word "abomination" broke out. The angel straddled the fallen boy, one leg on each side, and lifted his arms. Fingers spread, his hands plunged downward. She heard the crack of bones before a gargling scream reached her, the Sider's rib cage split wide, the angel's fists groping inside. In her horror, she stepped back into Luke.

Bright white light shone between the angel's gore-covered fingers. Kristen squinted, trying to figure out what she was seeing. Fire burst from the center of his palms and fell like drops, hissing in the snow. A moment later, the flames dimmed and then went out. What was left of the Sider disintegrated, nothing more than a gray mark marring the snow.

"*Seraphim* means 'burning ones.' Fitting, no?" Luke's arms were still tight around her, his voice barely a whisper in her ear. "They've learned to pull out your soul. Destroy it. No chance to go Upstairs or Down." The house was still full of screams.

"You got me out," she said in awe as Luke turned her toward him. "You saved me."

"Instead of warning you." He ran a finger down her cheek. "I guess that makes us even."

The horror of his words slammed into her.

From the corner of her eye, she saw the angel's head snap up, twist toward them. He came toward them at a loping run. She flinched, and Luke leaped in front of her, a snarl rumbling through him.

The angel slowed. "Only when the boy was dead could I taste her terror." His words shivered through her like nails on a chalkboard. "Her kind is unclean. She spreads seeds of plague. Stand aside, Lucifer."

"No closer, slave." Under the leather jacket he wore, Luke's shoulders rippled. Black steam hissed from the seams, out the collar and arms, and then sunk to the snow like a low, heavy fog. Rolling and bubbling, it reached Kristen and oozed over her shoes. She kicked, trying in vain to keep it off as it climbed up her legs in tendrils of darkness.

The angel didn't stop. "The orders of a Fallen mean nothing."

The bottom of Kristen's dress disappeared under the inky blackness. Luke pressed his hand against her stomach. "You'd let them all escape for the sake of this one?" he asked. "Are those *your* orders?" He jutted his chin toward the house. A group of four Siders was tearing across the yard.

The angel in front of her and Luke wavered. "Our orders are to end them on sight. I've seen her."

"You've seen them now, too."

The black fog crested over her hips, coating her with a liquid warmth. *Luke wouldn't save you only to kill you.* She couldn't trust him, though. She brushed at one of the tendrils, and it wrapped around her wrist, spiraled up her arm. Wisps stretched toward her neck, her jaw. Kristen fought to move, but at her feet the dense fog felt more like tar.

Luke's voice stayed calm and collected as he spoke to the Bound. "My wrath surrounds her. You won't break through before the others are gone." He pointed to two more Siders sprinting across the lot. "You've allowed four to escape already. Four to spread the plague instead of one. There go two more." For the first time, the Bound angel looked uncertain. "I wonder," Luke mused, "if you'll be punished?"

With one last glance at Kristen, the Bound disappeared. The Sider across the yard stumbled as the angel popped into existence beside him.

At Kristen's feet, the black fog dissipated, releasing her. Luke took her hand as it gathered back into him. From the house came the sound of a window breaking. "Some party," he said.

The screams were louder now, and with them came a crackling. A glimmering orange glow shone from beyond the shattered glass.

Kristen took a step toward it in disbelief.

"Is that fire?"

A ball of flame burst from the second story of her house.

CHAPTER 14

Madeline checked her watch, annoyed and jittery with anticipation. Any second now, Kristen would show, and Madeline would tell her what she'd done, the glorious leap of faith she'd taken. God, how it'd paid off.

She peeled the dress up her leg, revealing her thigh and the gash stinging fiercely there. Maybe Jackson had been right about cutting too deep. Unhealed, it wept fresh blood through three Band-Aids.

She slipped her cell phone from her cleavage. Jackson hadn't been happy to stay home and guard the girl, but there wasn't simply Kristen's reaction to worry about. Luke had only yesterday told her he wanted the Siders kept around. And Madeline's discovery would make Luke, too, an enemy.

She flipped the phone open and keyed in a quick text to Jackson, trying to calm her nerves. *Not missing anything.*

Muted through the door, the music from the party was

bordering on creepy, the singer's wail fading in and out. The beats stopped suddenly, but the stricken cry went on.

Music's worse than normal, she texted.

At the base of the stairs, the door to the outside opened. A frigid draft teased her curls as Madeline stood. The hemline of her dress slipped down, the fabric catching on her Band-Aids before draping her ankle again. "Kristen?"

A footstep creaked on the old boards, then another at the same time. Madeline froze. "Who's with you?" she asked. Her voice echoed in the tiny space. She couldn't see around the spiral of the staircase. She lowered herself a step, bracing on the wall to get a glance around the bend. *Please don't be Luke.* She hadn't seen him, had counted on talking to Kristen before he and the Fallen made their appearance. If he'd shown, and she'd missed him, it would explain Kristen's delay. *He can't know what I've done,* Madeline thought.

Run. Now. The thought beat harder with each moment she waited. In a few steps she could be out of the enclosed staircase and in the upstairs hall.

The wailing music had gotten louder, more off-key. It sounded almost like . . .

Screaming.

Launching up the stairs, Madeline grabbed the knob, but the door was ripped out of her grip. She dove forward, past the figure in the doorway. He grabbed her by the neck and lifted her.

"Please," she choked, hanging helpless. She clawed at the hand, but her gloves made her nails useless. "Please, I can't breathe!" She pointed her toes, trying to find ground. Maroon irises bored into her. *Bound.*

With a dramatic choking noise, she rolled her eyes back and went limp. Her limbs twitched to fight, punch, survive as he shook her once, hard. And then his fingers loosened. With everything she had, Madeline swung her leg into his crotch.

The angel tossed her backward. Flying down the steps, she slammed into the wall, her shoulder popping out of place. When she hit the landing, pain radiated through her rib cage, so intense she couldn't get air.

The Bound who'd grabbed hold of her descended the stairs even as two others came up from below. "End her," he rasped, still bent from her kick. "Quickly. They mustn't be allowed to escape."

"Stop!" she croaked. "I'm not one of them." She held a hand up, agony shooting through her chest. "I'm not. A Sider. I swear."

A face appeared suddenly before her. She flinched, jarring ribs that must be broken. She could smell the angel, a thick scent like wood smoke that tickled at the back of her throat. She clenched her jaw, didn't dare move.

"We know what you are. We watched you well, Madeline."

The broken sound of her name made her cringe. "Don't hurt me. I helped Gabriel. Please. Ask him. I'm on your side."

Silence. The angel she'd kicked plodded down the stairs.

"See to the others," he said quietly. His two companions loped past. When the door at the top of the stairs opened, a cloud of acrid smoke rolled across the ceiling.

"Oh my God," she whispered.

"No." He tottered closer, his steps uneven. "Not your God."

Panic knotted in her stomach.

"Madeline." A low, sharp crackle came from his mouth. "Tell me how the plague began."

I don't know, she thought. *Should I lie?* A thump shook through the floorboards above her head. Something hammered against the door. She curled up, hiding her face. If he was going to kill her, she didn't want to see, didn't want to know it was coming. Cold sweat poured off her. *I'm going into shock,* she realized. The angel kneeling next to her made a pitying noise.

Fingers stabbed into her shattered ribs, squeezing. Madeline screamed. Black dots sparkled in front of her as she fought against losing consciousness.

"Stop!" she sobbed. Warmth spilled down her side.

"Brief pain, then nothing," he said as if to console her.

"Gabe will speak for me!" Blinking away tears, she grabbed for his wrist. "I'm his friend. Tell Gabe. I fixed everything," she said. *I'm mortal now.*

The hands on her froze, and she let her own fall away. They'd bring Gabe to her and he'd make the pain stop and it would be okay. *Where's Luke?* she thought. He'd save her. She'd make a deal with him. Anything he wanted.

"You *dare* ask Gabriel to speak against his own kind while you stay loyal to *Lucifer?*" She tried to lift her head, but the angel pressed down on her shoulder. "You'd brand Gabriel a traitor to lure him back to darkness? It will never be."

He shoved her hard. The back of Madeline's head cracked against the wood stair. Her vision swam as the Bound angel drew back a hand.

"Please," she said.

His fist plunged down.

CHAPTER 15

Gabriel walked down the street alone. He'd tried to ride the subway, hoping the constant swaying of the cars would settle him. But once he'd gone through the turnstile, dark thoughts from when he'd been Fallen surfaced, fragmented and out of focus. He couldn't explain the cold sweat he'd gotten from standing on the platform. Before the train even pulled into the station, he decided to walk.

He couldn't bear to stay with the other Bound, knowing the Sider in the prisonlike room was there because of him. Gabe had heard screams, tried to tune them out, but what his ears had blocked out, his conscience kept loud. *Don't break,* he'd begged Zach without saying a word. *Don't tell them where Eden is, if you know.* When they finally decided Zach had given them all he knew, Gabe had taken off.

He looked up to find he'd walked almost twelve avenue blocks and wound up in front of Milton's. A sheet of plywood covered a window. The door was locked, the establishment closed. He rested his forehead against the iron gate over it for a beat and looked in through the glass of the door. Inside, the tables had been tossed around, and a dark splotch of dried blood stained the entryway. Gabe turned away.

He crossed the street and headed through the alley, drawing out his walk to Eden's. Checking the apartment without her there to report back to the Bound should take some pressure off. Yet, even though it wasn't a lie, he felt like a liar. The faint taste of sulfur hadn't left him in almost a day.

When he came out of the alley, a girl looked down at him from above. She'd sprawled out halfway up by the time he made it around the side of the stairs.

"You a Sider?" He said it without thinking.

"You need Touch?" she asked. Gabe hesitated only a second before nodding.

Her braids bounced with each stair as she came down to meet him. "You pay me first, then I lose the protection," she said, holding out a gloved hand. "Twenty. Unless you want to double up. That's thirty."

Gabe reached into his pocket. "What is Touch exactly?" he said, without taking out the money. "How does it work?"

She snapped her gum. "Magic."

"No, really," he pressed.

For the first time, the girl seemed to be sizing him up. She took a step back.

"What'll forty bucks get me?" he asked quickly, and just like he'd hoped, her eyes met his. The fear dropped away from her. Gabe eased closer. "There we go," he whispered as the girl's eyelids drooped, the connection taking. "Whose crew are you with?"

"Madeline's," she slurred. A frown dug deep. "Madeline would want me to pass to you because you seem so sad."

Gabe flinched, almost broke eye contact, but stopped himself. "Were you on Touch before you became a Sider?" She didn't answer. He gave the girl's shoulder a gentle squeeze, and forced himself to use the information she'd given him. "Did the Touch make you sad like me, and then you became a Sider?"

"I was alive once," she said. "I had so many things I wanted to do. . . . So many things and then it all kind of just . . ." She wiggled her gloved fingers in front of her and then splayed them. "Poof. And now there's nothing. I have to get rid of Touch." The vacant misery in her invaded him, gripped his bones like a parasite and dug in. He slammed his eyes shut, so unnerved he almost missed her whisper. "It has nowhere to go because I can't use it."

Gabe snapped alert. "You can't use it yourself," he said. "All those things you were *supposed to do* . . ."

On the stair, the girl seemed to be coming out from

under the influence of his sway. "It's twenty bucks for a dose," she said, an edge to her voice that hadn't been there seconds before.

"Forget it," Gabe said distractedly, tossing the cash he had in his pocket to her anyway. "Take this and get out of here. Don't come back, understand?"

"Hey!" she called after him, but he didn't turn back.

Mortals' paths led them from one event to the next, their whole lives planned out in branches of choices. And without paths, the Siders seemed paused. "And all that potential has to go somewhere," Gabe said to himself. "That's what Touch is."

A thought sparked in his mind. The Siders Eden had sent Upstairs had gone on passing Touch, passing potential to souls that shouldn't have had any. The souls Upstairs then disappeared. *They're not* disappearing, *though,* he realized. *They're reincarnating.*

"Holy shit," he blurted.

A disgusted sound just behind him broke through his stupor. "Such unbecoming language," Raphael admonished.

Gabriel stared at him, face blank. *He saw me let the girl go,* Gabe thought. *I'm screwed.* "Please, let me explain," he said. "It's not what you think."

"And what do I think?" Raphael asked. "What *should* I think? That you're not acting like one of us? That you're

releasing Siders instead of ending them? An offense pun-
ishable, Gabriel."

Fear lanced through Gabe. He was so close to figuring
it all out. Could feel it. "No. Don't turn me in. Please," he
said, grabbing for Raphael.

"There are others who have given up on you, Gabriel,
but I refuse. Perhaps to a fault." Gabe shook his head as if
to reassure him, but Raphael went on. "You must end the
death breather, Gabriel. The time has come."

I can't.

"You can," Raphael said. "She'll be weak when you get
to her."

Gabe froze. "What did you do?"

"Her injuries will be enough that she won't escape you
again."

"No, you don't understand." Panic sped through him.
They were hurting Eden, knowing he wouldn't be able
to resist his promise with her weakened. But from what
he'd seen at her apartment, even bruises had the potential
to kill her. "Tell me where she is," he demanded. When
Raphael didn't answer, Gabe took him by the shoulders.
"I'll be Damned if I don't get to her in time."

Raphael nodded sadly. "Indeed you will. And that
choice is yours, Gabriel. Choose wisely."

"I will! I *will*! Tell me where she is," he begged. When
Raphael rattled off the location, Gabriel's heart sank. He'd

never been to the alley Raphael named, so he couldn't travel there instantly. Gabe drew up a mental map of lower Manhattan, searching for the closest place.

The abandoned building. Eden was only a few blocks from where the Bound gathered. *What the hell is she doing there?* he thought, but it didn't matter. From the building to that alley would be a two-minute run. *I can save her.*

If I make it in time.

CHAPTER 16

Az didn't look up when someone knocked on the door of his cell. Instead, his hand went under his thigh. Tucked there were the crumbled pieces of three keys. Though each was stronger than the last, the metal had still broken apart when he'd tried them in the lock. "You come to gloat? To tell me she's dead?" he asked. "Or did Gabriel Fall?"

"I've come to talk," Michael said through the small barred window. "I've been made aware of certain *theories* you harbor."

The comments were vague. If any of the Bound were seriously debating Gabriel's intentions, they weren't speaking it aloud any more than necessary. Az didn't look up. Though the connection couldn't take unless he wanted it to, he wouldn't be trapped by Michael a second time.

"He has the strength to end her," Michael said.

"He'll never forgive himself if he does."

"A fact that unfortunately bears more credence," he said finally. "I do not wish Gabriel lost to me again. Not when I can save him pain. If he's prevented from killing her until she dies on her own . . ."

Careful to keep his expression empty, Az lifted his head. Michael gripped the bars of the window. Blood coated his fingers, ran in smears up his wrists. "What have you done?" Az whispered.

"The Siders are being exterminated. Your death breather can't go on without them," Michael said. *She's still alive,* Az thought. The blood on Michael's hands proved others hadn't been so lucky. "Death comes no matter what foolish sacrifices are made in her name. You would truly relinquish glory for the temporary pleasure of her, Azazel?"

"She's smart. She'll escape. Survive." Az didn't waver. He met Michael's gaze. "And she's never been temporary to me."

Michael rotated his head slowly to the side, studying Az.

"Just like Gabriel's never been temporary to you," Az said. The slight flinch from Michael was all he needed. Az stood. "He will never be the same after. You know it as much as I do. Don't make Gabriel do this."

Michael's grip tightened on the bars. "Yesterday, we snared a Sider who knew your precious death breather.

Plucked thoughts of her from his head like grapes. We learned much before we gave him his peace."

"Who was it?" Az asked shakily. Jarrod's face swam into his thoughts. It could have been anyone.

"He made her beverages and gave her shelter. She and her two Siders hide within his walls. We'll use her sickness to draw her out. Inexistence creeps nearer to her every moment."

Zach, Az realized. His shoulders slumped. The Bound had been at Milton's. *I'll destroy them if they lay a finger on her.* "If anyone ends Eden but Gabe—"

"I tell you of what we know," Michael said, cutting him off. "So that you may take my words to heart. Gabriel stays in the mortal realms for *you*, Azazel. He feels duty bound to keep you from Falling fully." Michael lowered his voice to a whisper. "Yet your death breather held you balanced while Gabriel was blackmarked, did it not? You don't need him. I want him returned to glory." Michael's eyes danced with his fervor. "What is your love worth?" he said with a sneer. "You seek freedom; you desire your Eden? Then cut loose the ties binding Gabriel to the mortal realms." He dropped his hands. "If you wish a chance to save her, the price is Gabriel. Is she worth it to you?"

Az ran a hand through his curls. "I . . ."

Rust red swirled in Michael's irises. He stepped farther back into the hall as if he didn't want Az to see. "How can you hesitate?" Michael pressed. "Choose to save her, and give me back my Gabriel."

A tremor passed through Az. It felt like a trick. "What about what Gabe wants?"

Michael went on as if he hadn't spoken. "She'll be attacked. Weakened. Once he's close to her in that state, Gabriel won't be able to resist the compulsion."

Az knew his irises must be crimson at the rage inside him. *Let him see,* he thought, but Michael showed no reaction. "Why are you doing this?"

"They're already luring her, Azazel. Moments until she sheds blood."

Az's wings flared. Feathers scraped against the walls as they spread to fill the room. "Open the door, Michael," he said.

"A promise Upstairs is binding, even if you're not Bound."

With a single pump of his wings, Az was across the room. He slammed his fists against the metal. "Open the door!"

"You're to convince Gabriel to return Home permanently." Michael went on, urgency in his voice. "Swear it, Azazel, and freedom is yours. Stay silent, and she'll be ash in moments."

"Gabriel will leave the mortal realms," Az said, cautious. Curling his fingers around the bars, Az made his choice. "He'll come back Upstairs. Permanently. You have my promise or my life."

Michael dug for a key as he spoke. "The rest of the Bound are slaughtering the Siders at a soiree in the Bronx," he said. He held up a bloodstained hand. "Gabriel is too late to save them, but you can use the information to send him away. Break his compulsion long enough for you to escape with your death breather."

"It's done? They killed the Siders there?" Az asked, his heart in his throat. "Kristen's dead?"

Michael looked nonplussed as the lock clicked. "Such an effort to tell them apart, and no gain. The genocide is in progress."

He swung the door open.

"How fast can those wings carry you, Azazel? Faster than fate?" Michael asked.

A thousand curses rushed to his lips, but there wasn't time. Az rushed past Michael and into the hall.

From just behind him, he heard Michael's whisper, a single word. "Fly."

CHAPTER 17

The phone call had caught Eden off guard. She'd been expecting Madeline. But it was a Sider on the other end, one who'd sounded ragged and desperate, too scared to come to them. He'd given her somewhere to meet, an alley off a street in the Financial District. A short subway ride away.

Every corner they came around, Jarrod stopped her and Sullivan, insisting on checking ahead. If the Bound spotted them, no amount of running would help this time.

"Clear," he said, keeping a few yards in front of them. They took a side street, then another before heading down the alley. The Sider had told her it hooked right in an L shape. They wouldn't be bothered. He would meet them there. Halfway down, a single light shone to guide their way. Rats scurried without fear. The patters of their feet against plastic trash bags set Eden's skin crawling.

"Let's hurry," she said to Jarrod.

Eden glanced back at Sullivan and noticed her clutching

her stomach. When she realized Eden was watching, she dropped her hand and gave her head the slightest shake, a silent plea in her eyes.

A good twenty feet in front of them, Jarrod looked back as he went around the corner. Eden waited until he was definitely out of earshot before she spun on Sullivan.

"How long?" Eden demanded. She grabbed Sullivan's hand and twisted it over, but even in the creases, the palms were free of ashes.

"It's just a stomachache. So far." The note of panic in her voice told Eden otherwise. Sullivan's skin looked clammy, almost green. She hissed through clenched teeth.

"What's it feel like? Stabbing?" Eden asked. She glanced down the alley to be sure Jarrod hadn't ventured back. "How long, Sullivan?"

"Yesterday, I promise. That's it."

Eden squeezed her shoulder gently. She knew all too well the agony Sullivan was going through. "It'll pass. Give it a second."

Hugging her stomach, Sullivan doubled over. "I have to tell him," she whispered. "I just don't know how."

"Don't panic." Eden rubbed Sullivan's palm again. "We'll tell him after we're done here. You've got at least a few days, though. The pains won't get much worse unless you're injured."

A crunch of footsteps echoed through the alley. Two

figures passed under the dim light ahead of them, but neither was Jarrod.

Sullivan straightened. "Where is he?"

"I don't know," Eden said. Something was wrong. "Stay calm. We've got this." She spotted a fist-sized chunk of asphalt against the wall. Toeing it, she said Sullivan's name and drew her attention to it. Eden shuffled forward until the broken asphalt was behind her.

"Eden?" Sullivan's whisper was cautious.

Eden had been alone in the alley at the apartment nearly every day, brought Siders she didn't know into it for months without feeling any danger. as she stared at the guys creeping toward her, something inside her shifted. *They're not Bound,* she thought. *But are they Fallen?*

The two guys stopped just in front of Eden and Sullivan. Eden met their steely gazes, and one of them sneered, skin crinkling around predatory eyes. The reaction wasn't what she was used to. Usually the Siders who found her seemed grateful, or afraid, or desperate. On the phone, his voice had broken.

She waited, but neither said a word. She fought the urge to avert her eyes, knowing it would make her look weaker.

One of the guys was tall and reeked of trouble, from his baggy jeans to the tattoos decorating the visible skin of his neck and knuckles. A cliché street thug. The other was younger, and looked naïve enough to seem out of place.

Almost timid. And then he opened his mouth. "So you're the little girl with the good shit? They say you're picky about who you give it to."

Eden froze.

"You're not gonna be picky with me, are you?" he asked.

They weren't Siders. Or angels. They were junkies, the way Sullivan used to be. Eden curled her hands into fists and shoved them into her pockets, grateful for her gloves. She couldn't afford to give up any Touch. In her peripheral vision, she saw Sullivan bend down to pick up the asphalt and hide it behind her back.

Eden shrugged her shoulders, trying to keep the attention on her. "You misled me on the phone."

The tattooed one laughed, but the younger one silenced him with a punch to the shoulder.

"Look, I'm sorry," she said, trying to keep her voice even and nonchalant. "We're not selling. It's not—"

The younger one leaped at her.

"Jarrod!" Sullivan screamed.

Fingers dug into Eden's cheeks. "Give me the fucking Touch," he snarled. Droplets of spit dotted her face. "I was told *exactly* where to find you. I don't have time for your games, bitch!"

"I don't have any to give." She tasted blood as his grip ground the inside of her cheek against her teeth.

"Bullshit." He shoved her against the wall without

warning. Her back hit hard, the air rushing out of her. If he'd been a Sider, her exhale would have killed him.

He didn't even flinch. Against a mortal, the powers that made other Siders fear her were worthless. He heaved her from the bricks and slammed her against them again. This time Eden didn't hold back her cry. Where was Jarrod?

"I have some!" Sullivan screamed suddenly. The tattooed guy turned to her. Sullivan swung toward his temple with the rock. He ducked and caught the blow in the shoulder. His fingers slid across Sullivan's bare hand as he knocked the rock away. It clattered across the ground to Eden.

"Give me more," he said. Sullivan backed away slowly.

Eden shook her head. "Don't."

The word barely escaped before a punch whipped her head sideways, dropped her. Her vision blurred as she struggled to her hands and knees.

The tattooed guy grabbed Sullivan by the arm. "Dose me again!" he demanded.

"She lied. She doesn't have any more," Eden ground out. A boot met her stomach in a swift kick. She moaned as she curled reflexively into a ball even as the younger guy ruthlessly pried her limbs apart. His weight crushed low on Eden's hips. Snagging her wrist, he ripped the glove from her hand, splitting her knuckles open as he grated them against the iced ground. Touch passed from her fingertips.

Eden felt him change position on top of her, fumbling lower, digging at her thighs. She wanted to fight, to push him away, but he was too strong. "Where is it? I know you've got cash."

Her stomach clenched hard. She retched, but all that came out was a cloud of ashes. *They're going to kill me*, she realized. *They're going to kill me and they don't even realize it.* "Please," she begged. "Please, you have to stop."

To her surprise, the guy on top of her froze.

Eden raised a hand to her face, wiping cheeks smeared with a mix of blood and ash as she turned her head. Feet away, where no one had been a second ago, stood Gabe. Her mind blanked out, short-circuiting between fear and relief. Something was in his hand, a bat or a crowbar. It glinted viciously in the weak light. "Don't touch her," he snarled.

"You don't wanna make this your problem," the one on top of her threatened.

"Oh, yes I do." Gabe's eyes flared red as he disappeared, then he flashed back just in front of them. "Don't touch her."

His thug friend bolted past them. Scuttling off her and to his feet, he took off after.

The instant they were gone, Gabe dropped down next to her. The last time she'd seen Gabe, he'd given Jarrod a note. *Don't leave Eden alone with me*, it'd said. She tried to turn, to claw away from him, but she couldn't get her limbs to move. Everything felt so heavy. "Jarrod," she croaked. "Help."

"You're okay," Gabe said. "Eden, it's me." The chunk of broken asphalt dug into her hip. "You're . . ." His voice lowered, a slow swirl starting in his eyes as he took her in. His breaths came faster, cut off as he curled his hands into fists and dropped them at his sides. "Sullivan," he called over his shoulder, "you all right?"

"Bruises," she answered. "Is she okay?"

For a split second, Gabe seemed to come back to himself and turned to Sullivan. "Jarrod's around the corner. He wasn't moving. Go to him."

Eden heard her struggling, but kept glued to Gabe, afraid to look away. "Don't leave me," she said weakly, but already she heard Sullivan's footsteps fade.

"Shhh, I won't leave you," Gabe murmured to Eden, his fingers gentle on her cheek. "You're hurt bad." His stare blanked out, the words barely a whisper. "I couldn't let them kill you. I don't want to. . . ."

She curled her hand around a rock. She didn't know if she had the strength to hit him hard enough to get away. *I can do it,* she thought. His gaze dipped to her side. *He knows.* With the slightest nod, he leaned forward, tilted at an angle that would give her the best shot. She could feel him trembling.

"Don't, Gabriel!" The voice echoed off the buildings.

It can't be, Eden thought, stunned. Gabe didn't turn toward where she'd seen Jarrod disappear. He looked up. Eden followed his lead. She couldn't make out anything in the darkness, and then suddenly Az's wings flared wide enough to fill the alley, breaking his dive. His legs swung wildly as he pumped the wings again. Hitting the ground in a crouch, Az used the momentum to shove Gabe and knock him off her.

Gabe skittered back, staring at Eden in horror. "I didn't." He glanced up at Az, his eyes yellowed and wide. "I didn't do it."

She tried to say Az's name, but nothing would come. *He's here. He's really here.*

"You're alive," he said, almost as if he couldn't believe it. His thumb stroked her split lip and then broke away to brush her bangs back.

"Oh my God," she whispered, covering her face. Her hands shook against skin slick with blood. Az's arms wrapped around her, pulling her against his chest. She clung to him.

"Shhh," Az whispered, cradling her. "I'm here. It's over."

She dropped into the crook of his arm as the horrible taste of ashes and rot filled her mouth. *No,* she begged. *Ten seconds. Just give me ten more seconds with him.* But already everything inside her writhed in agony. Eden heard Jarrod and Sullivan coming and moved just enough to see them. As they came closer, she saw how Jarrod limped, leaning heavily on Sullivan. *They're both all right, though,* Eden thought.

Gabe cowered against the brick wall.

"I know you didn't do this," Az said to him. He held out a hand. With a sigh of relief, Gabe took it. "The Bound betrayed you. They set you up to find her hurt and to keep you from—"

"How did you get here?" Gabe asked. His eyes wavered back to Eden, broke away again.

"They attacked Kristen's," Az said.

Gabe's grip tightened. "No. When?" he asked as Eden fought to sit up.

"Help them," she wheezed.

"There was a ball tonight," Jarrod said from next to them. He clamped one arm to his chest. His wrists had bruises so dark they were black. He'd fought hard. "Everyone went."

"Go to Kristen's, Gabe," Az said. "I've got this."

With a pop, the air swirled a tornado of snow, and the space where Gabriel had been was empty. Eden fought to get enough air to speak. "Are they all right?" she asked.

When Az loosened his grip, Eden's head drooped back before she could catch it. Her vision blurred, gritty with ashes.

"I'm here. I've got you," Az whispered, lifting her up again. She knew he still held her hand, but things had gone fuzzy. Her lungs felt like they'd been dipped in drying concrete.

"Oh, Eden, no." The terror on Az's face almost broke her, but she wouldn't let herself look away. "No, I made it on time. You're okay!" Az juggled her into his arms. "We have to get somewhere safe."

Leaning in close to his chest, Eden listened to his thudding heartbeat. It took all her strength, but she got an arm around his neck, felt his skin, cool beneath her feverish fingers.

"They knew you guys were staying at Zach's," Az said. "The Bound are in the Bronx. They won't expect us to go back to your apartment." His grip on her tightened as he lurched to his feet.

She felt a tremor pass through Az's shoulders as he unfurled his wings. "Sullivan, can you and Jarrod make it there yourselves?" he asked.

Eden heard Jarrod arguing, but the words seemed to skip and bounce, unrecognizable. Blinking, she tried to focus, but everything blanched to gray.

For a moment there was nothing, and then Az's voice pulled her out of the darkness. "Stay with me!"

It's too late, Eden thought. She lost her grip on Az, her hands falling away.

There was a scream. A rush of air when Az launched into the sky.

And then there was nothing.

CHAPTER 18

The orange glow of flames lit the hazy smoke-filled lawn. Half of Kristen's second floor was engulfed by the fire. *I'm too late.* Gabriel's stomach curdled.

He pictured himself near the door to the back stairs. Cold air rushed through him, and he materialized there with his face nearly pressed against the hot glass. He cupped his hands and stared in between them. The stair-well was pitch-black.

When he opened the door, smoke swirled out, burning his throat, but Gabe could see no fire on the wooden stairs.

She's dead. A terrible thought crossed his mind, that he'd run over what was left of Kristen as he searched the house, grinding the ashes of her into the carpet as he passed. He tucked an arm over his mouth and nose, and started to climb the stairs as he heard distant sirens. He'd check her room and whatever else he could before the firefighters arrived. He rounded the corner, feeling his way in the dark the same as he'd done a dozen times before.

He kicked something that bounced against the trim with a hollow thunk. When he stooped down to pick it up, he was surprised to find a phone. *Light,* he thought, pressing the buttons so that the display illuminated in a pale glow. He swept it out in front of him. Just around the turn of the stairs, a heeled shoe hung over the edge of a step. Gabriel jumped toward it. The light found a face, eyes open and staring blindly.

"Madeline!" he cried out in surprise. He fell to her, swiping curls from her face. The skin under his finger was slick. She didn't move. Didn't blink. "Oh no," he whispered. "Madel—" A choked gasp caught in his throat. The middle of her chest was caved in, a jagged hole where her breastbone had been. Gabriel stared in horror. *But she's not ash.*

"Come on, Madeline. We have to go." Sliding an arm underneath her neck, he tried to move her, to lift her. Her head lolled. The blood that had pooled in her mouth spilled onto his legs. "Oh no, sweetheart."

He tried to wipe her cheek clean, but his own bloody fingers only made things worse. *They took her heart out. They took her soul.* She couldn't be alive. *But why is her body still here?* When Siders ended, they disintegrated.

Above him, he could hear the thump of water spraying the roof, the hiss as it hit hot coals.

He had to go.

Tucking the phone into his pocket with a shaking hand, Gabriel closed his eyes and pictured Kristen's room. Madeline's fingers were still laced in his when he phased out. He came back a second later alone and leaning against Kristen's bed. "Hello?" he whispered.

"She's not here." The voice startled him. He turned toward the angel behind him. The face he knew so well, had once delighted in seeing, now sent sorrow coiling through him.

"Were you with them, Michael?" Gabriel collapsed onto the bed. The blood on his hands, Madeline's blood, smeared onto the comforter. "Did you kill my friends?"

Michael hissed a warning as he arched his neck toward the closed door. "Careful words, Gabriel. There are others about. You're being foolish."

When Michael took a step toward him, Gabriel bolted off the bed and stumbled against the dresser. "Raphael sent me after Eden. Because you didn't want me to stop you here!" He wiped his hand across his cheek and nose without thinking. His sticky fingers skipped across the skin. "Madeline risked everything to help me when I was Fallen. She's the reason I knew everything I told Raphael about Downstairs. You killed her, didn't you?" Gabriel's eyes flicked down to Michael's hands. They were still covered in blood.

Michael's own gaze fell to Gabe's fingers. "You, too." A thrill of what seemed like hope trilled in his voice as he asked, "Is the death breather finished?"

Gabe flexed his hands. The drying maroon near his knuckles cracked, showing clean skin underneath. Outside the door, fire crackled. He had a vision of Kristen in the very room in which they stood, painting her toenails at the vanity, her long dark hair running down her back.

"I thought I had done you a kindness by not allowing you to participate here. It seems you don't see it as such," Michael said, his voice awash in disappointment. "You look at me as a monster for doing pleasing works. For cleansing the Earth of a plague threatening the mortals. The Siders *will* be driven to extinction, Gabriel. They are not your friends." Michael shook his head slowly. "Your part ceases with the completion of your task. End Eden. Come home. I can't shelter you any more than I have."

"Shelter me?" Gabe blurted in disgust. Anguish bubbled inside him, threatening to take over. *Gone,* he thought. *Madeline's gone. Kristen's gone. How many others?* Michael had taken them away, just as he'd tried to take Az away so long ago. "Tell me if Kristen still exists," he whispered.

"Shhh."

Gabriel stilled. Michael would relish telling him she was gone. *So why isn't he answering?*

Hope tried to burrow in, but Gabe wouldn't let it, wouldn't be able to stand it if he was wrong. *Please let her be safe.* Gabe sent out a thought. *Please, tell me where she is.* He grabbed Michael by the neck. He smelled the same as he had centuries ago, like a fall breeze. *Did you spare her for me?*

"The answer will only cause you pain," Michael said, leaning in to brush a delicate kiss against Gabe's cheek.

I thought you'd help her. I thought you'd do that for me.

"She did escape, Gabriel."

Gabe jerked back.

"With Lucifer," Michael finished.

Hope and horror left Gabe stricken. "At least she's away from you," he said.

"Gabriel, you are dimming. Is it not enough to act as if the Sider plague is somehow salvageable, now you endorse one who takes up with *Lucifer*?"

"This," Gabe said quietly, "is not right." He walked past Michael to the sounds of glass and wood breaking, the firefighters entering through the front of the house.

Michael snatched his arm. "Gabriel, you must let them go."

The truth passed Gabe's lips before he thought to stop it. "I can't."

He closed his eyes, smoke passing through him as he transferred to the backyard, near the bushes. Red, blue, and white lights burst across the burning house. Flames crackled through holes burned in the roof. He took the thin path through the ivy covering the lawn. Behind him, a window in the attic shattered from a burst of fire. In the sudden brightness, Gabe saw a glimmer of pink tangled in the bushes. It trailed into the shadows, trimmed in lace. A dress.

He crouched, hoping against hope that Michael wouldn't come after him. He'd seen no other Bound. "I'm not going to hurt you, but they will. Run," he whispered.

A sob of relief came from the bushes. "Gabe?"

He pushed aside the branches. The girl tucked inside had a deep scratch across her cheek. Her thoughts were scattered terror. "Erin? You've got to get out of here," he said, but she shook her head, grasping his arm.

"Everyone's still inside. Help them!"

"They're ash, Erin. I got here too late." His voice broke.

"Oh God. Maddy." She let out a staggered sob, the last hope draining from her. "Sebastian, he . . . he lowered me out of the window, and I ran. I thought he'd be right behind me, but he went after Kristen."

At a sudden yell, Gabe spun around. A team of fire-fighters circled the side of the house.

Gabe charged into the bushes and grabbed Erin under

the arms, dragging her out the other side into the neighbor's yard. In the open, he could see her grotesquely swollen knee. "Can you walk?" he asked as he lifted her to her feet.

She limped a few steps and then shook her head. "Not without help," she said. Her eyes searched his.

If the Bound catch me helping her, I'm done, he thought. *If Michael tells the rest of the council what I just said to him, it's over for me anyway.* "Okay," he said, staring off down the street. "Okay, come here," he said, scooping her up.

CHAPTER 19

Sebastian was gone. Madeline, Vaughn, Erin. All the Siders she'd taken into her home. The Bound had destroyed them and burned down her house. Those should have been the things Kristen thought about as Luke pulled her down the street. But every time she tried to concentrate, the image that popped into her head was of the jar on her mantel, the tiny black monkey preserved in formaldehyde. "Petri. My monkey. They boiled him."

Her voice sounded strange, even to her own ears. She'd been quiet in the town car Luke had summoned, but once it had dropped them off a block from his apartment, she couldn't seem to stop talking. Luke's grip tightened on her wrist at the words. "Yes. The dead monkey is gone, and we're very sad. I got it the first ten fucking times you mentioned it," he snapped.

"But they just burned him, and all my things, and they tore open that boy. He was on my lawn. And Petri. He was

in a jar and— You told them about the ball, didn't you?"
He'd wanted to punish her. Have the Bound take out as
many of her friends as possible in one fell swoop. "You
bastard," she said as she swung at him.

He hooked her wrist before her blow could connect.
"The loss was great," he said. "Take the grief inside you.
It will make you stronger."

"You did this to them!" she said.

His eyes caught the glare of a streetlight, red and burning. "Quite the opposite, my little orchid. All blame for
this falls on the Bound."

The fight ran out of her. "I don't believe you."

"No?" His laugh grated on her. "They aren't fools.
They've captured dozens of Siders and questioned them
all as they learned how to turn them to ash. One spilled
about your tinderbox. Fortunately, I, too, have my own
sources. I just don't torture Siders for information."

Luke curled his fingers though hers. To any passersby
they would look like a couple out for a stroll, but she
winced at the tightness of his grip. When he spoke, she
expected cruelty, for him to cut her deep while he knew
she was fragile. Instead, he gently plucked a leaf from her
sopping, tangled hair. "You *will* make the Bound pay,
Kristen," he promised.

He pressed her hand between his palms and rubbed.
She could barely feel his touch, let alone any heat he

generated. Her feet were numb in her heels, soaked with slush. She slipped her hand out of his without responding. They walked in silence, her heels crunching the salt scattered on the sidewalk.

Luke's coat dropped over her shoulders. She looked up, surprised. "Put it on," he said.

She slipped her arms into the sleeves. The thick leather wasn't the best for warmth, but it cut the wind. Luke's scent of spices filled her head.

As they walked the last feet to his apartment building, she watched him beside her. "There have to be others who survived. I need to go back."

He stopped in the middle of the sidewalk, staring into the shadows of an alley. His head dipped.

"Luke?" She shivered. "What is it?"

A shadow behind the Dumpster lengthened up the wall. It broke off and skittered up to the gutter, slipping onto the roof. It was followed by a dozen more. Kristen stumbled backward. "What the hell?"

"I've sent them to check. Don't expect much."

The shadows were his . . . minions or demons. Dark things. "Thank you," she whispered.

"Don't." He reached for her, but only to dig into the pocket of the coat for his keys.

She didn't look at him as he pulled his hand out. "No," she said. "Thank you for getting me out."

Don't thank him. He let the others be annihilated, she thought. *I'm only here because of him,* her consciousness warred. *Don't be stupid. He must have something to gain. You're a toy to him.* She started to shake her head, but caught herself. *Hold it together.*

When they got up to his apartment, the usual draft of the penthouse had been banished, the heaters raging. Luke ran a hand through his wet curls and shook off the last of the snow melting into them.

"Stay here." He headed down the hall to his bedroom without looking back.

She reached down, clawed open the straps holding on her shoes, and kicked them off. Stumbling toward the couch, she stripped the blanket off the back of it. A violent shiver made her teeth chatter.

They're gone. She dropped her head into her palms. She thought of the boy on her lawn, the desperate backward crawling. The crack of his bones. Somewhere in the house, the Bound had found Sebastian. A silent sob racked through her, then another as she felt herself finally breaking. Her jaw ached from clenching her teeth to keep everything inside. It wasn't until she heard the creak of the bedroom door a few minutes later that she reined herself in again.

Behind her, Luke cleared his throat. "You need to get out of that dress. It's soaked."

She sniffed hard and nodded, but kept her head down and her face hidden.

"Here." He reached over her shoulder and handed her a thin sweater and a pair of leggings. "I bought these for you before you left."

She stood and turned. He'd changed into charcoal grey sweatpants and a matching thermal top. It struck her how normal he could look when he wished, how human. "May I use your phone?" she asked.

He strolled to the island separating the living room from the kitchen and picked up the cell from the counter. "To call whom? I doubt many escaped, Kristen."

"Sebastian," she admitted. "I need to try."

He tapped the screen and held it out to her. When she reached for it, he pulled it away at the last second. Her anger seemed to amuse him, though he hid it well. "Tell me why you left Aerie," he said.

Kristen hit him with a level glare. "Tell me who told you about the ball. Was it really a Sider, or did Gabriel send you to get me out? Did he know what was going to happen?"

"That," he said, "is not something I'm willing to share. Why did you leave Aerie?"

"I am not having this conversation with you, Luke."

The grin spread. "You are if you want to make any calls."

She didn't have time for his games. Nor for sugarcoating

and tiptoeing. "Because you're a liar." Crossing her arms, she kept her face blank, gave him nothing. The material of her ruined gown pressed against her skin and sent a chill through her. "The dresses you bought me? The books? The look in your goddamned eyes and that pathetic seduction attempt. Every moment I spent here was manipulated. Twisted. You saned me up just enough to force your own delusions down my throat." She held her hand out. "Now give me the phone."

Luke closed the space between them. She froze, her hand pressed against his chest. "Forced?" he growled. His forehead knocked against hers. "Now who's the liar?"

She was dimly aware of her mouth opening and closing, a truth she shouldn't voice trapped there. *This is everything you wanted*, Luke's voice said in her memory of that night.

Luke pressed the phone into her palm as he pulled away. It wasn't until he'd stalked off down the hall that she let out the breath she'd been holding. "Glad to be back," she mumbled to the closed bedroom door.

Just as her thumb lowered to enter Sebastian's number, the phone vibrated in her hand with an incoming call. Instead of a number or name, a set of symbols popped up on the screen. Code. For who? She accepted the call.

"Hello?" the person on the other end said hesitantly. "Luke?"

She would have recognized the voice anywhere, almost said his name in reflex.

Gabriel. Her heart drummed, but Luke's door stayed closed. *He told Luke to get me out,* she thought. *And now he's checking on us.*

"Are you there?" he said.

"You knew," she cried, her voice breaking. "How could you?"

Luke's door opened. Before Gabe had a chance to say anything, she thrust the phone at Luke. "It's for you," she sneered.

He ripped the phone from her hand and glanced at the screen.

"You made it out?" Then his grip tightened, disgust and anger flooding his face. "What do you *think* happened, Gabriel? The Bound laid them to waste. Why do you have Madeline's phone?" Luke's brow pinched as he turned away. "Obviously." A sudden humorless laugh burst out of him. "Of all the things I never expected to hear from you . . . Tell her yourself if you're serious. She thinks *I'm* a liar."

He passed her the phone without so much as a glance and wandered into the kitchen. Shaking, she raised the speaker to her ear. In the other room, Luke pulled down a box of hot chocolate and set about making two cups.

She didn't want to hear Gabe's voice again, wasn't sure

she could bear it. Part of her wanted to hang up. "I have nothing to say to you."

"Kristen? You really are safe?" The relief at hearing her seemed to take his breath away, though she couldn't bring herself to answer him. When he spoke again, his words were hard. "Listen to me. I want you to stay with Luke. Hide from the Bound as long as you can, okay?"

At the sink, Luke filled two cups and put them in the microwave, his casual indifference masquerading as privacy.

"I can't think of any place I'd rather be," she said, her voice trembling. "Now that my house is gone. And nearly everyone I know was *slaughtered*."

She heard Gabe swallow. "Were you there?" he asked. "When it happened?"

"Of course I was! Luke . . . ," she said. Her eyes stung. *He was there,* she wanted to say. *He was there* again *when you weren't.*

"I thought you were dead. After Madeline, I was so sure I would find you next."

Kristen stilled. "What do you mean, after Madeline?"

"Her body. On the back stairs. Her ribs were . . . I couldn't save her. I found her phone."

"Madeline's gone?" The strength ran out of her legs. She slumped to the floor.

Luke took a step toward her but caught himself.

"I thought you knew," Gabe said. He sounded broken. "I was too late to stop—"

She threw the phone against the door with all her might. It shattered into pieces, skittered back across the floor to where she sat silent and shivering.

When Luke made his way to her side, she didn't look up. He lowered himself carefully to his knees, set a cup of steaming cocoa down in front of her. When she didn't react, he picked up the mug and wound her fingers around it. They ached with the heat. Luke kept his hands over hers.

"I'll make him suffer if you ask," he said quietly.

She thought of Gabriel, how he'd found her in the chapel years ago. His loyalty and friendship had been the only things that kept her going. Had Gabe really been responsible? When he'd Fallen, she'd thought he'd abandoned her out of anger and cursed his name. But she'd been wrong then. *Could Gabriel really have done this?* she wondered.

Luke scooted closer and traced a finger down Kristen's cheek. "When you begged for Gabriel back without saying a word, he was my gift to you. I can make him go away if you'd like. Things can be as they were."

Fury coursed through her veins. "A *gift?*" When she tried pulling away, Luke grabbed her wrist. Cocoa sloshed over the rim of her cup. "You wanted him Bound for *your* benefit. Don't try to spin this."

Luke was near enough that his breath lent a bit of warmth to her cold lips. "And you used me to get well."

"So what is it this time?" she asked. "What happens when I'm of *no* use to you?"

"I imagine the same thing that happened to me when Gabriel came for you."

I left him, she thought. *As soon as Gabriel was back, I just walked away.* Tentative, she tilted her head just enough to rest against Luke. "And if I say I should have stayed?" she asked. He jolted suddenly, his shoulder cracking against her chin.

"What's—" she started, but a knock interrupted her.

"Go change," he demanded. "Now." He was already making his way to the door. He turned back to her, a finger raised for silence before he jabbed it toward his bedroom.

She raced down the hall and through the bedroom door. Just before it slammed, she splayed her fingers against the jamb, blocked it from closing. She pressed to the crack, gritting her teeth against the sting in her hand.

Luke had opened the door a few inches and then slid his boot up against it, double security for the thick chain lock. ". . . were supposed to report back, not bring me remains," Luke was saying. She heard his soft curse at whoever was outside. "Oh, for fuck's sake, is he *alive?*"

She bit her lip. Whoever was outside had brought a Sider. Kristen was sure of it.

The hinges creaked as her weight shifted, and Luke's hand shot out behind him. She froze. He held up a single finger to keep her from moving. No other part of him acknowledged her in any way. For a few moments, his voice dropped too low for her to hear. "Take two others with you and go," he said to the visitor through the three-inch gap. "Let me know who you see there."

A muffled reply.

Satisfied, Luke closed the door and engaged the dead bolt. His other arm was still cocked back toward her, the finger held up. For a long moment he only stood, silent. Finally, he relaxed his stance. "You can come out," he said, motioning to her as he took a seat on one of the bar stools.

"Where's the Sider? Is he hurt?" she asked, rushing toward the door.

Luke grabbed her as she passed. "It wasn't Sebastian."

"You say that like he's the only one who matters." She dug in with her bare heels, straining against his grip. It was then that she noticed the strange smell. Wet smolder. "Let me go! I can dose him! Help him heal!"

"There's no one out there anymore, Kristen."

She stopped fighting.

"That Sider was burned terribly and suffering." He met her eyes at the hurt sound that broke from her. "My demons took him away before you even made it out of the room."

"Took him where?" she asked.

"To Eden. He'll be out of his misery in minutes if she has an ounce of compassion in her." Luke ran his fingertip around the rim of her abandoned mug.

The piece of mercy wasn't like him. She didn't trust it. "Why would you do that?"

"Eden's Siders are still poisoning Upstairs. With the Bound so busy down here, maybe he'll slip through, take out a few souls before they catch him."

She dropped back onto the chair. The night had been too much. "Madeline's really dead?" she asked. Luke nodded. "Maybe you should have saved her, instead," she said, struggling to hide how distraught she was. "After all, she was loyal to you. Feeding you information. Why save me and not her, Luke?"

He went back to the mug, circling the rim. "Because you were enough," he said. "And what I wanted."

She watched his finger, the slow, calculated turn. Whatever plot Luke had set into motion, she wasn't naïve enough to believe she was the endgame.

CHAPTER 20

$\mathcal{B}$y the time they'd gotten back to the apartment, the fog in Jarrod's head had dulled. Sullivan still helped him up the four flights of stairs. When Az opened the door, Jarrod plowed past him.

"Eden!" he yelled. He turned back to Az, shaking with fury. "Where is she?"

"Bedroom," Az said, already making his way back there. "We got lucky. There was a kid waiting on the stairs. She's still rough, though."

"And now she's weak and in a place the Bound know. We need to leave. It's not safe," he said.

"Nowhere is safe," Az shot back.

"You don't get to just whisk in here and fuck everything up." Jarrod strode forward, but Az didn't back down.

"I got her out of danger," Az said. "I brought her here. Where were you when Eden and Sullivan were getting the shit beat out of them?"

"Screw you," Jarrod spat, inching closer. *I can take him,* Jarrod thought. Adrenaline pumped through him, all the helpless rage he'd felt. Just as he started to clench his hands into fists, fingers entwined with his. He looked at Sullivan in surprise.

"Please," she said quietly. "This doesn't help anything. Az didn't do anything wrong."

Az stepped back, his voice careful and apologetic. "She wouldn't be able to kill any Siders if she stopped breathing, right? I was worried she wouldn't make it."

Jarrod shifted from foot to foot, knowing Az was right. "At least agree with me that we need to get out of here," Jarrod said.

Az crossed his arms. "Look around the apartment. Is anything different? Out of place? A door open that you know you shut. Anything."

Jarrod glanced around. They'd left in a rush, but everything looked the same. "Not that I can see," he answered.

"I don't think the Bound have been here," Az said. "Which means they can't get in without using the door." He turned toward Eden in the bedroom, his back bare, his wings tucked tight into two hollows on either side of his spine. "Just give her a little time."

"But Gabe can get in," Sullivan said. "He said we had to leave."

Az looked back over his shoulder, his irises ringed red.

"The Bound just massacred his friends. I wouldn't exactly be worried about Gabe right now."

The faint sound of Eden calling took Az back into the bedroom.

Dropping into the armchair, Sullivan picked up the remote and turned on the television.

"What're you doing?" Jarrod asked.

"I want to see what they say." After flicking through a few channels, Sullivan stopped on the news. On the television, the reporter's face was grim beneath the fur lining of her hood. The pillars of Kristen's porch gleamed white against the blackened house in the background.

Half of the second floor was entirely gone.

Jarrod sunk onto the arm of the couch. "Oh my God," he whispered.

"Neighbors have stated a party *was* taking place at the time of the fire, Tom, and police are still searching," the reporter went on, turning to give the camera an opportunity to get a dramatic sweep of the steaming wreckage, "but as of this time no bodies have been found."

"Fire's the perfect cover for a hell of a lot of ashes," Jarrod mumbled. He clicked over to the next channel. Another news crew, this one on the other side of the lawn. ". . . are now saying one body, that of a young woman, was found near a back entrance at the property. Police have stated the cause of death is being investigated but is not—again, is not—believed to be related to the fire."

In the armchair, Sullivan snapped to attention. "What's that mean? How could they find someone?"

Jarrod dropped his head, drove his forehead against the heels of his palms. "Does it matter?" he burst out, throwing down his hands. "We've got to get the fuck out of here! The Bound hit Milton's. They hit Kristen's. We have to get Eden and leave before—"

The loud buzz of the intercom cut him off. Sullivan jumped out of the chair. Another buzz droned.

Eden's bedroom door opened. Az stood on the threshold. Jarrod took a hesitant step toward the intercom and then broke for it. "Who is it?" he yelled into the box.

Instead of a voice, there was a series of clicks.

"Oh God, it's the Bound," Sullivan whispered.

Jarrod hit the intercom again. "Who the fuck is this?"

The clicks sounded. *Tickticktick*—a pause—and then three long shudders, almost as if someone had scratched over the slots of the speaker —*tickticktick*.

"Code." Eden's rasp barely made it out of the room. "Morse code."

Sullivan ripped her coat from the hook beside the door and grabbed for the knob, but Jarrod blocked her.

"No."

She stared up at him. "Eden's right. Three short, three long, three short. It's SOS. Someone's hurt, Jarrod!"

"You're ready to just rush out there?" he asked. "You don't think it could be a trap? Seriously, that never crossed your mind?"

She met Jarrod's glare. "And if it's not?"

Az had come back into the living room. "Then it's a Sider. One more, and Eden will be strong enough to move. Maybe there are two." When Jarrod glanced over at him, Az's eyes flicked to Sullivan pointedly. Jarrod turned just in time to see her rubbing her palm. He grabbed her wrist, saw the black on her fingertips.

"When did this start?" he asked in disbelief. Everything else faded away. He searched her face, her pallor, looking for signs he'd missed. *She's sick. She's dying.*

"It's not bad yet," she said, as if it would be some consolation.

"Damn it, that's not the point." Jarrod jammed on his shoes. He rushed down the flights of stairs, but stopped just before the bend that would let him see out the windows beside the security door.

Sullivan and Az had followed right behind him. Together, they stepped around the corner. A scream tore out of Sullivan even as she tried to squelch it.

Faces.

They pressed against the glass, three of them, heads swiveling as if they rolled on broken necks. Across their cheeks, black smears stood out against pale skin. One tapped his finger against the glass and then curled it, calling them closer.

The girl was the same demon they'd seen at Milton's, but this time her features seemed to shimmer slightly in and out of focus. Her lips came closer to the glass. She blew an oval of steam. *For*, a claw of a finger squeaked out, *Eden*. The steam evaporated. She pointed down, below the window, where Jarrod couldn't see. *Come out*, the thing mouthed.

At the sight of Sullivan, the demon raised a hand and gave a slight wave, a smile cracking a horizontal split across its face. It faltered as it caught sight of Az.

"They can't be near me," Az said, slowly taking a step down. "I'm only half Fallen, which means to them, I'm still half Bound." For every step they retreated, Az moved forward one. Jarrod watched Az's wings spread, slide up over the railing, and spill across the stairwell. Slowly, the demonic trio backed off the stairs and onto the sidewalk, retreating until they were down the street, out of sight. Only then did Az open the door.

"Jarrod," he called out. "Come on. I need your help."

On the stoop, leaned against the building, was a hulking mass of blackened . . . something. *Oh God, that can't be a person.* Then the smell hit him. Smoke and meat. Cooked flesh. Jarrod gagged.

It moaned.

"Jesus Christ." Sullivan pushed around him and

dropped to her knees beside what was left of the Sider. When she looked up, Jarrod saw her horror, but her voice came out unwavering. "We have to get him upstairs."

"Az, get Eden. Bring her down."

"No." Sullivan's demand stopped Az before he could take off. "Help me. We've got to get him up." The Sider screamed as she slipped her arms under his. "I'm so sorry," she whispered.

Four flights of agony. Stifled moans, as if the Sider knew he had to keep quiet, couldn't let the neighbors hear and come to investigate. The smell was awful. *What the hell are we doing?* he thought. Twice he stopped, but Sullivan urged him on. "Please, just help me," she said.

Finally, they got the Sider inside the apartment and set him on the couch.

Sullivan lowered, worked slowly, pulling strips of what used to be a shirt off the shoulder. The cracks in his skin wept pink liquid. A mix of fluid and blood, it ran like tears over his bumpy skin and dripped off to soak into the cushions.

"I need cold water," she said. "Any towels you can find me. Fast."

Jarrod squeezed her shoulder. This was only drawing out the burned Sider's agony. "Eden will take away his pain a lot faster than—"

"Now!" she snapped.

Jarrod gestured for Az to follow him. In the kitchen, the tinny splash of water filling the mixing bowl covered his words. "Get Eden," Jarrod told him. "I don't know what Sullivan's doing. It would take a dozen Siders' worth of Touch to heal him, and even then . . ." He couldn't figure it out. Az took the bowl and a clean hand towel from the cabinet.

When they came around the corner, Sullivan's fingers hovered, shaking, just above the Sider's blistered black skin. "Hang in there," she said. "I'll fix you."

Az set the bowl beside her. It sloshed over the edges onto the carpet. "We're not torturing him anymore."

"You don't recognize him? Jarrod." Her head snapped up. "Please. It's Vaughn."

The room was silent except for Vaughn's cries as she laid the sopping cold towel on him, the steady plop of dripping water. Every drop, every touch seemed to drive him further into agony.

Suddenly, Az stood.

"Don't make Eden kill him!" Sullivan begged, catching his hand before he could leave.

Vaughn croaked out a whisper. She leaned closer, dabbing at his wrecked face. Blisters burst in her wake. His charred fingers rose suddenly, clamped around her wrist. She froze, staring down in horror. The touch dropped her glamour.

Her skin molded over, sores opening on her arms. Her mouth opened wide in terror.

"They killed us," Vaughn rasped, oblivious. "They killed us all."

"Get him off me." Sullivan's words sped up as she spoke, slurring together. "Jarrod, get him off me. Get him off me now!"

Before Jarrod could move, Vaughn let go, one split and crumbling finger snapping off.

"Please," Vaughn moaned. "Make it stop."

Sullivan staggered backward. Just before she bumped into Jarrod, she turned. Gray tears streamed down her cheeks. "I can't help him. I can't do this," she whispered, her fingers gripping fistfuls of Jarrod's shirt even as his arms came around her. "I have to get out of here."

He looked at Az helplessly, stroking her hair. Seconds ago she'd been strong, determined. Now she melted into his shoulder, barely holding herself up.

"I'll get Eden," Az said, already heading in that direction.

Sullivan ripped away, heading for Jarrod's bedroom, leaving him behind, unsure what to do.

"Come on," he heard Az say to Eden. "I've got you." Az came out, Eden hoisted in his arms, balled up tight. "Jarrod, go after Sullivan. Close your door," he said as he passed.

In his room, Sullivan sat on the bed with her back against the wall, her knees pulled up against her chest. Through the door, sounds came from the living room, Eden's voice breaking and all the awful sounds Vaughn was making.

Jarrod swallowed hard. "Even if you'd been able to pass to him, it wouldn't have . . ." He trailed off when she looked up at him, tears trickling down her cheeks. He moved a foot closer, still keeping enough space between them that it was her choice if she wanted to come to him. He didn't know whether to touch her or not, what would help. "This isn't your fault. You know that, right?"

Something in her gaze hardened. "Don't patronize me."

"Patronize?" Jarrod cocked his head. "This was the Bound, Sullivan. They did this. They would have tried to kill us, too, if we were there."

"But I . . ." Her shoulders shook, her eyes wide and confused and afraid. "I wished for it. I wished it so many times, for him to die. Even before I took off. I just never thought. . . ."

He deserved that and more for what he did to you, Jarrod thought, his confusion slowly edging into anger. How could she be crying over Vaughn after everything he'd done to her?

He remembered what it was like when James died and

they'd found him in a doorway. Adam, killed by Libby on the roof. Neither death compared to waking up in the alley, his head screaming and Sullivan and Eden gone. He'd thought for sure they'd both been ash. He'd never lost anyone he'd *loved*. There was a knock on the door.

"Yeah," Jarrod said, his voice weak. Az's head popped into the room.

"It's done," he whispered, peeking at Sullivan's back, his face clouded with worry. His fingers curled around the frame. "There's something you need to know. About Gabe."

"Now?" Jarrod said.

Az dropped his eyes to the floor. "You know how on the roof, when we were fighting Luke, Gabe couldn't keep from confessing what he'd done to Eden? How it was just a compulsion?" Jarrod nodded. "Well, Upstairs it's the same way for promises." Az hesitated. "Gabe promised he would kill Eden."

Jarrod's arms fell away from Sullivan as he stood in surprise. "What?"

"It's not what you think!" Az said quickly. "Gabe set up the Bound. Once he made the promise, *he* has to be the one to fulfill it. None of the Bound can kill her but him. It was all he could do to protect her."

Jarrod shook his head, trying to wrap his brain around the idea. "You angels are fucked up."

Az didn't bother to deny it. "It would be better for him if he didn't know where she was," he said, his brow furrowed. "Eden told me how he came here. That he wants her to find out how the Siders started."

Jarrod nodded as he made his way to the doorway.

"I think that's a good idea," Az said, stepping back into the hall. He glanced over to where Sullivan had curled up in the bed. A muscle in his jaw twitched. "She's like Eden now, isn't she?"

"Luke. In the park," Jarrod said quietly. "We were looking for you."

Az's frown deepened. "I'm so sorry."

Jarrod shook his head. There was nothing to say. "If Eden's good to move," he said, changing the subject, "when do we leave?"

"Now. If you want to grab some stuff, this would be the time."

"Right." Jarrod started to move toward the closet but stopped. It was the worst time for the question to pop into his head, but once it did, he had to ask it. "Hey, how did you get back here?"

Az locked eyes with him. "I was let go for a favor requested in return. I won't say what, so you're just gonna have to trust me."

Jarrod called out when Az started to walk away down the hall. "Do you know how to kill the Bound?"

Az stopped, one hand on the wall. His wings swelled in and out with each breath he took.

"Is there a way?" Jarrod asked.

For a long time, Az didn't answer. "Metal forged of fire and sin," he said finally, without turning around. "Blades made by the Fallen."

"Where would we get them?" Jarrod pressed.

Az's wings shuddered. A feather drifted slowly to the carpet. When he turned to Jarrod, Az looked grim. "Luke," he said. "I wouldn't count on getting your hands on any."

Jarrod gave him a slight nod.

"We should pack some stuff," Jarrod said to Sullivan when Az had gone. He sat beside her on the bed, and she leaned onto his shoulder for a beat as if drawing strength. He wrapped an arm around her and stroked her back.

Jarrod glanced around the room. It felt weird to know he'd only lived here a few months. It was home. He pulled away from Sullivan and headed to the closet. He knew there was an old backpack of Adam's buried in the back. He grabbed that and a duffel bag and stood staring.

He ran a hand over the hangers that held Adam's old tattered band T-shirts. The few flannels that James had worn. *I'll probably be with you guys soon,* he thought. But the thought didn't bring him any comfort. Libby had killed both James and Adam, and sent them Downstairs.

They didn't get some afterlife relief. If they still existed at all, they were in Hell. Suffering. He pulled a few flannels out and tossed them to Sullivan.

"Here, these should fit you," he said as he crossed over to the dresser and opened a drawer. A minute later the bag was full. He slid out a small side drawer full of old receipts and wrappers, kept pulling when he got to the end of it. Holding the drawer in one hand, he swept his hand along the back.

He took out a tightly wrapped roll, the few bucks he'd managed to hole away, mostly tips from Milton's. It wasn't much, maybe forty or so dollars. "Ready?"

Sullivan looked up at him from the bed, her brown eyes glossy. He hooked a thumb in the waistband of his jeans and slung the backpack over his shoulder.

"We didn't have rent," he said quietly. "We would have gotten kicked out anyway."

He thought she'd say something. Tell him it was going to be all right. He didn't know why he expected it—it was such a terrible thing to ask of her after what had just happened—but when she didn't, he got a sinking feeling of dread. "You all right?" he asked her.

"Nope." She stood up, the duffel in her hands only half full with James's shirts. "But it doesn't change anything. We still have to go."

CHAPTER 21

Luke kept his bedroom black, the windows so blocked out that not even the city lights stole through. When Kristen moved against the covers, she heard the crackle of flames. Fire. She rolled herself into a tight ball on the bed, tucked into the corner near the headboard and against the wall. Clamping her hands over her ears, she tried to keep out the horrible sound of the flames that had eaten them all.

But in the darkness, her terror only grew.

"'I have been here before/But when or how I cannot tell,'" she cried, the words instinctively rushing out of her. The cadence of the poetry was off, though; it did nothing to settle her. Bits of nightmare tortured her—Sebastian cresting over the side of the mattress, his face melting, an eye boiling and bursting as he used the blanket to drag himself closer. The glowing coals of his finger bones singed into the fabric.

"'I know the grass beyond the door.'" Kristen's voice shook. "'The sweet keen smell'!" she screamed.

The door swung open, flooding the room with sudden light. Luke stood silhouetted against the glare from the hall. "Kristen? Are you all right?"

She stared around in confusion, soaking up every detail. The deep maroon of the walls. Luke's dresser. The closet was open, the clothes he'd bought her hanging neatly. *I never left,* she thought suddenly. It was a dream, *all* a dream. Not just the fire but so much more—Luke and how she'd left him at the club, Gabriel being Bound again, everything.

With a violent shudder, she threw off the covers and leaped for him. She curled her arms around his neck. Luke stiffened.

"I'm hallucinating." She pulled back and stared up at him, her heart raging. "A fire, and Gabriel . . . I'm going mad. You have to help me. I'm giving you permission. *Please!*"

Luke looked at her for a long second before slowly drawing her back against him. "It wasn't a hallucination."

Kristen slumped.

If I'd stayed with Luke, there would never have been a ball, there would never have been a fire. "I didn't know what would happen. If I'd known the price," she started.

"Come to the kitchen with me," he said, brushing her

hair back. "I already have the kettle on. We need to talk."

Still shaken, she let him lead her down the hall, half-way there before the wording struck her. *I already have the kettle on,* he'd said. A trickle of paranoia leaked in at the back of her thoughts. Had he given her the nightmare to wake her up? Could he do that? The comfort of his hand in hers dissolved.

When they got to the kitchen, Luke headed for the stove, where, just as he'd said, the kettle steamed lightly, two mugs sitting on the counter with tea bags already in them. Kristen took a seat on one of the bar stools. He glanced over at her.

"Nothing," she said in answer to a question he hadn't asked. She shook her head, turned her attention to the rings decorating her fingers. Instead of staying on his side of the counter, Luke passed back into the living room, to her stool, setting both mugs down next to her.

"Have you begun to imagine your revenge yet?" He dropped a sugar cube into one of the mugs. "In your nightmare, did you hear your friends screaming?"

"Why would you say that to me?" Like a fingernail scraping a match, a flame of hate sparked to life inside her. "Why would you ever—"

"Sebastian, Madeline, the others? Fists were plunged through their chests. The Bound *murdered* them," he said. "And so I'm asking if you've begun to plan your revenge yet, that's all." Fury coursed through her. Luke's words were low. "You don't need to shy away from that darkness inside you." As an angry heat flushed her face, he took the tips of her fingers, kissed each one until she dropped her hand. "Not with me."

Backing slowly away from him, Kristen worked her face into a mask, pushed her roiling emotions down deep. "What you did to me last night? Making me watch them turned to *ash*?" *They wouldn't have been there if I hadn't invited them.* She wrenched the thought from her mind. "What you did was unforgivable."

Luke's grin was unexpectedly playful, dangerous. "Then don't forgive me."

Just out of her view, he reached onto the counter and slid something across it. She couldn't see what he held behind his back. "What is that?" she asked, walking backward.

Luke paced her step for step. His arm stayed cocked, whatever he had, hidden. "I have something for you."

"Show me," she said, nodding toward his hand. Her back bumped against the apartment door.

"This will be useful to you," he said, bringing an enormous knife out from behind his back. The slight curve of the eight-inch blade shimmered with the light stealing in from the hall. Luke continued his slow saunter toward her. His eyes smoldered like spent coals.

"Do you wonder where you would be without me?" he said as he reached her. He flattened his hand against her breastbone. "Heart torn from this exquisite chest, your soul burned into nonexistence? You'd be just like the others. Nothing."

Her shoulders tensed, she was sure any moment she'd feel the searing pain of the knife buried in her side. Instead, it clattered to the floor. Without warning, Luke's fists slammed against the door on either side of her. The loud bang rattled her. Through her thin sweater, the door leeched away her warmth, her back against the metal.

She froze as Luke's hands slid down. He grabbed her chin and wrenched her face up. "When we first met, you didn't dare tell anyone about us. I was your darkest secret. Because you wished it, I told no one," he said, enunciating each word. "The second time we met, I came for you when you were sick, fixed the broken parts of your mind when no one else could." Kristen tensed at the memories, praying he'd stop, but Luke went on. "I gave you dresses. I gave you poetry. Anything you wished. Yet when Gabriel came for you, I was banished from your world yet again, wasn't I?" He waited for her to answer. "Wasn't I?" he asked again.

"Yes," she admitted.

His fingers on the back of her neck eased her gently away from the door. "Tell me, what you would give. What would you give to trade your grief for their pain?" he asked.

She gasped as Luke's body pressed against hers. Her arm curled around him almost in reflex. It was that touch, her fingertips on the soft cotton of his shirt, the sharp shoulder underneath, that undid her.

"What would you give for vengeance?" he whispered as she let her head fall back just enough to expose her throat.

He'll consume you.

Let him, she thought as his mouth, hungry, met her skin.

"Claim me," he murmured, "and I will tell you how to get the revenge you seek."

She fought to quell the hate he kindled inside her, seemed to grow stronger from. *Why are you fighting him? This is what you want.* The fires he fed crackled, raged. *Don't listen,* her mind screamed, but her heart drowned it out, thudding hard and fast in a pounding static hiss.

"Can you picture it? Cleaving the Bound apart." He went on. "Their blood on your hands. How badly do you ache for vengeance? Tell me." His teeth grazed her neck before the bite softened to a kiss, his lips warm, like the blood of the Bound would be. Something inside her sighed. "Carve out their hearts," he said, "with the knife I sharpened for you." At her harsh intake, he bent to pick up the blade. "It's special, this knife. It will kill them when nothing else will," he said, pressing it into her hand. His breath hit her cheek, hot. "It's my gift to you."

At what cost, she thought. And did she care? Images played in her mind, a slide show of murder, maroon streaming from corpses at her feet.

"All I ask is your loyalty. All I ask . . ." He curled his hand tight, pressing his fist against the wall. "Twice you've denied me, Kristen. Still, I am yours. Your secret, your pleasure, your darkest dream. Give yourself to me, and I will give you everything." She stared up into his eyes, his irises mottled with uneven rings of green. *Hope,* she thought, the color a mixture of blue for happy and yellow for fear.

"I belong to no one," she said, her chest heaving, need searing her insides. She latched an arm around his neck. Her mouth opened to form single-word excuses. *No. Wrong. Run.*

"But I want," she said slowly, not quite believing what she ached for. "I want their blood." The green flecks had gone from his eyes. They'd darkened with desire, an oily black that twisted her stomach, but not her heart. "And I want you at my side when I get it," Kristen said.

A sound escaped him, between a sign and a moan. Ice flashed through her, so cold it burned, but she didn't care. She drew Luke closer. *They'll suffer for what they've done,* she promised herself.

On the stove, the kettle started to scream.

CHAPTER 22

"And I said, she's not available." Az's voice roused Eden from a fitful sleep. She stretched on the threadbare sheets of the cheap hotel they'd found. Daylight brightened the window, the thick curtains open and tied back. Az was silhouetted in the sunshine, bracing himself as he leaned forward against the heat register. His wings were hidden again under a thick sweatshirt. Eden fought to focus and made out a phone pressed against his ear. "You have my word, she's alive. She just . . . she can't come to the phone."

She struggled to prop herself against the headboard. "I'm up," she croaked.

Az spun toward her. "You're at this number?" he said into the phone. "I'll call you back."

"Who—" She coughed hard before she could get out the rest. He crossed the room in two steps and crawled into bed with her. He passed her a glass of water from the nightstand. "How long have I been out?" she managed after draining it. She leaned into the crook of his arm, just enough to stare up at him.

"A few hours. It's a little after nine." His eyes drank her in as he shook his head. "I'm sorry, I just . . . When they let me go, I thought it was a trick. I don't know what I would have done if . . ." He pulled her into a loose hug as if she were delicate, breakable. "I thought you were already gone."

"You *were* gone. And I couldn't handle it," she said. Az being there didn't seem real. Not even with her arms around him, not with his heart beating against her shoulder. "You asshole," she whispered as she tightened her grip on him. Her voice came out thick. "I don't care if you did it to save me. I don't care. If you ever leave me like that again, I will drag your ass back from Upstairs and kick it myself."

His laugh shook them both. He kissed the tip of her nose. "I love you, too," he said.

"How did you get back?" She had so many questions she hadn't thought to ask him last night.

She felt his hesitation, but he didn't slip into their familiar patterns, the lies and half-truths of protection. Az started talking.

"Gabe, he . . ." Az played with her bracelet, not looking at her. "Gabe promised to kill you, Eden, because if he has to do it, none of the other Bound *can*. Michael knows Gabe's resisting. The rest of the Bound might be coming after me because I stopped him. I promised Michael that if he let me out, if he let me go, I would get Gabriel to go back Upstairs. For good. No one else knows."

"Oh God," she whispered, horrified.

Az looked pained. "While you were sleeping, Gabe called me. He's got Erin with him. She was hurt trying to get away at Kristen's." The words came out slow, as if he were gauging how much she could take. Last night faded in and out of clarity, but she was pretty sure it was all there.

"Kristen?"

"Is with Luke," he said softly, taking her hand. "But . . . "

She steeled herself, tucking her head against his shoulder again. His scent, cold, snowy crispness, drifted over her. She wanted it to settle her much more than it did. "Tell me."

"Gabe said he saw . . . He said Madeline didn't make it."

She shook her head slowly, tears welling in her eyes. Madeline was ash. Gone. "Oh God."

"That was Jackson on the phone. Her Second," Az said, continuing when she nodded. "All he knows is that Madeline never came home. He's called you seven times.

He's a wreck, Eden. He keeps saying he has to talk to you. I tried to get him to tell me why, but he wouldn't have it." He shrugged. "I even offered to give the phone to Jarrod. He said only you."

She held her hand out, and Az passed her the phone. "Where is Jarrod?" she asked, suddenly looking around the hotel room. Sullivan was missing, too. The comforter was spread on the floor where they'd slept, an abandoned pillow a foot away.

"Down the hall. Sullivan said she needed air, but Jarrod wasn't looking good so I think she was trying to figure out what's up with him."

Biting her lip against the ache in her bones, Eden tried to straighten while she pulled up Jackson's number on her phone. Az looped an arm around her. She sighed against his chest as she hit Send.

When Jackson answered, she realized just what Az had meant by him sounding wrecked. His voice shook. "If this is Eden, say so. I'm not talking to anyone but her."

"It's me." She'd seen Jackson only once, briefly; he'd been with Madeline the night Jarrod had stayed out with Sullivan and they'd thought he'd been taken. She barely remembered what he looked like, but his agony and fear were clear.

"Madeline made me stay home last night with some of our Siders. They found out about her. I don't know how."

Eden frowned. "Found out about who? Madeline?"

"No!" Jackson shouted loud enough that she had to pull the phone from her ear. "The girl. She's one of us! They're making her do it, spreading the word to any Sider they can get hold of. She's changed a dozen of them already. I can hear her down there begging for help," he said, his voice falling to a desperate mutter.

"She's a Sider? One like me? Who made her, Jackson, the Fallen or the Bound?"

"Neither," he answered. Through Jackson's frantic sounds, she could hear pandemonium in the background. Sobs and slams and then Jackson yelling unintelligible words. She plugged one ear and pressed the phone tighter against the other.

"What's going on?" Az asked. She shook her head, unsure even what to tell him. A sharp bang made her wince. There was a shuffle.

"Are you there? Hello?" Jackson called.

"What's going on?" Eden demanded. She eased away from Az and lowered her feet to the carpet. Black flashes nicked at the edge of her vision. Az touched her shoulder as she swayed slightly, but she caught his hand instead and used it for leverage to stand. "Jackson, tell me. Now."

"On the news," he blurted. "They found a body. It was Mad, I'm sure of it."

He wasn't making sense. "But there wouldn't be a body,

just ashes," Eden said. She thought of Vaughn, burned beyond recognition before she'd given him a merciful end. "Do you think she was just too hurt to run?"

Az squeezed her shoulder. "Gabe saw her," he said in a low voice. "Dead. A body."

"That's impossible," Eden said. "Why do you think it was her, Jackson?" she said into the phone.

"I told her not to go. We could have run. We could have . . ."

She made a scribbling motion to Az. He nodded and snapped a pen and a pad of paper up from the nightstand, tossing it to her. She bent her knee, paper and pen poised. "Can you give me your" —a tremble coursed through Eden— "your address, Jackson." She started again. Her vision blurred as pain shot through her. "Az, help."

His arm instantly came around her shoulder. "You're okay," he said as he eased her onto the bed.

She heard Jackson's sharp gasp. "Az? He's one of them!"

"No! He's on our side!" she argued, but Jackson drowned her out with his angry screams. "It's not what you—"

The background noise went suddenly silent as he hung up.

"Fuck." She dropped the pen, cradling her stomach. Az rubbed her back until she sat up and wiped the corners

LEAH CLIFFORD

of her eyes. Despite the pain, there were no ashes. The discomfort ebbed, but didn't quite leave her. "There's another death breather. From the sound of it, she's taking out too many Siders. She's going to be overloaded on Touch soon. Do you know where Madeline lives?" *Lived,* she corrected mentally, but couldn't bring herself to say. Az's face fell as if she had. He nodded. "We need to go there. I can take the girl's extra Touch. Sullivan, too."

He leaned and rested his forehead against hers. "You're sure you can make it?"

"I have to make it." She hung her hands around his neck. His closeness felt like a gift. "When I asked Jackson if it was the Fallen or Bound who made the Sider, he said neither." She pulled away enough to gauge his reaction.

He raised a cautious eyebrow. "What's that mean?"

"I have no idea." The wording of it unnerved her, though.

"Then let's go. If there's a new kind of Sider, Gabe will want to know about it. Maybe it can help him."

"Why's he so set on figuring out how we started?" she asked. It seemed like a colossal waste of time. Dangerous for no purpose. Eden leaned down and shoved her shoes on, fumbling to tie the laces. She realized she couldn't remember taking them off last night.

Az stared down at his hands, tangled up in his lap. "Finding out how it started means there's a chance he can

198

figure out how to undo it." He sighed hard. "So says Gabe, anyway."

She let the idea spin around in her brain. "But we're dead," she said. "What's to undo?"

"Well, he has a theory," he said, sounding uncomfortable. "That without your paths, you *can't* die. That the Siders are *paused.*"

They both looked up as the door opened, and Sullivan and Jarrod came through. Sullivan slid the chain into place. "Hey!" she said cheerfully. "You're awake!"

Eden smiled back. When she looked at Jarrod, though, he seemed sullen.

"Eden finally talked to Jackson," Az said as he helped her up. She had to lean on him more than she liked. "Something's going on with him. If you guys are ready, we can explain on the way over there."

"Sounds good," Sullivan said, her voice chipper. Beside her, Jarrod said nothing until she squeezed his hand.

He glanced up. "Ready when you are."

They stood for a moment, Eden and Az on one side of the room, Jarrod and Sullivan on the other. It was only when Sullivan turned, slid the chain, and opened the door again that Jarrod looked at Eden. Gone was the determination in him she'd always taken for granted. "Let's get this over with," he said.

CHAPTER 23

Last night, when he'd carried Erin into the apartment he used to share with Az, it had been ransacked. Part of Gabriel wondered if he'd done the damage himself in the first days he'd been Fallen, come home like some sort of muscle memory and torn apart everything left of his old life. He tried not to think about it. Tried to keep his head out of the dark place his nightmares inevitably slithered to.

He hadn't slept last night. Instead, he'd watched over Erin while she whimpered in fitful dreams, listening for any little noise to indicate that the Bound had come after him. But it seemed Michael had deemed it best to leave him alone. How long the reprieve would last, Gabe had no way of knowing.

His mind spun around the Sider girl on the stairs before Raphael had found him. Was Touch really unused potential, replenished as their futures struggled to catch traction, like spinning tires? Could that potential reform their own paths if he found a way to unstick them? *I have to find out what caused them,* he thought. *That's the key.*

Gabe reached down and shook Erin's shoulder lightly. She launched up, instantly awake. "It's all right," he reassured her. He reached into his pocket and pulled out the phone he'd taken last night. A bloody fingerprint stained the screen.

"I need your help," he said as he scrolled down the contacts. "Madeline knew how to get in touch with everyone, in every borough. Who is in Brooklyn?"

Erin stared at him, her eyes swollen almost shut from the tears she'd cried last night. "Maddy *really* never told you?" Gabe shook his head. He let the phone fall to his lap. "Erin," he whispered. "I need to know how the Siders started. Do you know? The Sider in Brooklyn. Is that the *first* Sider?" He took her hand.

"Gabe, they might be the only safe ones left. I can't give them away."

"Please." He didn't know what to say to convince her. "They'll get you—all of you—if I can't figure out a way to stop them. Please. Help me."

She bit her lip and took her hand out of his. "I don't have a number for them. I doubt they're in Maddy's phone, either," she said slowly.

"Wait. Them?" Gabe asked, confused.

Erin glanced up, a hesitant decision in her words. "I can take you there."

Even before she'd led him to the Brooklyn neighborhood where the mysterious Siders lived, Erin had seemed like she was trying to back out. Every question he'd asked her on the subway had gone unanswered. They'd already lapped the block once, and now they were standing on the sidewalk, wasting time. Finally, Gabriel threw up his hands. "Which house, Erin?"

The look she gave him was caustic. Erin twisted away.

"Wait, I'm sorry," Gabriel said, stopping her before she could take off. "You *can* trust me, Erin! What do you need me to do? How can I show you?"

Erin slowly raised her hand. "She usually doesn't like visitors," she said. "Looks like she decided to see us, though."

Erin was pointing to the fancy columns adorning the front of the home they'd been standing in front of. Now, though, the door was open, and a girl leaned on the frame.

She didn't look more than eighteen. Her hair was done up in a delicate plait, surrounding her head in a thick, dark halo. On her hands she wore silk gloves, their color a perfect match to her tailored gray pants and blouse. Everything about her screamed money, sophistication.

He took the steps one at a time, never taking his eyes off the girl.

"Hello, Erin," she said, her voice clipped. "You've brought a friend."

Something about her voice was so familiar.

"I know you, don't I?" Gabe said before he could stop himself. He racked his brain to place her but only came up with a memory of lightning striking in the distance. "But how?"

Was it something from when he was Fallen? Nervousness skittered through him. Had she been with Madeline? He barely remembered that time—only snapshots of the forbidden things he'd done in back hallways of clubs, glances cast over his shoulder at the mortals he left behind when Madeline found him, guided him back to the strobe lights of the dance floor. *These are not memories you want to think about.* Gabriel shook his head to rattle them away before what came to the surface was worse. *Leave the darkness behind you.*

He held out a hand. "I'm—"

"Gabriel," she said, ignoring the hand he offered. Her voice was stilted. "I'm very curious to know what brings you to my home."

Erin stepped in front of him. "Annalise, please. It's important. He's one of the good—"

"Don't be naïve, Erin. None of them is *good.*" She

took a step back inside. "Go away, and don't bother coming back because I won't be here," she said, grabbing for the knob and starting to close the door. "I'll let Madeline know where we are. Eventually."

Erin jammed her foot into the frame. Gabe's heart sank. This girl didn't know about Kristen's, about the extermination.

"It's a war, Annalise," Erin said.

"So you brought it to my doorstep?" Annalise let go of the door and leaned close to Erin. "If you say pretty please, I'm sure your good friend here will tell the Bound to play nice." She turned her nose up at Gabe. "After all, they're known for being compassionate," she spat.

"Madeline's gone!" Erin blurted. "The Bound know how to destroy us. Permanently." She stepped back into Gabe, as if needing him to hold her up. He could feel her trembling. "They attacked us last night, at a ball. They obliterated us. You have to help Gabriel. He's the only one on our side."

Annalise paled. "Madeline's . . . gone? Everyone is . . . ?"

Gabe tried to catch her thoughts, but the cacophony was an indecipherable mix of colors and memories, fragments of words. *She's hiding what she's thinking.* Alarm bells sounded in his head. She shouldn't have known how to do that.

"Who are you?" Gabe demanded. He moved closer,

but then a guy's voice called out from inside the house.

"Annie?" Gabe heard the thud of footsteps clomping down an unseen staircase. "What's going on?"

The door yanked back, and behind Annalise stood a guy who could have been Az's brother. The curly brown hair, the blue eyes. The high cheekbones. Gabe stared as the guy took them all in, lingering on Annalise. Finally, he nodded to Erin. "Long time no see," he said to her cautiously. He held out a gloved hand to Gabe. "And you are?"

"Very confused," Gabe managed.

The guy looked at Annalise, rigid beside him, then past Gabe and Erin to scan up and down the street. "Well," he said, putting his hand on her shoulder, "it's freezing. Can you be very confused inside?"

"Good idea," Gabe said. Focusing on the guy's thoughts, Gabe picked up nothing unusual: worry about what Gabe and Erin's presence meant, the calm he was trying to push to Annalise, an ache to spread Touch. He may have looked like Az, but this boy was a Sider.

Annalise flinched as Gabe brushed by her. There was no chance he was leaving without answers. "I'm sorry," he heard Erin whisper behind him.

Inside the house, gorgeous wood trim lined the hall and wound up a spiral staircase. The guy opened a set of carved pocket doors leading into an elegantly furnished living room. "I'm Donavan," he said, and gestured to an overstuffed couch. "Make yourself comfortable."

Annalise reached for Donavan as he started to sink onto a love seat.

"This is just Sider drama. You don't have to stay." Through the static of Annalise's thoughts, a dram of panic oozed out.

"I don't know what was going on outside, but it looked a little more serious than that. I'm not leaving you alone right now, Annie." Donavan sat and pulled her down with him. "So what did I miss?" he asked.

"There's something both of us are missing, apparently. Talk," Gabe said. "Who are you?"

When no one said anything, Erin spoke up from beside him. "Donavan ran Staten Island before Vaughn."

Annalise gave her a look that swore murder.

Donavan took Annalise's hand almost unconsciously. "Right, but Annalise is here, and the commute is killer. So I opted out. Did something happen to Vaughn?" Gabe saw Annalise's hand clench on Donavan's. Donavan glanced down at her and then back to Gabe. "I'm sorry, but who are you again?"

Annalise's tone was resigned. "Gabriel's not a Sider. He's Bound."

Fear crept onto the guy's face, and Gabe's frustration boiled over.

"I'm not like them!" he yelled. "They slaughtered everyone at Kristen's and burned their souls. I am trying to help you!" He stood there shaking as the others watched him in a stunned, nervous silence. "There's still time," he said, lowering his voice. "I'm trying to find out how the Siders started. If I can trace it back, if I can find a way to fix your paths, or—" He shook his head, at a loss as to where to start, what to ask first.

Erin's voice was quiet. "*Were* you the first Sider, Annalise?" The other girl bit her lip, but Erin went on. "Please. He really is trying to help us."

"That I know of, yes," Annalise said simply.

For a long moment, no one said anything. Donavan raised his and Annalise's clasped hands and pressed her fingers to his lips. "Listen," Gabe said, no longer pulling punches. "You know how to hide your thoughts, which takes at least some sort of practice. And I recognize you. Was it an angel? Did we cause this somehow?"

"You and I met once, in passing," she answered.

Blue-black storm clouds fought their way up from Gabe's subconscious. Annalise above him, her arms held out for balance. "Where?" Gabe asked. "When?"

Donavan, too, seemed bewildered. *Is that why she's fighting this?* Gabe thought. *He doesn't know how she became a Sider, either. She doesn't want him to.*

Gabe watched Annalise, her face pinched with whatever

memories tormented her. "Promise me you won't kill us," she whispered. She looked up at Gabe. "And if you can't, promise me you won't kill Donavan. Say it."

Beside Annalise, Donavan's eyebrows drew together.

"I promise I will not harm you or Donavan," Gabe said without hesitation. A week ago he would have worried that the words would bring a punishment. Now, he was surprised to find how little he cared. *I'm seeing this through.* "How did you become a Sider?"

She swiveled to Gabe as if daring him to act. "I'm a Sider because of you, Gabriel," she said, heat behind the words. "Without you, none of this would have happened."

CHAPTER 24

At the door of his apartment, Luke tangled a lock of Kristen's hair around his finger. "You know," he said slowly, "Gabriel can't guarantee your safety. Or your sanity."

"Oh, darling, such sweet things you say." The sarcasm covered the sting she felt at his words. She wrapped a cashmere scarf around her neck. "Afraid once I head out into the big bad world I'll realize what a mistake I've made choosing you? Maybe make a run for it while I can?"

"Maybe." He gave the lock of hair a sharp tug and then tucked it behind her ear. "I'm not sure what your word is worth." She didn't know whether his smug smile was meant to set her at ease or infuriate her.

The thick jacket she had was nothing she would have chosen herself, not a style the Bound would expect her to wear. It smelled like Luke. The scent enveloped her, stealing deeper inside. Her body hummed.

She took a breath before giving him an indulgent look. "You're not going to have me followed by those minions or whatever I saw last night?" she asked. In the light of day, the not-shadows seemed improbable. Luke's expression went whimsical, his voice dropping low.

"They've always been with you, Kristen. They'll obey you if you call to them, though they can't hold form around the Bound," he said, spreading his hands out at his sides. He curled his fingers slightly as if in invitation, fixated on a spot just over her shoulder. "It'd drive a weaker girl mad to know how close they are. To see how easily they whisper to you from their dark corners. Once you hear them, it's hard not to listen."

Kristen fought the urge to turn. "You think I'd fall for that? There's nothing there," she snapped too quickly. Luke twitched just enough to let her know he'd picked up on her bravado. For a split second, she thought she felt a sigh against her skin. Behind her, a floorboard gave the slightest creak.

A corner of his mouth tweaked up in a grin. "I'll tell them to keep their distance," he said as he stepped aside so she could open the door.

"The Bound will pay for what they've done," she said. For a long moment, she only stared into Luke's eyes. "'For I have sworn thee fair, and thought thee bright,/Who art as black as hell, as dark as night.'" She kissed him, as close to his lips as she dared, but he didn't flinch. "My love," she whispered, "is a fever.'"

Despite the layers she wore against the cold, Kristen felt exposed. Standing alone on a Queens street corner, she had every reason to be afraid, but fear had nothing to do with the tremors that battered her insides. Her skin was raw and roughed over from Luke's kisses, her cheeks blush burned. Already she felt the absence of him.

Her nearly knee-high boots crunched ice and salt, the left one tight and aching on her calf. Luke had promised other weapons like the one she carried tucked in that boot. He would only give them to her one at a time. They were precious, rare. This one would be given to Jackson. She had never thought to memorize his number, but he hadn't been at the ball, so she was hedging her bets that he was alive, staying out of sight in Madeline's home.

What was she going to say to him? Her ball had laid the Siders out on a platter. Kristen shook her head, thrusting the guilt away. Today, she'd right her wrongs. Help Jackson and anyone else who was left. If Kristen had been the one dead, Madeline would have done the same for her.

Kristen scanned the street for threats. Bells rung as Salvation Army workers collected change in front of stores. The clouded, heavy skies were a portent of snow to come.

She turned at the small bodega on the corner and headed up the street. Every few minutes, she glanced behind to be sure she wasn't being followed. She circled back of the nondescript, run-down house and lifted a cracked flowerpot. The dead plant rattled as she set it aside. Underneath was the spare key. She slipped it into the door.

"Hello?" she called out softly, her hand on the knob.

No one answered. Two stairs led up to a kitchen. There was food on the counter, none of it spoiled, as if someone had made a late breakfast and then disappeared without cleaning it up. The cupboards were open, paint peeling from them.

"Jackson?" Kristen yelled.

She imagined Madeline bounding around the corner, half expected her, but no one came. Kristen passed into the hall, up the stairs. Every crack and creak echoed through the emptiness. A shirt hung, looped around the rails of the banister. Another lay discarded in the hall. She froze, listening.

Silence, save for a ticking clock, the wind groaning outside. The door to every room lining the hall was open. She gave each one a cursory glance, padding quietly on. Most of the rooms were untouched. A very few were ravaged, dresser drawers hanging askew, clothes ripped half off hangers and then abandoned. The floors were hardwood;

any ashes should have been easy to spot, but there were none. Jackson must have taken whoever was left and run. Which would explain why most of the rooms were perfect. They had belonged to Siders who died.

"Jackson!" she yelled louder. "Anyone?"

When she got to the last room, there was something on the scuffed-up floorboards. She swallowed hard and cast a glance back at the stairs before she took a step forward. Her face wrinkled in disgust. Vomit. Old and dried.

"What the hell went on here?" she whispered. Madeline's house might have been run-down, parts of it falling apart, but she wasn't the type to leave something like this. The puddle had been there long enough to crack and split as it dried.

A knock sounded at the front door. Kristen pressed herself against the wall, frozen. Jackson had clearly left in a hurry; what if they'd gone because they knew the Bound were headed to Madeline's next? The knock came again, louder and more insistent. *Relax*, she commanded herself. *The Bound wouldn't exactly be knocking.*

The knob squeaked as it turned.

"Hey, it's open." Eden's voice. Dizzy relief spilled over Kristen, a second ahead of frustration. As long as Eden was around, Siders would be dying. But Eden would fight against the Bound. With everyone else dead, Kristen wondered if it was time to rethink her position.

"It looks like he's already gone," said a second voice. Male. *My God,* she thought. *That can't be Az?* One set of footsteps, then another, crossed into the living room below.

"Coast clear?" And Jarrod. The whole crew. Which meant she was outnumbered three to one. There was a whisper of nylon, coat sleeves brushing against each other. "Come on," he added a second later, his tone softer.

Who else was with them? Kristen eased backward into one of the rooms and tucked herself into the wedge between the wall and the door.

The voices were less distinct, but she could still hear them milling about down there. *Go away,* she thought desperately, but the fates were not in her favor. The quartet went back the way she'd come in, to the kitchen. A moment later, there were murmurs at the base of the stairs.

Eden sounded angry. "We're checking everywhere. Even if they're not here, maybe they left some clue where they were going, or what Jackson was talking about."

Kristen held her breath, torn between hoping Eden would go on about whatever Jackson had said and praying she'd leave. She got neither. Four sets of shoes clomped up the stairs.

"You and Sullivan take that side," Eden commanded. *Who is Sullivan?* Squeaking hinges marked their progress.

They closed the doors as they searched room by room, minute by minute.

"Clear," she heard Jarrod yell from across the hall.

In her hiding spot, Kristen swallowed hard. Everything had gone absolutely wrong. If they discovered her now, Eden would never trust her. All that was left was pleading mercy if she was found.

"Should we just stay here?" Az asked.

A shadow darkened the floor. "I don't know," Eden said slowly, stepping into the room Kristen hid in.

Go away, Kristen thought. The floorboards creaked as Eden moved further in. Kristen cleared her mind, readying herself for what she was about to do. *Nothing a little acting can't fix,* she thought.

Kristen shoved the door hard, then slammed the lock. Whipping around, she faced Eden. "Don't scream, it's me!" she pleaded.

Eden stood, arms spread out and ready to fight.

Kristen amped up her false terror. "Please," she whispered. "You have to help me. Tell Az and Jarrod not to hurt me!"

A bang rattled the door against her back. Kristen held her hands up.

"Eden?" Az yelled from the other side. "What's going on? Open the door!"

"Kristen's in here! She's locked the door." Eden stared

at her, desperate and full of fear.

Someone kicked hard enough to rattle the door in its frame.

"What do you want?" Eden demanded.

Kristen let her bottom lip quiver for just a fraction of a second. "I . . ." She counted off two seconds of hesitation. "I had nowhere else to go."

To her surprise, Eden looked unaffected by the show of emotion. *So help me, if I have to give her tears, I'd rather just kill her,* Kristen thought bitterly.

"Save it. You were with Luke last night," Eden said.

Kristen didn't flinch. "And you were with Gabriel?" she guessed.

"Hey!" Az yelled, pounding hard. "Open the door or we're kicking it down!" A heavy boot rattled the door.

Kristen dropped the hysterics. "I'm sick of playing games, Eden. Yes, I'm with Luke," she said. Eden blinked once, enough to let Kristen know how well the act had worked. "Look, I know we've had our differences. But we trusted each other once. Enough that I helped you get Az back, and you tried to help me get myself back." She jumped as the boys kicked the door again.

"Madeline said you want me gone." She was beyond pale, her cheeks almost gray in the winter light stealing in through the window. "You left me out of any plans. You left us to fight alone!" Eden said, real pain in her voice.

Kristen softened. "I had to. Things have changed, though," she said, coming to a decision. "You'd have been done for if I'd invited you to that ball. Let bygones be that. Fight the Bound with me." Another kick to the door. "Impatient, aren't they?" she said as the lock finally splintered. She darted out of the way just as Az burst through.

"Get away from her," he growled. "Now."

"I'm fine!" Eden insisted.

Jarrod's eyes were cold and trained on Kristen. "Block the door," he said softly, and a new girl stepped into position. "Eden, take her out."

"You're not serious," Kristen said.

"Why shouldn't she?" Jarrod said. "You wanted *her* dead."

Az glanced up. "What?"

Her first instinct was to back away from Jarrod, but that put her farther from the exit. Instead, Kristen skated along the wall. "Eden, call him off!"

"You store Touch, don't you?" Jarrod asked. He tracked her, his shoulders arched forward, movements calculated. A predator stalking prey. "With everything that's been happening, you must be loaded up from your Screamers."

Now Az was edging toward her. She glanced at Eden. There was pity in her eyes. *She really means to kill me.*

"Wait!" Kristen yelled, holding up a hand to fend them

off. "Just wait!" Madeline had told her Eden grew sick when she'd stopped taking out the Siders, but she'd forgotten about it. "I can pass to her."

"Back off, Jarrod," Az said quietly.

Kristen gave him a grateful half nod and then turned her attention back to Eden. "God," she whispered. "Look at you."

Now that she was actually paying attention, the difference in Eden was striking. Not only was her color off, but there were dark circles under her eyes. Her skin was odd, almost translucent.

"How bad are you?" Kristen asked. To her credit, Eden didn't look away.

Jarrod rocked forward on the balls of his feet, nervous and twitchy. "Don't answer that," he said. "She's with Luke again. Anything you tell her, count on it going straight back to him."

Between the halfhearted attempt on her life and Jarrod's attitude, Kristen had run out of patience. "While your concern is no doubt appreciated by Eden, trust me, Luke isn't interested in killing her off. Not when her Siders are going Upstairs."

Suddenly, Jarrod rushed her, slamming her against the wall. Kristen gasped as his forearm pressed against her throat. "You're not here to hide," he said. "You're after Sullivan."

Kristen swallowed hard. "You're Sullivan?" she asked the girl at the door.

Instantly, Jarrod leaned, his arm pressing harder. Who *was* this girl? Why was Jarrod being so overly protective?

"Did you call Luke already?" Jarrod snarled. "Is he on his way here?"

"Hey!" Az yelled. "Ease up!"

"Jarrod, there's no way she could have known we were coming here," Eden said. Something about her voice was strange. Kristen looked past Jarrod. Clutching onto the side of a short dresser, Eden had her arm laid out across the wood and her head resting on it. She used the other to push Az away while he tried to soothe her. Black smeared his skin where she'd touched him. Her eyes didn't leave Kristen. "With all the Touch you're carrying, taking you out would buy me a week," she said, her voice gravelly. "You dose me, and I get a few hours. What would you do?"

"You know what I'd do," Kristen answered. "But you're not me."

Eden's head knocked gently against the wall as she lowered to the floor. "I just figure sooner or later you'll make yourself useful again," she said, amusement in her voice. She waved Jarrod off.

"I heard you say you talked to Jackson," Kristen said.

"He called me." Sweat broke out on Eden's forehead.

She coughed into her sleeve, her lungs rattling, wet and full. Ashy flecks speckled her lips. She wiped them off with the back of her arm. "He and Madeline were up to something. We can find him faster if we work together," Eden wheezed.

Jarrod stepped behind Kristen. "Dose her," he demanded.

She sidestepped, a look of warning crossing her face. "I don't like you where I can't see you."

"And I don't give a shit," Jarrod shot back. "Dose her, now."

Eden wasn't being dramatic; that much was clear. Kristen slowly moved to sit next to her. "You try to take me out and all Hell will break loose," she said. "Literally."

Eden nodded, grimacing as she leaned forward. Kristen passed her the dose. Only when Kristen had pulled back to a safe distance did either of them let loose the breath they'd been holding. Eden's choked out in a half sob of exhaustion. "Thank you," she said, her voice shaky. She opened her eyes. They were bloodshot, but she seemed less . . . gray. "Jarrod, can you get me a glass of water?"

Kristen stared at her, silent. It was an obvious ploy to get him out of the room, and clearly the boy knew it. He set his jaw, ready to argue.

"Take Sullivan," Eden added.

"We'll go," Jarrod said. "If you promise Az stays here with you."

"Done," Eden said.

Amused, Kristen watched him waver before he snatched the girl's hand and crossed the room with her.

Once they were gone, Eden faced Kristen. "Are you after Sullivan?"

Confused, Kristen leaned forward. So the girl was important. "Why would I be?"

Eden held her gaze. There was strategy in the look. *She actually thinks she can toy with me.* The thought gave her an edge, a moment to clear her mind before Eden went on.

"The demons saw Sullivan, so Luke knows about her," Eden said. "I would think if he accidentally made another Sider, he'd be pretty keen on taking her out before any more got sent Downstairs. You're sure you aren't here to find her?"

Another death breather. Kristen struggled to keep the emotions from her face, but Eden's twitch of a smile told Kristen she'd blown it. *Why wouldn't he have told me?* Not knowing about Sullivan was a detail that could've gotten her killed.

"Kristen, talk to me," Eden said earnestly. "What's really going on? You can't trust Luke."

"Yes," Kristen said, before Eden could go on, "I can." One hand itched absently at her boot before she caught herself. She betrayed nothing more than she already had. "When did Luke kill the girl?"

"The night Sebastian and I came to Aerie looking for you, but way later."

Had that been why Luke didn't tell her about Sullivan's existence? He never would have made a Sider on purpose. Was it possible he'd lost his temper and made a mistake? "Luke was so angry when I left," she said, grim.

Two minutes later, both sides of the story were out on the table. Jarrod and Sullivan came back just as Kristen got to the part about Luke having Madeline suggest masks so he could be there and get Kristen out.

"So Luke used Madeline and then left her to die," Jarrod said, his voice emotionless. "Nice."

Instead of being angry, Kristen turned to him calm and controlled. "Gabriel's Bound. He obviously knew what was going to happen and did nothing. I don't see you vilifying *him*."

"How could you think he'd just let that happen?" Az said. Disgusted, Kristen rolled her eyes, but Az went on. "*I* told Gabe about your party. I sent him to help as soon as I left Upstairs. He didn't know. The Bound kept him in the dark."

Her face fell. Suddenly Gabriel's relief at hearing her voice took on a whole new meaning. "He called Luke to be sure I'd gotten out. But who told Luke?" she asked. "He said it was a Sider."

"Maybe it was Madeline?" Eden asked with a raised brow.

"She was acting strange," Kristen acknowledged.

Kristen went quiet, lost in thought, remembering Madeline, the emeralds around her neck and her reaction to Kristen's nearing hand. Bits of the conversation with Gabe floated back. *Her body,* he'd said. *On the back stairs. Her ribs were . . . I couldn't save her.*

Kristen rolled the rings on her fingers one at a time, shaking her head for a moment before she spoke. "I saw the Bound destroy a Sider." She swallowed to give herself a chance to collect her words. "They tore out his heart and stole away his soul, and he disintegrated into ashes."

"So why didn't Madeline?" Sullivan asked. Kristen's unease grew.

Az, too, seemed unsettled. "When Gabe told me about Madeline, he said she was . . . ripped open. The same way that Sider must have been. She was definitely dead," he said.

Kristen tilted her head back, concentrating. "You're right. She and Jackson were up to something. She was excited, nervous. She said she had to tell me something huge. That it was going to change everything." Kristen lowered her voice to a whisper, hesitant to put her thoughts into words. "Jackson told you on the phone that there was another Sider. And when you asked who made her, the

Bound or the Fallen, he said neither, correct?"

Pity made its way onto Eden's face. "Kristen . . ."

Kristen stabbed a finger into the air. "No, listen!" she shouted, her careful mask of indifference finally cracking apart. "She didn't want to be touched, and she still had a body after she died. And a death breather not made by angels." She kneeled down beside Eden and helped her to her feet. "What if Madeline wasn't a Sider anymore? My God, Eden . . . what if this girl, this Sider, can make us mortal again?"

CHAPTER 25

Jarrod closed the door to the room and turned into Sullivan's arms. They'd stolen away for just a few moments across the hall. He could still hear Kristen on the phone. She'd used his phone to call Jackson, knowing he probably wouldn't answer a call from Eden. Now she was trying to get him to explain what was going on. He cracked the door back open, but he couldn't hear any words, just the sound of her voice.

Even with Kristen's dose, if either Eden or Sullivan were hurt, they were all in trouble. And he'd never trust that Kristen wouldn't turn them over to Luke in a second if it was to her benefit. The sooner he convinced Eden and Az to split from her, the better.

"How do you feel?" he asked Sullivan.

She shrugged a shoulder. "Not bad."

"Want to try the truth?" he said, and then softened his tone. "Look, Eden and Az lied to each other so many times. They think they're helping each other or protecting each other, but it's stupid. It screws them over." He lifted her head with a finger. "We're not doing that."

She tucked herself under his chin and let out a heavy sigh. "I can feel it in my bones," she said. "Like it's breaking them apart from the inside."

"Can you hold up?" he forced himself to ask. Already he heard Kristen promising Jackson they'd come to wherever he was. As long as Sullivan could make it there, someone could dose her and things would be okay. If she couldn't, he'd have to come up with a plan.

"I can make it," she said, determination in her voice.

"Hold your breath," he said as he leaned in slowly. Their lips met. He felt the minuscule amount of Touch that had built in him pass to her. Sullivan ripped away.

"Take it back!" she demanded. "What if the Bound get you?"

Every part of him wanted to lie, but instead he looked her right in the eye. "If the Bound get me, there won't be anything left to heal."

Someone called his name from the hall, and he opened the door. Eden looked relieved when she saw him. And more than that, there was a glow of intense excitement about her. "Apparently, Madeline and Jackson *were* doing some sort of experimenting. All the Siders staying here passed to the same few mortals. One girl bore the brunt of it."

"Oh God," Sullivan whispered.

"She lost her path." She paused to let it sink in. "But with one key difference. *Madeline* killed her, Jarrod."

His jaw dropped. "What?"

She glanced at Sullivan. "Sullivan and I, we're both tied to angels, Fallen and Bound. But this girl, she's tied to a Sider. Madeline . . ." Eden trailed off, shaking her head in disbelief. "I don't know how she figured it out, but she did. Jackson said they tried it on a volunteer first. They had the death breather Rachel do her thing, expecting ashes. The Sider didn't crumble like normal. There was a body. And a few hours later, he woke up."

"Eden!" Kristen called sharply from downstairs. "Come on!"

She glanced back. "When Gabe found Madeline at Kristen's ball, she *was* dead. She didn't turn to ash because she was already mortal, Jarrod. Mortal!" Eden backed toward the stairs, gesturing for them to follow.

It took a second before Jarrod found his voice. "You mean . . . we can all be mortal again?"

"Where are they?" Sullivan burst into motion, running down the stairs after Eden. "Did they tell you?"

Az and Kristen were already waiting by the front door. "Yeah, we got an address," Eden said. "It's not far, but we've got to hurry. The Siders Jackson had with him made Rachel turn them all. That's what was going on when he called before. She's carrying way too much Touch. Jackson took some from her, but it wasn't enough. Sullivan and I can help."

Sullivan grabbed Jarrod's hand, practically skipping down the stairs. "I knew it would be okay," she said.

Jarrod didn't answer. At the door, Kristen looked nervous. Az wasn't smiling, either, something haunted and lost in his eyes as he watched Eden come down the stairs.

Before Jackson even answered the door to the apartment, a scream rang out through the hall.

"Jesus," Eden whispered.

Jarrod started to wonder why no one had called the cops when the cry was smothered into a barely audible moan. He glanced around, his hand on Sullivan's back. Eden pounded on the door again. The place was a shithole. Riding up the elevator, he'd been sure the cables were going to snap and plunge them to the basement. It didn't even have real doors, just retracting gates that made it feel like a cage. Down the heavily stained hallway, he spotted a staircase. *Thank God*, he thought. There was no way in hell he was getting back in that elevator.

A hollow clink sounded against the door as a chain was released. The dead bolt clunked. Finally, Jackson opened the door.

"Where is she?" Eden demanded.

Frantic, he pointed behind him. "Kitchen."

"Jackson," Kristen said. She took him by the elbow and moved him out of the way enough to let Eden storm by. "You tried to help her, didn't you?"

He nodded, running a hand back and forth over his shaved head. The skin was raw and red. He was wired, carrying far too much Touch. "I couldn't pass. I couldn't leave her alone." He shuddered and lowered his pinkie to gnaw on the nail. "She just keeps screaming."

Az closed the door and redid the chain and dead bolt. "There's no one here but you and her, right?" he asked.

Jackson nodded. A sliver of blood showed on his fingernail where he'd bitten the cuticle too deep. He grabbed suddenly for Kristen. "Mad's dead!" he cried. "She's dead!"

"I'm so sorry, Jackson. Sebastian, too." As Jarrod watched, she seemed to shake it off. "You did so well," she said as Jarrod led Sullivan past. "Madeline would be proud."

They entered the kitchen just as Eden tipped up and away from the girl. "Okay, you can breathe, Rachel," she said.

Though Jarrod didn't see a bedroom, a mattress had been dragged from somewhere and was wedged between the wall and the front of the stove. The girl on it trembled, her arms twitching and jerking. With a shaking hand, she wiped her mouth.

Eden squeezed her shoulder. "Any better?" she asked.

The girl nodded absently, but it was the change in Eden that stopped him dead. She looked healthy, the gray color gone from her skin. Her cheeks glowed rosy. With her free hand she waved over Sullivan.

"This will be just like you did with Jarrod, only you're going to be getting a lot more Touch," she coached. "Be sure to hold your breath." She kept her hand on Sullivan's back as Sullivan leaned forward and took the dose.

Az pressed in behind Jarrod. "How are you?" he asked Eden.

She winked at him, and he seemed to relax a bit. "Ready, Jarrod?"

Jarrod moved forward. "Should she be losing Touch that fast?"

"Can you imagine what would happen to me if I took out twenty Siders? Especially twenty paranoid Siders, who've been storing instead of passing? She's way over-loaded. And I don't think anyone even told her any-thing." Eden rubbed the girl's back. "Jarrod, take a dose," she said. He hesitated. The girl, Rachel, already looked glazed, like she was well on her way to being out of her mind. "She needs to get rid of it," Eden insisted when Jarrod didn't move. "What happens if later Sullivan and

I need to be dosed and you didn't take it?"

"That's not playing fair," he said, crossing his arms over his chest. "Why don't you just have her turn us mortal now?"

"No!" Az blurted. "Eden and Sullivan can help her regulate if she's turning Siders mortal. We can save them from the Bound. If she does it to Eden now, though, she'll just take back all the Touch she got rid of."

Eden stared down at the girl. "You're right," she said. "Jarrod, take the dose from her. We need to keep her levels as low as possible so she can help Siders as we find them." Eden motioned for Sullivan to switch with him.

Rachel didn't move when Jarrod kneeled next to her, just kept staring off into space. He turned her face toward him without thinking about his ungloved fingers. Instantly, her glamour dropped away. Jarrod jumped back in surprise. One of her eye sockets was hollow. The other oozed, part of the rotting eyeball dripping down her cheekbone.

Sullivan's scream pierced the silence. On the mattress beside him, Rachel's jaw dropped open, tendons stretching, and she wailed and then went quiet. Her bones creaked, the fabric of her shirtsleeves swaying as she wrapped her arms around herself and started to rock. Jarrod couldn't believe she'd dosed both Eden and Sullivan and still carried so much Touch.

"Jesus," he managed. "Yeah, I guess she won't be running out any time soon."

The Touch thrummed into him, his mouth going numb, his throat tickling with vibration. The dose was bigger than anything he'd ever gotten from Eden. On her lips, he could taste salt. "Rachel?" Eden said suddenly.

Jarrod found the girl staring at him. Not blankly, but actually making contact as he pulled away from her.

"It hurts," Rachel moaned, and he thought she was done until she swallowed and added another word. "Less."

Eden smiled at her. "We're gonna have you give us more, okay? We'll keep going until it stops hurting at all."

Rachel stiffened, backing herself against the rusted stove. "I don't know you. What's going on?"

Eden didn't have a chance to answer before Kristen's voice grew louder in the living room. Footsteps crossed to them, and she poked her head around the corner.

"We need to go," she said. Eden started to argue, but Kristen shook her head. "We need to go *now*, Eden. Do you know where we are?" Her voice pitched up. "This was where Gabriel stayed when he was Fallen. It's not safe here."

Eden swore, stumbling to her feet. "We can't keep running like this!" She glanced down at the girl. "We can't get caught. She's everyone's chance to survive."

"But what happens when there're no Siders left? Who changes her?" Az asked.

Eden helped Rachel to her feet. "That's a bridge we'll cross when we come to it."

Jarrod slammed his fist into the wall before he spun on Kristen. "If you screw us over . . . if us having to leave again is some plan to turn her over to Luke, I swear to God . . ."

He didn't bother finishing the threat, instead wrapping Rachel's arm around his neck. Her legs wobbled and gave out. "Son of a bitch," he muttered, and dropped to a knee, throwing her over his shoulder.

She gave a surprised "oomph."

"If we're going, let's go," Jarrod snarled.

Az backed out of the way and headed into the living room. Jackson already had the door open.

"Stairwell," Jarrod said. "We'd be sitting ducks in the elevator."

"Good call." Eden passed him at a jog, opening the door to listen down the stairs. After a second she gave them a thumbs-up, and the rest of the group charged down the hallway. "There's no need to panic," she said as they clomped down, her words almost lost in the pounding echo of their feet. "We don't even know that they're coming. This is just a precaution."

"Right," he heard Az mumble from behind him. Jarrod could feel him wanting to get by, to get closer to Eden, but with Rachel over his shoulder and the stairs steep, Jarrod didn't dare stop to let him pass.

When they reached the bottom, Eden slammed into the push bar and swung the door open wide, spilling them onto the street. She turned back to Jarrod as soon as they were out. "I want Rachel to dose us again," she said. "We might not get another chance, and we need her functioning. And me functioning."

He could hear how short of breath Eden had gotten just from the few flights. She was better, but not nearly as strong as she needed to be. He slipped Rachel off his shoulder and leaned her against a brick wall.

"Thank you," Rachel said.

Jarrod bent over, resting his elbows on his knees. The Touch she'd passed him was still settling. He could feel it, slithering through him. Already he was itching to pass it off to any mortal they found, but he had to hold on, save it in case one of the girls needed it. Which meant he had to keep his head clear. No dark thoughts.

When he stood up again, Sullivan was next to him. "What's wrong?" she asked, worried.

"Too much Touch makes any of us sick, crazy. You and Eden can hold much more than I can." Even as he said it, a wave of pain washed through his abdomen. He clenched his teeth until it passed. "When Eden used to dose me, I'd pass it off to the mortals pretty quick so it didn't affect me."

"But now you're keeping it for us, in case we get hurt?" she asked quietly.

He gave her a quick nod. "Can Rachel dose Sullivan again?" he called out to Eden.

Rachel seemed more animated, coming around with each dose she gave. If it was true—if she *could* make Siders mortal again—Eden and Sullivan would have to stay with her, drain her of the Touch she accumulated with every Sider she took out. And if they were getting massive doses of Touch from Rachel, they wouldn't need to take out Siders.

Kristen sidled up to her. "I'm first." She glared back at the look of uncertainty Eden gave her. "Do you have any idea how much time I've put into training myself to store? After you two, I'm the most capable person in this group to help her."

"We need to find out how to get the Siders to come to her," Eden said as Rachel dosed Kristen. She turned to Jackson. "Or better yet, we can have her go to them. Stay on the move."

Suddenly, Kristen's whole face shifted, going pale. Jarrod turned just in time to see someone with an odd, loping gait walk the last few feet of the cross street they stood on and disappear behind the edge of the apartment building.

"He was in my yard." Venom filled Kristen's voice. "I

saw him last night," she said, stepping forward. "I'll kill him for what he's done."

Az grabbed for her arm. "Are you crazy? We go. Now," he said as he snagged her. "Do not run unless they see us."

"Shit," Jarrod whispered, knowing it was probably too late already to make an escape. The Bound were like roaches; spotting one meant they'd already infested a place. His eyes skipped around, taking in roofs and fire escapes and cars parked on the side of the street. They could be anywhere. Beside him, he heard Sullivan's frightened breaths.

Eden wasn't bothering being inconspicuous. She slowly walked backward. "Az, stick close to Rachel. They can't get to her."

"Understood," he said as he moved to the girl's side. "If we get split up—"

A foot slammed into Jarrod's chest. He flew back as the angel finished materializing, and landed hard. He rolled out of the way just as a fist plunged into the gravelly snow.

Even before he finished the roll and was back on his feet, he focused on the blur of Eden's black coat. Still alive. Another Bound popped into existence beside him. He threw a punch and heard the thing's nose crunch under his knuckles.

"Az, get Rachel!" he called, praying. Jarrod took the split second to glance around. Their group had scattered.

Four Bound—including the one he'd punched—had Az and Kristen flanked, backing them slowly toward a chain-link fence.

Rachel ran for him instead of Az. "Who are they?" she gasped beside him.

"Angels," he answered distractedly. Where was Sullivan? He swept across the scene again. Panic surged into him. Where the hell was Eden?

At the fence, Kristen drew something out of her boot. She dropped a sheath and brandished a curved blade. It glinted evilly in the winter sun. "No closer," she commanded.

A gasp rippled through the Bound. *A knife?* Jarrod wondered. He'd let her get close to Eden and never thought she'd been armed. He expected the Bound to laugh. One eased closer. Jarrod watched, torn between getting Rachel out of there and staying to help. *Would the Bound hurt Az?* he wondered, knowing even as he thought it that they would. He was half Fallen. To them he was nothing. And he was with the Siders.

For the moment, it looked like the angels were trained on Kristen, or, more accurately, the knife. She held it in front of her with both hands on the hilt.

One of the Bound made a horrible metallic sound. "You struggle valiantly but in vain. Weapons mean nothing in weak hands."

She carved the blade through the air, stopping it near

the angel's neck. "Don't," she warned, "call me weak."

The angels stumbled back a step.

"Who would give such a weapon to you?" Another step back. Whatever the knife was, it had them ready to run.

"Lucifer," Kristen snarled. "You will leave me and my friends. If any of you harm us, it's his wrath you'll have to fear!"

A murmur of dissent went through them. Even Jarrod couldn't look away. A blade forged in Hell. The only thing that could kill one of the Bound. Kristen's hair swirled around her in the breeze, wild, her eyes flashing. She looked badass. She looked terrifying.

One of the angels winked out of existence.

Then two more.

"We are many," the last growled. He backed slowly away. "Your kind dims."

And then he, too, was gone.

"Kristen!" Az shouted. "Do you even know what the fuck you're holding?"

"Angel antidote." Kristen waved the blade from side to side like it was a toy. "Handy!"

Az stared at it like it was a snake. "Luke wouldn't trust you with it. Did you steal it from him?"

She stilled. "Why wouldn't he trust me?"

Az didn't answer. "Jarrod, where's Eden?" he asked carefully.

No. Jarrod whipped around, scanning the alley, praying Eden and Sullivan would be climbing out from behind a Dumpster or in an alcove.

"Jackson's gone, too. And your girl," Kristen said.

A whoosh of air swirled beside Jarrod. He heard the pop of one of the Bound coming back and ducked instinctively. Arms appeared around Rachel's middle. She looked down in surprise.

The angel zoomed backward down the street before Rachel could even scream, her shoes skipping across the pavement. One came off, tumbled to the side as she whipped around a corner out of sight. Jarrod took off after, though it was hopeless. There was no way he was going to be able to keep pace, let alone catch up. He got to the first street but hesitated in the crosswalk. Az and Kristen dashed up behind him. *Don't panic, think,* he commanded himself.

A scream drifted through the air. Everyone froze. Distorted, carried by the wind, it was still full of agony.

"No," Az whispered. He took off after the source, not waiting, not looking back. Like Jarrod, the second he'd heard it, he knew who it belonged to.

Eden.

CHAPTER 26

I *made the Siders?* Gabe thought. That was impossible. There was no way he could have caused something so catastrophic, so horrifying, without knowing it. "You're lying," Gabe said. He tried again to read Annalise's thoughts. Again, she blocked him effortlessly. "Who are you?"

Her eyes bored into his. "You're not going to jump, are you?" she said. Gabe shook his head, not understanding. "That's what you said to me. 'You're not going to jump, are you?' Do you remember me now? I'd gone to the park, overlooking the river, and—"

"The concrete pilings," Gabriel whispered. He pushed his fists down into the couch cushions. Suddenly, he remembered. How long ago was it? Five years? Six? It had been sunset, the sky oscillating with oranges and reds, and from the west a storm was rolling in. He'd been restless, and wanted to go to the park, just to get outside. Az hadn't, but Gabe had convinced him. Thunder was rumbling in the distance when they got there, but he hadn't wanted to give Az the satisfaction of leaving so soon. Finally, Gabe had gotten tired of his friend's sulking and told him to go home.

He'd gone on alone. The gravel path had split, one branch straight, the other curving around to the water-front. He'd been about to go the shorter way when he'd seen her red tank top bobbing ten feet higher than a person could walk. She was up on the concrete pilings there to keep bikers from taking the curve too sharp and plunging over the cliff. She'd been balanced, the wind in her hair, staring out at the water.

"I used to go there all the time to watch the storms roll in. I could see everything. The water, the bridges, the city." She fell silent.

"You made me nervous so close to the edge," Gabe said.

"It wasn't supposed to rain, but clouds and the sunset and it was so perfect. I couldn't remember a better day. And I turned around and you were behind me."

Gabe'd caught her thoughts, seen the excited shine coating them. He remembered the moment her happiness had hit him, so overwhelming he'd felt drunk off it. Her mind, singing and blissful. When she'd faced the water again, he'd made his way back to the main path. He searched his memory for more, but there was nothing.

"How did that make you a Sider?" Erin asked.

Annalise's eyes were wet. "I heard someone else coming. I turned, but I caught my lace and tripped." She leaned forward and put her head in her hands. "I hit my head when I landed and must have blacked out for a second. When I came to, a boy had his arm around me, starting to lift me up."

"Az?" Gabe guessed, but Annalise didn't acknowledge him.

"For a minute, I was worried about how hard I'd hit my head, because he looked so much like you," she said, looking at Donavan. "You were supposed to meet me that day. Those pilings were our spot."

Donavan shook his head. "But when I met you, you were already a Sider," he said. "We met at that same park. Walking on the path." Gabe watched as Donavan pieced it all together. When he spoke again, his voice was measured. "You came up to *me* the day we met. You knew me? So I . . . forgot you when you went Sider?"

Annalise took his hand. "You never could remember why you loved that park so much," she said.

"Jesus Christ, Annie," he said, ripping away from her. Her hand hung in the empty air. "If I knew you when we were mortal, why didn't you ever tell me?"

"Because Az wasn't the last one to show up! And I

never wanted *him*"—she spat the word—"to know you existed. And I never wanted to have to talk about what happened next."

So focused on Donavan, Annalise let a few snapshots of memory slip through to Gabe. Az helping her to her feet. His back as he rounded the corner. Another angel approaching once he'd gone. And Gabriel saw that angel's face.

"No," Gabriel whispered, and Annalise's attention snapped to him, her thoughts garbling once more, but it was too late. "What did he do to you?"

She shuddered. To his surprise, at seeing her upset Donavan seemed to forget his own anger and sat back down, putting his arm around her shoulder. "He thought I was with Az," she said. "He told me he needed to check my pupils, since I'd hit my head. I assumed he was a doctor, but when I looked into his eyes . . . Well."

Gabe made himself sit still and wait for her to continue despite the sudden rage flooding through him.

"When I woke up, we weren't in the park anymore and he was babbling. Things I didn't understand about paths and love and how I didn't have to be afraid. That Az and I could be together forever." Her voice dropped. "I kept trying to tell him I didn't know who he was talking about, but he'd seen us together right after I fell. And he had my memories of Donavan. He thought I was confused from hitting my head, or that Az lied to me about his name, or . . . something."

Annalise picked at a thread on her pants. Then she opened her mind to Gabe.

A barrage of fragmented memories slammed into him. *Kept me in a room—locked—promised not to tell anyone what he'd done—"keep Az from Falling"—and then we could all have what we wanted—* "He told me that he would fix me," she said aloud. "I felt like I was going out of my skin. Every day it got worse, this feeling building inside me, and then one day, I couldn't take it anymore. And I took a sheet from the bed and—"

"Stop," Gabe said, his head hanging low. "That's enough."

Donavan rubbed his hand up and down Annalise's arm, his thoughts stricken.

"I woke up on the floor," she said, finally. "I thought I'd failed." She stared ahead, focused somewhere far beyond the room they sat in now. "The door was open and so I ran. I ran home."

She didn't say any more. They all knew what happened, how without a path, any life the Siders had led as mortals was as if it had never existed. They were forgotten.

Donavan brought his hand up to her head, stroking her hair. "And me?"

Annalise sniffed. "I thought it would be okay if we just

started over. I wasn't sure what I was, only that I was different. I thought maybe you could still love me. Every time we touched—I'm sorry, I didn't know what I was doing to you," she got out before she burst into tears.

Donavan pulled her against him. "Is that enough?" he asked Gabe, an edge to his voice.

"Why me?" Erin asked as Annalise lifted her head from Donavan's shoulder. "I met Madeline shopping. Did you send her after me? Did I know you?"

"No," Annalise said, a bitter twinge to her words. "You were friends with Madeline when she was mortal. You forgot her when I turned her, just like she forgot me. After Donavan, Madeline was the first of my friends I recruited. She mentioned how much she missed you, and so you were my gift to her."

Erin blanched. "Kristen?" she whispered.

For a long time, Annalise said nothing. "A girl Donavan and I had gone to school with," she said. "She'd always seemed kind of out there and fascinating. We started passing her Touch. Then we realized in the time since we'd been mortal, she'd started to fall apart at the seams. We knew something wasn't right, so we stopped. Too late. We didn't know she'd gone Sider until she reintroduced herself to Madeline later." She wouldn't look at Erin, her chin quivering as she met Gabriel's gaze with feverish intensity. "For two years, that poor girl suffered for what we did to her. But you saved her, Gabriel. You'd been watching Madeline and Erin. I was terrified you'd seen Donavan and me. That if you knew where to find us, eventually, *he* would come. So we split into territories, and I went into hiding here."

"Did he come after you?" Gabe asked.

She shook her head. "I'm sure he thought I was dead. I'm not sure what he thought when he came back and my body was missing. I don't even know *if* he came back. I have no idea why he was so adamant that I end up with Az."

"I've got an inkling," Gabe said.

Erin was staring at her, her lips parting just enough to speak. "The others?"

Annalise spun back to her. "Vaughn was Donavan's friend. They grew up together," she said quietly. "It was a game once I figured out how to do it. We brought our friends in. Vaughn was supposed to be the last. We didn't know he started to sell Touch almost immediately. He didn't realize he was inadvertently making Siders. At first, I even thought it was the same angel doing to others what he'd done to me. By the time anyone figured it out it was Vaughn, things had already spiraled so far out of control."

A ringtone startled them all. Gabriel dug Madeline's phone out of his pocket. The number wasn't one she'd saved. "Hello?" he said as he answered.

Heavy breathing. Running and then a gasped "Gabe!" Gabriel shot to his feet. "Jarrod?"

The response was breathless. "They took them. All four of them. I didn't—"

"Took who?"

"Az is gonna lose it. You've gotta get here, Gabe, like, *now*. The Bound took Eden. Sullivan." He panted into the speaker. "Jackson. They got them all."

"Where are you?" Gabriel demanded.

"Your place," Jarrod said. "When you were Fallen. Two blocks from there. Running." He heard Jarrod begging Az to slow down. "We found out how to make the Siders mortal," Jarrod said a second later.

Gabriel motioned to Erin to get up. "Don't leave, do you hear me?" he said into the phone. "You keep Az with you and don't leave."

"They. Have. Eden. He's wigging the fuck out. Black eyes, whole bit."

"Damn it," Gabriel spat. "Do what you can. I'll be there in a second."

He hung up the phone and slid it back into his pocket. "Gabe?" Erin said.

"I have to go," he replied.

"I started the Siders. I know you have to tell the Bound." Annalise stood, fear bleaching her face. "What's going to happen to me?" Donavan gripped her hand.

"Nothing if I can help it," Gabe said. He caught her in a hug. "Thank you for what you've told me." Her mortal life had been snatched away through no fault of her own. She'd suffered, not knowing why. He patted her back before he pulled away and turned to Donavan. "Stay here. If anyone comes besides me, run. Do not be a hero. If I'm not back by nightfall, disappear. Go away and you do not come back, understood?"

He left them without waiting for an answer. Halfway down the front stairs, he pictured the apartment complex, the shaded nook of the laundry room near the front door. *Go,* he thought.

CHAPTER 27

$\mathcal{E}$den had memorized what she could of the building the Bound dragged her into two hours ago. She'd counted eight flights of stairs before they'd marched her out of the stairwell. The center of the building was open, the empty space surrounded on each floor on four sides by a balcony that led off to rooms. Eden and the other Siders' dragged footsteps sent chunks of debris tumbling beyond the railing, falling to the floor so far below. Above, an impressive atrium of glass and metal let in the late-afternoon light. Bound angels had lined floors and floors of railings like sentinels. *You hurt us and I'll rip your throats out.* Two of them flinched at the viciousness of her thought, and she was surprised to find pity in the eyes that dared meet hers.

Then they'd dumped Eden and the others down here in this pit.

The floorboards underneath her were wet and warped.

The door and windows had been covered over with thick crisscrossing layers of barbed wire, cemented to the walls to hold them in place. Eden's fingers bled where she'd tried to rip it loose. The ceiling was partially collapsed, making it the only opening in the room. The Bound had taken their phones, their jackets, and their gloves.

Jackson hadn't made a sound in almost an hour. Sullivan cried quietly. Only Rachel seemed alert, staring at Eden as if expecting her to have some sort of escape plan. *Yeah, right,* Eden thought.

Just out of sight, one of the Bound paced in the room above. She heard him, making his rounds every few minutes. Eden had tucked everyone into the alcove underneath what remained of the ceiling. She lay still, a hand between the floor and her cheek. *I've got to do something.*

"Get up, guys," she said through chattering teeth. "We need to walk."

No one moved. She forced herself to stand. "Sullivan, now."

The sobs slowed to hiccups as Sullivan got to her feet. Eden limped to Jackson. He didn't acknowledge her, just stared out from his spot against the wall. Dried blood ran a broken trail down his face. She gently flaked off what she could. The wound itself had healed quickly with all the Touch he carried, but he seemed disoriented. "Just a little longer. Az will come for us," she said. "Jarrod, too."

He hadn't responded to any previous attempt to draw him out, but this time he focused. "Maddy won't."

Eden wrapped her arms around him, and was surprised when he hugged her back.

"You really think we're going to get out of here?" he asked. His expression was bleak.

"Az will come for us," she repeated. No matter how bad things got, she knew Az and Jarrod wouldn't rest. She squeezed Jackson tighter. *I will not die here*, she promised herself.

When Eden stepped back and started pacing, Jackson followed a few steps behind. Rachel stayed at his side, helping him along. The room wasn't large, but doing something—even walking in circles—would keep them from feeling so utterly hopeless.

"Stay around the edges," Eden said as she fell in beside Sullivan. Sullivan nodded, and Eden lowered her voice. "The Bound are keeping us alive for a reason. If they wanted us dead, they would have done it already."

A sudden chuckle echoed through the room. In the threshold above, an angel glared down at them. "Such a foolish deduction," he said.

Eden recognized him as the one who had tormented Az at Rockefeller Center. It seemed like months ago they'd run into him at near the tree, but it hadn't even been two weeks. *Michael*. He blinked out above and reappeared in the room with them. Sullivan pressed against Eden, and they backed away slowly.

"You." Eden's voice wavered. Michael jutted his head out, crooked it to the side. The movement was reptilian, horrible. "Gabe's our friend. He'll be upset if you hurt us."

His lips peeled back in a grimace. "Do *not* call him unproper. *Gab-ri-el.* Once your kind is exterminated, he will be whole again. And when you fall to ash, he will be mine."

Eden held an arm over the others, keeping them behind her. "He's no one's but his own. And he'd never be with *anyone* who would hurt his friends."

Michael's agitation only worsened. "Silence. You speak aloud of things you know not."

"We didn't do anything to you!" Jackson broke in. He pushed in front of Eden as Michael twisted around. "Why are you doing this? You're supposed to be the good guys!"

Michael sidled closer. "Your kind is born of corrosion and putrescence. Souls perish at your touch and you celebrate with pageantry and fine dresses?" He sneered, incredulous. "You dare beg mercy?"

"You were at Kristen's," Jackson said. Eden didn't like the violent, reckless edge to his words.

"Jackson—" She seized the back of his shirt as he stepped toward the angel, but he ripped away.

"Did you kill Madeline?"

"I don't answer to you," Michael said. It was all the answer Jackson needed. He let loose a primal scream and leaped, but Michael was ready. His fist slammed into Jackson's jaw, dropping him before he had a chance to react.

"Stop!" Sullivan cried, but the plea only brought on a kick that cracked Jackson's ribs.

"Do you not see the chaos your kind has caused?" Michael took a step back. "The fate of mortal souls at your fingertips and still you seem to think this unholy existence is your privilege?"

In one lithe movement, his fist plunged, breaking through Jackson's chest in a spray of gore. Shock froze Eden as Michael yanked his hand free. Something glowed in his hand. Then flames broke out and fire dripped between his fingers. The drops hissed as they died on the cold floorboards.

As the last bits dimmed, Michael vanished, reappearing a split second later looking down at them from the room above. "I won't be led astray," he said, his voice echoing through the silent room. "I'm stronger than the others."

Eden didn't dare release the cry she was holding in until she was sure he was gone. On the floor, a pile of ash was all that remained of Jackson.

Behind her, she heard Rachel collapse. And beside her,

Sullivan hadn't moved. Eden stepped in front of her. Her eyes were glassy. "Sullivan," Eden said. "Hey."

Eden sank slowly and pulled her knees into her chest. Already, she'd started to shiver again. "Az is coming," she whispered.

I will not die here.

Someone shook Eden awake. She drew a breath to scream, but a frigid hand slammed over her mouth.

"Someone's coming!" Rachel whispered.

Eden listened. Footsteps. *Don't be Michael,* she thought. *Please don't be Michael.*

Sullivan's hand found hers. "It's Jarrod. I know it."

None of them dared move. Eden concentrated on the noises. *At least two of them,* she thought, but there was another sound. *Are they dragging someone?* Her heart thumped hard enough that she heard it echo in her ears. *Don't be him,* Eden begged silently, hoping Sullivan's wish for Jarrod would go unanswered. If they'd caught him, then that meant they'd gotten Az, too. And Kristen. What if Jarrod and Kristen were already turned to ash?

"Please don't hurt me," a boy cried. Eden hated herself for the relief she felt when she didn't recognize the voice.

Rachel started to move, but Eden stopped her. A muffled argument drifted down to them.

Then a body hit the floor at Sullivan's feet. It was a guy,

his face hidden as he struggled to his knees. He spotted them and froze.

"For the Sider who poisons Downstairs." The words thundered. She felt Sullivan tremble. "We've been told you must be fed. The boy is yours."

Eden balked. She raised her hands, palms out, to the poor kid. *We're not going to hurt you.* He seemed to get the message.

A whispered argument bounced off the walls, layered, the words indecipherable. A Bound blinked into the space beside Eden. Before she could scream, he had her by the neck, dragging her across the floor, away from Sullivan and Rachel. "End him, and we'll spare your friend," the Bound told Sullivan. "For the moment."

"No," Sullivan said. "I don't *feed*. I don't need him."

Another angel appeared a few feet from Rachel. Gasping, she clung to Sullivan.

The arm around Eden's neck was slick with a thin sheen of sweat. The quick flutter of his heart pulsed against her shoulder blade and an idea stirred. She didn't hold on to it, so that none of the Bound could catch it from her mind. "Sullivan, listen to me. You can do this."

"The fuck she can!" the boy screamed.

The arm around Eden's neck tightened. She didn't struggle; instead, she kept as calm as she could manage and thought of sunshine and the ocean, the snow outside, the coldness of her toes inside her shoes.

Eden turned her head a fraction of an inch. "It's us or him, Sullivan!"

"No!" She stared at Eden in horror.

On the floor, the boy moved backward to put as much space between him and Sullivan as he could. One of the Bound strode toward him.

"Do it, Sullivan!" Eden screamed. The arm around her neck loosened just a bit as she strained forward. The extra inch was all she needed.

Without warning, Eden twisted and slammed her lips against the angel's. He jerked away, but not before she felt the tingle of Touch sliding out of her, into him.

Eden screamed and drove the palm of her hand into his nose. Back when she'd kissed Az, before they knew better, the Touch she'd passed him had overwhelmed him, the effect instant as his darkest thoughts multiplied. They'd almost lost him to the Fall. Now, she watched this angel's fear spinning out of control as she charged toward her friends.

The other angel backed away. "You poisoned him!"

"Get out!" Eden roared, clenching her fists.

The angel she'd dosed disappeared. His partner glanced from Eden to Sullivan to the boy, who was still on the floor, looking dazed. Rachel cowered in the shadows. Eden strode toward the angel. "You're next," she said.

And he was gone.

Holy shit, it worked, she thought, slowly relaxing her fingers. The last of her adrenaline drained away as the boy got to his feet.

Sullivan tiptoed closer, concern in her eyes. "They'll be back, Eden. They're going to come back, and now they're going to kill us for sure."

Eden sat down and crossed her arms over her knees. "They're going to try. And when they do, I will fight them with every breath and every bone left in my body," she said. A dizzy wave rolled over her, and she lowered her head. She wasn't sure if she should ask Rachel to dose her or if it was just the fight running out of her. "I'm not going out like this. Neither are you two."

There was an awkward moment of silence before she looked up again. "You either, kid," she told the boy.

He managed a smile. "I thought you wanted her to take me out," he said, pointing to Sullivan. "That was a trick? Badass."

"They can read minds. I just kind of went for it without planning." Eden turned her head to the side and laid it back on her arms. "It won't work again. So we'd better start thinking about our next trick."

CHAPTER 28

K̇risṭ꞉ꞔ꞉ dragged her fork through the plate of noodles in front of her. None of them had bothered to eat. They'd only picked the restaurant because of its lack of windows, the high booths that cut off any easy view of them from the entry.

Gabriel had met them on the street outside and pulled Az away without a word. They'd been too far away for Kristen to hear their exchange. She could only see Az shaking his head, horror-struck. *Is it Eden?* Kristen wondered. Finally Az came back, sitting in a sort of stunned silence. When Kristen had asked him what was wrong, he'd glanced up at her. His irises had gone nearly black.

She didn't ask again.

Now, they sat on cracked leather in some dive of an Italian restaurant waiting for word from Gabriel. An hour ago, he'd told them to stay there and left for Upstairs.

Across from her, Az sat on the edge of the bench, a

statue, his eyes dark violet. Every few minutes, the black center seemed to pulse, swirl out even as what was left of the iris yellowed. No matter what, they stayed glued to the sliver of door visible from where he sat.

"Anything?" Kristen asked.

Jarrod scoffed before Az could answer. "Yeah, Gabe walked in here ten minutes ago. He just didn't feel like telling you."

She glared daggers in his direction. "Unhelpful."

"Deal with it." He dunked his straw into the cup in front of him, nervously jostling the ice.

A waitress buzzed by the table, a tray balanced on one hand. "Can I get you anything else?" she asked, and then looked down at their three full plates. She frowned. "Is something wrong with the food?"

Kristen plastered on a grin, the fakeness of it aching in her cheeks. "Everything's wonderful."

"Well, all right," the waitress said, grabbing up a straw wrapper. "But you guys look like you came straight from a funeral."

"We did." Kristen watched the waitress squirm, enjoying the utter embarrassment in her face.

Across the table Kristen caught Az's eye. He took his phone out of his pocket and checked the display to get the time. His worry was clear. Not only was Eden missing, but Gabriel hadn't returned for them. Kristen wondered if, like her, Az wasn't sure if Gabe would be coming back at all. Which left them with one last person to turn to for help. "Let me know when you want me to call," she said.

Jarrod slammed his elbows onto the tabletop. "It's not happening, Kristen. Give it up."

She ignored him.

Az pinched the bridge of his nose and handed her his phone in defeat. "Do it," he said.

"No!" Jarrod made a grab for it. She leaned back out of his reach and put it to her ear. "Az!"

But Az's hand shot out, hooking Jarrod's collar. "Gabe said one hour. We gave him time. We need a plan B." He clenched his fist tighter. "I am not losing Eden, do you understand me?"

Jarrod held his hands up. "Don't let her lose you, either," he said carefully. "And don't forget: Luke will kill Sullivan if he gets to her first."

Az released Jarrod's shirt, sorrow on his face.

Finally, Kristen's call went through. "Let me guess," Luke said into her ear. "You've had complications."

Under the table, she slid a hand down her calf, into her boot. She gripped the hilt of the blade he'd given her. Safety. Security. Kristen struggled for words, uncertain how she wanted to play the situation with Az and Jarrod listening.

"My, my," Luke said as the silence went on. "I can tell

this is going to be good. Spill it."

Already she regretted making the phone call at the table, though she doubted the others would have trusted her if she'd gone out of earshot. She should have at least warned Jarrod of what she planned to say. Before she brought Luke in on the latest developments, she had bad blood to clear between them.

"Are you aware of her?" Kristen asked, already knowing the answer. "The new death breather?"

"Don't say *anything* about her to him. He knows enough." Jarrod's quiet words made the hair on her neck stand up.

"Yes, I know," Luke said, a new bite to his voice. "You're keeping some interesting company, Kristen. Send Jarrod my regards. He always seems to come out on top, that one. Is the girl there now?"

"I could have been turned to ash. Why was I not told about her?"

"She's not common knowledge. The Bound can read your mind, Kristen. I couldn't take the chance." He paused. "Am I missing something? It seems as if you've put your revenge on hold."

"I went to Jackson's. He'd already fled," she said. She made no mention of Rachel as she filled him in on how Az was back from Upstairs, how she and Eden's crew had found Jackson.

"Were you injured?" he interrupted when she got to the attack from the Bound.

"No, I used the knife you gave me," she said. "But both Eden and Sullivan were captured, along with Jackson and another."

"Captured? The Bound didn't destroy them?"

"Captured," she repeated. From the look on Az's face, the way she was drawing out asking for the favor was driving him mad, but he should trust that she knew what she was doing. That she knew Luke. *Stay with me*, she mouthed.

"I'm glad you had sense enough not to get yourself taken," Luke said. "I'm sorry to hear about Eden. As for the rest of them, I'd rather you didn't get involve—"

"You're going to rescue them," she said quickly.

"Am I now?" he murmured. "I do believe you're over-estimating your hold on me, *kitten*."

Kristen laughed. "The Bound have Sullivan. What better way to slaughter the Siders they've captured than to have her dispatch them Downstairs?"

There was silence on the line. A thrill trickled through her as she felt the power shift between them.

"You don't know where they're being kept?" Luke asked after a moment.

"No. I want you to find them," she said. "You'll help us get Eden back to Az. And then, instead of killing Sullivan, you're going to hand her over to a very worried Jarrod without so much as a scratch."

"And *my* reward is you?"

"We'll see. There's another Sider with them who is . . ." She taunted him with another pause. "Different," she finished.

"Different how?"

"Unlike anything we've seen before, and not something you want in the hands of the Bound. Jarrod and Az are here with me. Bring them weapons. I want the revenge you promised me, Luke. I want bodies."

Before he could respond, she heard a click of static. "Entertaining as always, Kristen," he said. "But there's another call I have to take. For now, stay put."

Kristen hung up without another word. She leaned back, satisfied, and slid the phone across the table to Az. "He's taking care of it."

Jarrod rubbed his hands across his head. "What's going to keep him from killing Sullivan?" The sadness in his eyes struck her until he started to speak. "You better pray whatever sick things you did with Lucifer got you enough pull to keep them alive. This isn't a fucking game, Kristen."

Her face went hot with fury, but before she found a retort, he turned to Az. "Let me out. Now."

Sliding aside, Az stood awkwardly while Jarrod scooted

past. "Come on, don't be stupid. Stay in here with us. If the Bound find you—"

"No worries," Jarrod said snidely. "I'm sure Luke will be happy to save my ass, too."

Kristen rose from the bench. "You have no right to treat me like this when I'm trying to help you!" she snarled. Restaurant patrons around her swiveled to stare. "I could have walked away!"

Suddenly Jarrod's face was an inch from hers. He didn't speak. He just stood there, nostrils flaring, fists balled at his sides. It took everything she had not to recoil.

Az's phone rang, the vibration bumping it across the table and breaking the tension. Kristen watched as his eyes went wide when he answered.

"You're sure?" It was impossible to tell if what filled his voice was hope or heartbreak. Kristen steeled herself. Az bolted up, shoving the phone in his pocket. "Let's go. Luke knows where they are."

$\mathcal{S}$he *has to be alive.* Jarrod's lungs burned as their group raced through the icy streets. *We're going to get to them in time.*

Unless Luke hadn't found them at all.

Jarrod's heart hammered in his chest. It could be a trap. Even if Luke had something to gain by helping them, he didn't have anything to lose by betraying them, turning them over to the Bound for what he really wanted. Sullivan.

They headed down Broadway, following Luke's directions.

"Hold up," Az panted behind him as they cut through City Hall Park. "He's there."

Sitting on the bottom lip of a fountain, Luke strummed on his guitar. A thin stream of pedestrians decked out in suits and dresses wandered past, occasionally dropping coins into a cup set on his guitar case. The fountain was gilded in gold and dry except for the snow filling it. A wrought-iron cross topped it. On either side of him, flames danced inside antique-looking lamps. Luke set the instrument aside as they approached.

His gaze skimmed over Az, paused on Kristen, and finally, stopped on Jarrod. A cruel smile curved Luke's lips. "Looks like your girlfriend got herself into quite the bloody mess again."

Rage ran raw through Jarrod's veins, but Az clamped down on his shoulder. "Yeah," Jarrod said slowly, his voice cold and controlled as he flicked his eyes in Kristen's direction. "Isn't that just the craziest?"

Luke's grin may have widened at the careful reply, but his eyes swore murder at the barely veiled insult of Kristen. "Do you need to be taught another lesson?" Luke asked lightly.

Do you need to be thrown off another roof? Jarrod's mouth opened, the comeback forming. *If you say it, he'll walk away,* he thought. *And Sullivan will be as good as gone.* Jarrod lowered his head without saying a word.

He didn't have to be looking at Luke to hear the satisfaction in his voice. "Wonderful. Now that we have the alpha male bullshit out of the way, let's get down to the matter at hand. Kristen, you still have what I gave you?"

"Of course." She bent to take the sheathed knife from her boot and hand it over, but he stopped her.

"Leave it," he said. "You'll need it again."

Luke took a single stride and drew his hand over Jarrod's coat near his waist, up his chest to his shoulder, across his neck. Jarrod tried to wipe the startled expression from his face. "Disembowelment," Luke said. "Sever the neck. Go for arteries. To kill a Bound, you need them to bleed out faster than they can heal."

"They just . . . bleed to death?" Jarrod asked, not quite believing. It was too easy. He glanced around them, suddenly conscious of being overheard. The cold kept the park from teeming with people, but a few still glanced at Luke with unsure expressions.

Oblivious or uninterested, Luke tapped a finger against his neck, his wrists, under his arms, near where his leg met his hip. Jarrod got a quick glimpse of a low-slung belt and a long knife holstered at Luke's waist, hidden under his coat. *"Ex sanguis,"* Luke went on. "Religion is obsessed with blood. Someone was trying to give you guys clues, just in case. Those assholes Upstairs needed a checks and balances system, so it got written into your holy code." He paused. "But it's not quite so easy. These blades are special. Sins melted into the metal as they were forged in hellfire. A wound from one of these weapons takes the Bound much longer to heal from."

"Are the Bound close?" Jarrod asked. Already the itch to fight twitched in his muscles. "Where're *our* weapons?"

"We don't get weapons," Az said quietly. Jarrod had almost forgotten he was there. "Yet. What are you offering, Lucifer?"

Luke put an arm around Kristen. He lowered to her ear and whispered. She eased against him, her brow furrowed. "I offer Kristen up as trust," Luke said. "In exchange, of course, for Eden. Are we agreed?"

"Kristen's not good enough," Az said. Jarrod watched the surprise and confusion cross her face, but Az went on. "Offer me Sullivan, too."

"What?" Jarrod demanded. He couldn't help the desperation in his voice, didn't understand what was going on.

Tapping his fingers against his lips, Luke stared off into the sky as if deep in thought. "Done. I offer up Sullivan as trust, if," Luke said, and pointed to Jarrod, "he offers Sullivan to *me*. Otherwise, we're done here." He picked up the guitar again. "Az, if you'd be so kind as to explain it to him."

He strummed on the guitar, singing softly as he wandered far enough to give them a chance to talk.

"Az, what is this?" Jarrod asked.

Az blew out a breath. "Did you trust him, standing next to you with that knife?"

"Of course not," Jarrod said, annoyed. They were wasting time. The girls could be dying.

"At times, the Bound and Fallen have had to work together, so a failsafe had to be invented. We need to concentrate on fighting our enemy, not each other." Az tucked his hands in his pockets, not looking at him. "If I turn on Luke, Eden will belong to him. Soul, body, everything."

Jarrod balked. "Jesus, Az! She's not yours to offer up like some prize. How could you do that to her?"

"I couldn't. That's the point." Az tilted his head at Luke, who'd turned at the end of the row of benches and begun to head slowly back toward them. "I will not cross Luke. And Luke won't cross me because he doesn't want to lose Kristen."

"Are you kidding me? He'd turn on her in a second."

Kristen glared. To his surprise, though, she didn't debate it.

"Which is why I asked for Sullivan. If Luke can't lay a hand on *her*, it hurts him where it counts." Az paused, met his eye. "It's also why he wants *you* to offer Sullivan. Luke has our weapons, Jarrod. He's the only way we can get past the Bound. And if he can't trust you and he walks away . . ."

Jarrod swallowed, feeling suddenly sick. It made an entirely fucked-up kind of sense. He would never go against Luke if Sullivan was on the line.

When Luke reached them, he bent down in front of his closed guitar case, the tip cup still on top, and balanced the instrument on one knee. "Well?" he said, his hands resting on the lid. He seemed amused by Jarrod's hesitation, the nod he finally gave. "Out loud, please?"

"I offer up—I offer up Sullivan as trust," Jarrod said, watching Luke for an indication he'd said everything right.

"*Now*, you get your weapon." Luke laid back the lid. The cup of change spilled into the snow, abandoned. Inside the case were three small backpacks. He handed one to each of them, looking around them at the smattering of mortals. "Keep them in the bags until we get inside the building," he said. "Az, you have two in yours."

Luke took a step toward Jarrod and studied him for a long second. "You follow my lead," he said. "You listen to me, without question. Are we clear?"

"Crystal," Jarrod answered, his tone sharp.

Luke's attention shifted to Az, then Kristen. "I don't want you to be surprised," he said. "Gabriel's inside. Went in about ten minutes ago. He wasn't exactly acting like the others were enemies."

Luke looked up, and the Walk sign cycled through. He led them across the street. Az followed close behind.

A moment later, Luke looked back, the glance timed for the moment Kristen would be in the middle of the street, most exposed. He didn't so much as look at Jarrod a few strides behind her. *He really* is *watching out for her.*

"Son of a bitch," Jarrod whispered.

Luke slowed to a stroll, heading them into a covered alley. He grabbed Jarrod by the arm and lowered his voice. "You're first. Climb the scaffolding. Fourth window's broken out. Be quick and silent."

Jarrod climbed.

"Faster," Luke said behind him. Jarrod slithered through the hole, holding on to the frame of the window, and then dropped to the floor. His feet barely hit before Luke was through. While Kristen poked her head in, Jarrod looked around. The sun had started to set, but plenty of light streamed in from the hallway. The room they were in was small. Old wooden office furniture molded to one side, wet from the leaking ceiling. The floor bowed uneasily underfoot with each step.

"Keep coming," Luke said. Jarrod turned back just in time to see Kristen slide through. When she dropped, Luke caught her waist. The ferocity in his gaze made Jarrod nervous.

"Do something for me?" Luke said to her. She tilted her head to look up at him, and he brushed her lip with his thumb.

Then his mouth pressed against hers.

Kristen ripped out of the kiss even as Luke doubled over and dropped to his knees. "Damn it all," she managed as she fell to him. "What have you done."

Neither of them seemed to notice Az climbing in,

his shirt gone, first one wing and then the next stretching wide. They buffered the eight-foot fall. "Tell me she didn't just pass him Touch."

Luke's shoulders and back heaved. A deep growl rumbled low in his chest, animalistic. Tiny hairs on the back of Jarrod's neck stood up. Unconsciously, he took a step away. Az grabbed frantically for the backpack he'd tossed in before him. He tore the zipper open and pulled out one of the two blades inside and threw aside the sheath.

From behind Jarrod came a pop as the air fluctuated. He tensed to run just as the Bound angel formed, but Luke vaulted up and over him, knife already drawn. He swung it in a hard upward arc, spilling intestines. A second slice nearly severed the angel's head.

"Get back!" Az yelled. At first Jarrod thought Az was talking about the angel. Then he heard the wet chop of metal on skin, saw Luke on his knees, slamming the knife down into the pulp of what was left of the angel.

"Oh my God." Jarrod couldn't look away.

With one last dramatic stab, Luke dropped his arms, his gasps the only sound to break the stunned silence. Without a word, he wiped the blade against his pant leg and tucked it back into the sheath.

Kristen was sprawled on the floor as if she'd been pushed out of the way. Her hair was falling out of her ponytail, strands hanging limp around her face. A discarded backpack and sheath lay beside her, a knife clenched in her hand. "Jesus."

Her whisper brought a sneer from Luke. "Am I frightening enough for you?" he snarled, crawling toward her.

Jarrod didn't dare move. Az was frozen a few feet to his left. Only Kristen reacted, ignoring Luke as she set her knife on the floor beside her. She snapped the elastic band from her hair and held it between her lips. "Of course I'm frightened of you," she mumbled as she gathered her hair back up, then looped the band around it. It was almost as if she wanted Luke to believe she didn't see him as a threat, though her words were a direct contradiction. She was standing her ground without challenging him. "You're a psychopathic Fallen with a machete. You're doped up on Touch. And," she said, licking her thumb as he reached her, "you've got blood on your lips." She smeared away the crimson.

Jarrod readjusted the weapon in his hand, staring at her in disbelief. "What the fuck is wrong with you?"

"One less Bound we have to fight later, no?" Kristen's smile was sly, her focus still on Luke. "Though kissing me probably wasn't the best choice. Try to rein it in. We don't have time for another hack job."

Horror washed over Jarrod, but then for just a split second, he saw something else in her. Revulsion. Terror, gone as soon as it came. Kristen's bravado was breaking.

"I knew him. He was my friend," Az said quietly, and then seemed to shake it off. "A long time ago."

"And now he's mush," Kristen said, jerking around to him as she stood. "Can you do what Luke did? Can you kill for Eden? Because you can't hover in the middle anymore, Az. Are you with us or them?"

Az stared down at what was left of the angel's face.

Finally, Jarrod reached out and squeezed his shoulder.

Luke got to his feet and rubbed a sleeve across his forehead. "If you're all ready, we need to move this along." He ran a finger down Kristen's cheek. "I'm feeling *quite* violent."

CHAPTER 30

Gabriel stuck to the shadows. He hadn't seen Eden yet. The longer he stayed away from her, the better. He'd heard there were other Siders with her, but didn't know who.

"Have you seen Michael?" Gabriel inquired as he passed a cluster of Bound. A few pointed up, but no one was helpful enough to give a floor. Sunset cast orange hues through the glass atrium. Instead of heading into the stairwell he faded out, materializing on each floor until he heard Michael's voice. In Gabriel's ears, the dialect Michael fought so hard to keep pure only sounded strange and foreign. *They're losing me bit by bit. I'm not one of them.* Again, that same thought, refusing to die.

He forced himself to study the cracked plaster on the walls, the old lath board showing through. Two rooms down, he could see a light in the direction the voice was coming from. His stomach churned.

Six angels lined the sides of a table with Michael at the head like some sort of high council. They were arguing when Michael spotted Gabriel on the threshold.

The emotions tumbled across Michael's face. "You've come back."

Gabriel fought not to react as six heads turned to stare. His eyes latched on to Michael's, refusing to acknowledge the others. "I've come on *my* terms."

A rippled whisper passed through the room. Michael raised a hand for silence, bowing his head toward Gabriel a fraction of an inch, his smile hesitant. "Name them, sweet prince."

In that smile, Gabe saw their first kiss, a tentative peck Gabe had surprised himself by initiating. Just as it had then, his heart swelled with hope. *Maybe he really will listen to me.*

Michael gave him a moment, waiting, before he swept the room with his eyes. "Leave us," he demanded.

"No!" Gabriel took a breath. "No, they need to hear this, too."

That same acquiescent nod. *Anything you wish*, it said.

"The Siders," Gabe said. "I want them released."

Michael's face turned to stone. His world worked without shades of gray, only right and wrong. He was a zealot, unshakable in his beliefs. He would never change. *Not even for me*, Gabe thought. Which shouldn't have hurt him.

Inside Gabriel, everything went cold. The happy memories with Michael split open and spilled out what Gabriel hadn't allowed himself to think of until now. Michael's lips against his lips, those same lips against Gabe's ear begging forgiveness after their last terrible fight. The shake started in Gabe's hands, and then it was everywhere.

"Their threat will cease. In such I trust. But what of your task, Gabriel?" he asked with false innocence. Michael leaned back casually, opened his mind enough for Gabe to catch one thought. *By my side or beneath my sword, Gabriel.* Without any warning, Michael was gone from the table and standing in front of him. "Shall I anticipate problems, or have you overcome your tremor of loyalty?" Michael said as he laid a hand on Gabriel's cheek. He dragged a fingernail down his jaw, digging enough to take off a thin layer of skin.

The air stung the trail where Michael had touched him. "My mind is settled," Gabe said.

"Well then . . ." The hand on Gabe's shoulder clenched. "The death breather is being held on the seventh floor. Remedy your mistake now," Michael said calmly.

"I don't know if I—" The fingers loosened and slipped from Gabe's shoulder to his arm. Around him, the room was silent, the others watching. Not one interfered. More hovered near the doorway, drawn in by the raw emotion in the air. *Still too few,* Gabe thought, being sure to keep it scrambled. *I need them all here.* He raised his voice. "Spare them, Michael! Some part of you *must* know it's the right thing to do."

Gabe gave no reasons, made no effort to back up his plea. The weakness of the argument clearly infuriated Michael. He leaned nearer to Gabe's ear. "You are being an embarrassment. Executioner or executed," he whispered before his voice grew loud enough for the others to hear. "We have not killed her because she awaits *you*. The other abomination we use to poison Downstairs. A third female is being evaluated."

The third must have been the Sider Az told him about at the restaurant, the one who turned Madeline mortal.

"And the boy?" Gabriel asked, but there was no need. In his heart he knew Jackson was dead. He couldn't even do Madeline the justice of saving him. "Will no one stop this madness?" He met each set of eyes in the room. "These are practically children! They're not demons! Let them go, and I promise you in time they'll be no threat to the mortals." The room swelled with Gabe's frustration and Michael's fury. More Bound gathered at the door.

"What mars your judgment, Gabriel? How can you not see the evil in them? They pull mortals from their paths, rob them of their lives, their chance at everlasting love!"

You hypocrite. He cloaked the thought without effort. Gabriel ripped his arm out of Michael's grip and stumbled backward. His heel caught on an uneven board, and his tailbone screamed as he hit the floor, the wood buckling under his weight. Pain flared up his thigh and hip as he sunk into the hole, broken splinters ripping into his skin.

Michael fell to his knees, his hand in Gabe's. "Are you injured?"

Without pausing, Michael helped him stand again. He gave his head a sad shake as if at a loss. "Gabriel, we've been patient," he said, a timid glance skirting around to the others. "Take him to the Sider. He fulfills his promise or . . ."

Rough hands drew him away as Michael trailed off. Gabriel swallowed his rage. *You deserve everything coming to you,* he thought.

Earlier, Gabe had called the only person left who stood a chance at saving the Siders. He'd thought of Az, Jarrod, and Kristen waiting for him at the restaurant, of Eden and the rest in that one-room prison, trapped. Gabe had known the Bound wouldn't give him another chance to walk away from Eden. And so he'd made the call to Luke.

It had surprised him how quickly Luke had come up with a partial plan, almost as if he'd been expecting the call. *Your role is small,* Luke had told him. *Tell me where the Bound are hiding out and, at the appointed time, create a diversion.*

There was a price, of course. Not trust or future favors.

Instead, Luke had asked for something so simple, Gabe had known it must be a trick. And yet what choice had he but to agree? Only Luke knew the full details of the plot; the Bound wouldn't be warned by any stray thoughts from the others.

"Let me go!" Gabe yelled now, jerking violently enough to keep the attention of the cluster of angels surrounding him.

Gabriel didn't fight as they hauled him out of the room. He dragged his feet just enough to slow their progression for a few more seconds, and then gave in. He'd played his part and drawn the Bound away. Az and Jarrod should be hidden somewhere in the building by now.

But as the Bound marched Gabe to the stairwell, a new fear took hold inside him.

You can resist killing her, Gabe told himself as they walked him up the stairs to where they kept Eden. *This can't all be for nothing.*

CHAPTER 31

In the shadows of a dark doorway, Kristen waited for Luke's signal. Jarrod and Az had gone to the left while she and Luke would take the stairs to the right. But Az and Jarrod had been gone two minutes, and still Luke stood, silent and unmoving.

Kristen licked her lips. "Are we going to—"

"Silence," Luke snapped. But almost immediately, he reached behind him and grabbed her hand, his thumb stroking the base of her palm as if in apology. From somewhere far off in the building, she heard yelling.

"They've been spotted," she whispered.

"They haven't."

He's on Touch. He's not . . . The thought trailed off. Well, on Touch he *was* himself. Even more himself. Dangerous. Deadly. He turned. His mouth skimmed across her jaw. "What are you doing?" she managed.

"The blood . . . you." His hands clawed into her hair,

shoved her head back roughly as he kissed a hard line down her neck. "I'm frenzied."

"Oh, for Christ's sake, get ahold of yourself!" She fought herself free, untangling him. "This is what you get for stealing kisses like a lovesick schoolboy," she said, and shoved him off.

"*I'm* lovesick?" He sidled up to her again, nipped at her earlobe. "Love," he scoffed. "A pathetic human emotion, designed to torture the weak creatures who give in to its charms. And it's *all* you crave."

"And what of it?" She refused to let him use her emotions against her. "Luke, this is neither the time nor the place." Her words were hardly more than a rush of air.

"You want the one thing I'm incapable of giving you." He tucked a finger under her chin and tilted her head up. "I will never love you." Those same oily black eyes devoured her, called to her. "But I possess you, inside and out. You feel it, don't you?" he said, a hand running down her side to her waist. "How I'm written into the pause you take between breaths, pumping through your blood. Etched onto your bones."

He's spiraling, she realized. The Touch she'd passed him was like chumming the waters before swimming with sharks. If she set him off, he might tear her apart before the Bound even got their chance. She knew better than to bait him. It didn't stop her. "*No one* possesses me. Least of all you, Lucifer."

She was too startled to scream as he twisted her around and against him. He cocked an arm around her neck. "I'm sorry for this, Kristen, I truly am. I suppose it's a mixed message to have saved you from the Bound," he said, walking them slowly through the hall, no longer bothering to hide their presence. "Only to hand you over to them."

No. It had to be the Touch. Some sort of mistake. "You wouldn't do this," she croaked out. "Not to me. Stop and think."

"I've used you before." He sounded coherent. He sounded like he knew exactly what he was doing. The arm around her neck squeezed. "Is this really so surprising?"

Sorrow crashed through her before it was burned away by fury. She clawed at his arm, shredding skin with her nails. "Let me go, you bastard!"

He pushed her toward the atrium. "I've brought a gift," Luke snarled, his voice echoing through the building.

Someone leaned over the balcony.

The air popped in front of her, and a Bound was inches from her face. "Lucifer?" he said. "The Morning Star brings presents in hopes of what exactly?"

Luke thrust her out in front of him. Kristen stumbled, would have fallen if it wasn't for his grip on her neck. "You have a traitor in your midst. This is Gabriel's. Use her to punish him."

I'm so stupid, she thought. She'd trusted Luke again,

and this time everyone would pay the price. Kristen unleashed an angry scream.

"In return, give me the Sider who poisons my realm," he said.

With a sound like fireworks, a dozen Bound disappeared from balconies above and reappeared all around them, drawn by curiosity and the scents of fear and rage.

One reached for her, but Luke snatched her against himself. "Stop fighting," he barked in her ear, and tightened his arm around her, though she hadn't moved. "Do you have authority to accept my offer?" he asked the angel.

The Bound turned to another beside him. "Michael. Find him." Then he stepped closer and touched Kristen's face.

Luke hissed at him, and he dropped his hand. "I want the death breather before I give her up," Luke said. "Take me to her."

The angel clicked its teeth. Kristen's blood ran cold.

Floor after floor, Luke kept her just in front of him. Most of the angels followed behind, others flickering in the stairwell above. Finally, they left the stairs and were led to a room.

"She's there," one of the Bound said, stopping them. Luke's hold on Kristen tightened as the angel reached forward to brush the tears from her face. "Don't worry. This will all be over soon," he cooed.

Five feet beyond the threshold, the floor of the room

was gone. Luke walked her to the edge and leaned over the lip to find Sullivan. Kristen almost fell in but recoiled back and up onto her toes at the last second. Luke nudged her again. The knife in her boot dug into her calves. *I still have the knife. He didn't take the knife. Why didn't—*

"What knife?" the Bound demanded.

Luke jerked the straps of the backpack from her shoulders. "She wanted revenge. I armed her to fuel her trust in me." He tossed the pack off to the side, his other hand on her waist. "Now," Luke said as his finger tapped once against her hip. His foot moved behind hers, braced against her heel. "Where's Michael?" Two taps. An angel stepped toward them. Three taps. "Back off!" Luke yelled. His tug sent her off-balance. Kristen tripped over his foot and fell backward into the pit.

She landed hard on her hip and shoulder, all her breath rushing out.

Above her, Luke screamed obscenities. "I never even *saw* the death breather! Where the fuck is Michael!" She heard footsteps as Luke stormed off into the hall.

Stunned, she lay there, pain radiating through her body.

"Is she okay?" The voice came from behind her.

Someone rolled her over gently. Kristen blinked hard to bring the face peering down at her into focus. "Eden," she choked.

Kristen tilted her head just enough to see the alcove the

rest of them were hidden in, the decayed ceiling overhead stretching a few feet from the wall.

Someone took her hands and dragged her into the false security of the cover. "Is she hurt?" a familiar voice asked. "Give her here."

"Gabe?" she whispered. He lifted her into his arms, hugging her with everything he had. She stiffened. "I'm okay." Was Gabe in trouble? Why else would the Bound have him holed up with the Siders they were keeping prisoner? Wait. *They can't* keep *him down here*, she realized. *He can just disappear. They know that.*

"You're right. But don't think it so clearly." He didn't let go, pressed his lips against her ear as his hand found hers. "He had to do that. Luke."

She faltered, unsure if it was a trick.

"Luke did not betray you, do you understand?" he whispered so there would be no doubt. Gabriel pulled back and kissed her on the forehead.

She could almost feel the soft taps of Luke's finger against her hip when they'd stood at the threshold above. Three times before she'd tripped over the foot he'd planted behind hers. *He was warning me, counting down.*

Gabe squeezed her shoulder. "Careful. I heard that. You've *got* to clear your mind, Kristen. He made me promise to tell you. It was the price for his help, but you cannot tip the Bound off."

She couldn't quite figure out the feeling that rushed over her. Relief, happiness, some part of her still disbelieving while vindication fought its way in. *Luke didn't betray me.* Kristen tried to get rid of the thought, surveying the alcove. Huddled in the shadows, farthest back, she saw Rachel. Sullivan, too, hid back there. Eden stood near the opening in the ceiling, looking up through the dimness. Kristen glanced around the rest of the room, suddenly aware of someone missing. "Where's Jackson?" she asked.

Only Sullivan met her eyes. "They killed him. And another boy when I wouldn't send him Downstairs. It was quick," she said with compassion. "Neither of them suffered."

You're lying. It was a kindness, one she didn't deserve from this girl Luke would surely have destroyed given the chance mere hours ago.

"Why isn't Az with you?" Eden asked. She was farthest away, and though she spoke to Kristen, she kept her weary gaze on Gabe. "Where's Jarrod? Were they both caught, too?" Kristen didn't answer. "Did you split up?"

"If they're dead, it's worse not to know," Sullivan said softly.

Gabe shook his head subtly. *Don't tell them.* "I was with Luke," Kristen said, but gave them nothing more. "Gabe, don't the Bound know you're down here?"

Shame dropped his shoulders. "I've been given a last chance to destroy Eden."

Kristen looked at Rachel. The girl stared back, but said nothing. "Can't Rachel just turn her mortal? The Bound won't kill us if we're mortal, right?"

Gabriel hesitated. "I don't know if I can keep you safe long enough for the change to take. Rachel said it takes time, like when you became a Sider."

Above them, a scuffle sounded across the floor. "They're back," Sullivan whispered as something slammed against the wall.

A scream cut short into silence.

A dark shape hit the ground behind Kristen. She turned toward it, instinctively, but realizing what it was, she backpedaled in horror. The severed head wobbled to a stop near her feet.

The body followed, hitting the floor with a heavy thud. Az landed in a crouch next to it, his wings spread wide for balance. He held his knife from Luke. Its blade dripped with blood.

"So I guess you chose a side after all," Kristen said as Eden dove forward with a shout.

Az took Eden in his arms, one hand cupping the back of her head. They swayed, together, Eden's fingers clutching and opening against his shoulder.

"Jarrod." Sullivan's whisper was almost lost. "Where's Jarrod?"

Kristen helped her up. Before the girl could walk into the open, Az caught her T-shirt, one arm still gripping

Eden fiercely. "He's okay," he said. "I'm staying with you guys. Luke and Jarrod are up top." He looked down at Eden. "Ready to get out of here?" he said with a grin.

She nodded. Kristen bent and slipped the sheathed blade from her boot. "Luke took my spare," she told Az.

"I've got one," he said, handing over the extra knife Luke had given him. Kristen gave to it Rachel. From another part of the house, they heard fighting and the sound of breaking drywall. Az let Eden go.

"Quickly," Az said. "Jarrod and Luke are distracting anyone they can while I grab you guys." He backed himself and Eden into the center of the room.

"No. I'm first," Sullivan said. The intensity in her voice kept anyone from arguing. Eden stepped away, and Sullivan moved into Az's arms. His wings swooped out, swirling dust through the air. He bent his knees, then leaped, pumping his wings once. He set Sullivan onto solid ground as Kristen heard something crash. "Hurry. Go help Jarrod," Az said, handing her his knife. Sullivan took it and spun on her heel, tearing through the doorway and out onto the balcony.

Kristen glanced over at Eden and laced her fingers together to make a stirrup. "Ready?"

"Yeah," Eden said, slipping her foot in. She bounced once before she pushed off. "Az!"

He rotated midair and gripped her forearm.

"Next," Kristen said, waving anyone over. "Hurry." From where she was, she couldn't see anything more than Az's nervous glances at the room behind him.

"Watch your back," he told Eden. "I gave Sullivan my blade."

"My backpack!" Kristen yelled up. "It should be right near there. In the hall."

The racket was getting louder. A howl of enraged agony drowned out the screams. *Luke.* Wrath burst through Kristen, hardening her insides into pure fury.

She forgot about Rachel and Gabriel, stretched her own hand out. "I'm next! Get me up there! Now!"

In a moment she'd be running to Luke's side. *Where I belong.*

But Az pumped his wings and shot out of the room. "Wait!" she yelled.

The room above her seemed empty. "Eden?"

Kristen took a tentative step back, raising her blade. Rachel had her weapon ready to go. Gabriel stood by her side. He motioned for Kristen to come closer, protect Rachel. "Stay here," Gabe told them before he disappeared.

He'd barely gone before a loud pop came from behind her.

"Kristen!" Rachel yelled. "Look out!"

She spiraled around, but only managed to give the angel a glancing blow. The momentum kept her swinging, and she sliced again. This time his blood gushed out and across the floor. She crept backward, the flood of gore chasing her as he slumped to the ground.

Three Bound appeared, coming toward her, two on one side, one on the other. A sputter, and there was another one behind her. She jerked, pointing her weapon at each of them in turn as if the threat would be enough to hold them off. Panic shook her hands.

"I need some help down here!" she called over her shoulder just as she felt someone press against her back.

"I'm still here," Rachel said.

They circled, back to back. A quick movement caught her eye just in time. She ducked a fist, but the motion split her from Rachel.

"Stay back," Rachel commanded, but the angel only laughed at her. He disappeared for a moment and then came into form again behind her. Kristen buried her blade between his shoulders, the cartilage of his spine crunching as she drove the knife deep. His scream was deafening. Rachel slit open his throat, ending the cry.

Kristen swiped at a splotch of blood on her arm. "Well, that was—"

"Behind—" was all Rachel had time to yell before arms wrapped around Kristen.

Flailing, she kicked her heels into the angel's thighs, but his grip only tightened, constricting. Rachel was already barely fighting off another. The angel holding Kristen threw her against the wall.

She slammed hard and dropped to the floor. The angel was on her immediately, flipping her over. He raised his fist above her chest.

Thwack. The angel's mouth dropped open in surprise. He stared down at the hilt of the knife now buried in his chest. His arm went limp as he crumpled forward. Someone grabbed her under the shoulders and dragged her roughly out. "How's revenge going?" Luke growled in her ear.

She collapsed against him, relief spilling through her. Squeezing his arm, she said, "I owe you one."

"Kristen," he chided. "Have you learned nothing about using those words?"

As she turned enough to see him, the smile forming on her lips stalled.

Luke was carnage. His cheek was split wide, ear to chin. Sweat soaked his curls, bits of gore and dirt stuck to his face. His irises swirled, black, hungry and mad with violent frenzy. She recoiled. He kissed her knuckles. "You wanted me at your side when you got your revenge. Do you still?" he said as he reached to rip his blade free of the Bound's chest.

Strangely, she didn't need to consider it. "Absolutely," she said.

"Good answer," he said, lacing his fingers with hers. "Because things are about to get messy."

CHAPTER 32

$\mathcal{E}$den kicked hard, but one of the Bound had her by the ankle and was dragging her down the hall. Skin scraped off her back where her shirt had pulled up. Splinters gouged into the heels of her hands as she tried to gain some hold on the uneven floorboards. She grabbed for one of the ornate metal spindles lining the walkway that surrounded the empty center of the building. Nine floors down, she saw Jarrod and Sullivan cross the open space in a mad dash before they ducked out of sight under the first tier.

The Bound let her ankle go, and she scrambled to wrap her arms around the spindles. A hand clamped down on her neck and pulled her up.

"Please, no!" she screamed as he pushed her against the railing. The open space seemed to spin as it yawned before her. She'd taken enough Touch from Rachel to survive a few injuries, but a fall like that would end her.

"Climb over or be thrown," the Bound said, his voice oddly calm.

Her lip quivered as she searched for Az and found him across the way, two floors down. Michael swung on him, Az's knife coming up just in time to block the blow.

"He's not likely to help you," the Bound said as he read her thoughts. "Now move." Shaking, Eden lifted first one leg over and then the other, keeping a death grip on the railing. A dozen scenarios burst through her mind of swinging wildly onto the balcony of the floor below her and to safety. Movie stunts.

The Bound exerted just enough backward force on her that her foot slipped. She scrambled, her heels hanging over into nothing. He gripped her upper arm.

"Please," she begged. "Cured. We can be cured."

"Gabriel!" the angel bellowed.

Eden hadn't seen Gabe, but a moment later he appeared next to the angel that had her, his hands held out in front of him. "Let her climb back over, Raphael," he said.

Raphael turned to him. "We burdened you with opportunities to kill this Sider. You used a promise against us, turned the words into protection for this girl."

"Exactly!" Gabe said. "She's just a girl. If you'd listen—"

"No. Long past is the time for excuses. Take my place and let her fall. Look away if you must. The drop will be enough to end her." Raphael adjusted his grip, and Eden let out a choked cry. "If she dies by my hand, your promise is broken and—"

Gabe sucker punched him. "Not happening!"

Raphael managed to stay standing for a moment before his eyes rolled slowly back. His hold on Eden weakened. Her toes slipped as the angel let go and went to his knees.

"Help me!" she screamed. The barest tips of her fingers curled for purchase on the railing as Gabe dove for her.

"I've got you!" he yelled, grabbing her forearm. She swung wildly as he clasped her arm. "Give me your other hand!"

His grip slipped to her wrist. Eden flailed to reach him, afraid to look down. "Don't let me go!"

She was level with the floor as he fought to hoist her up. She saw Raphael on his knees, shaking off the punch. He took in the scene, joy flooding his face.

"She'll die at your hands yet, Gabriel." He leaped for Gabe's legs and knocked him aside.

He lost his hold. "No!" Gabe screamed.

Eden fell.

Her ankle hit the next floor down, sending her into a somersault. Just before she smashed into the ground, a blur of white slammed her. *Wings.*

Az.

She groaned in pain. Everything hurt, but he'd taken the brunt of the landing. "Are you okay?" she asked, shuddering. Her ankle throbbed, but shock and adrenaline numbed the worst of it. Under her, she felt his heart beating wildly.

"I caught you," he choked out.

She got a hand beneath her. Pressing her palm into a puddle on the floor, she tried to push herself off him. The puddle spread slowly out from underneath Az, dark red. Eden scrambled up. "Oh God, you're hurt!"

She looked down and saw the wound on his chest where Michael had sliced him. It swelled from ribbon to rift with each rib it carved across. On either side of him, his wings shivered and twitched. The feathers smeared delicate threads of crimson. *He's hurt*, her brain screamed. *Bad. Deep.*

Eden rocked her head back and screamed, "Gabe!"

"It's bad," Az gasped. "Michael. You were falling and . . ." She heard the rattle of each erratic pull for air.

Eden brushed back his curls. "Don't try to talk," she said. "I've got this."

She tore the sleeve of her shirt and pressed it against the wound. There was a pop beside her.

Gabe dropped to his knees, horror on his face as he took in Az. "Oh no," he whispered.

"Fix him," she said. "Quick. I think they're coming. None of us have a weapon." The words tumbled over themselves, struggled out nightmare slow.

A wet cough broke up Az's words. "Eden. Where's Eden?"

"She's still here," Gabe told him. "I'm going to try to help you, okay?"

"Don't kill her, Gabe." Az moaned in pain, and Gabriel's face fell. "Don't kill her, please."

Eden could hear the tears in Gabe's voice. "I'll get her out of here. You just hang on."

This isn't real. This isn't happening.

She heard a rhythmic scraping noise—his foot, kicking out and back in a spasm. *We're losing him.* She pushed down harder on the already soaked bandage. "He's bleeding too much! We have to stop it!" Her fingers were slick. His eyes drifted closed. "Az?"

He opened them again and smiled up at her weakly. "They'll make you mortal again. You'll have a shiny new path and—" He cut off as the last of the blue in his eyes tarnished to a washed-out green. "I love you, Eden."

"I love you, too," she said, clutching his hand in hers, using it to add pressure to the wound. "You stay with us. I think it's slowing a bit." In her relief, she glanced up at Gabriel, saw the tears spilling down his cheeks. "No, it's going to be okay. He's gonna be fine." The bleeding had slowed to a trickle. "See? It's stopping."

"Yeah," Gabriel said quietly. "It's stopping now."

"We'll get you out of here, Az, okay?"

"Eden." She hated the way he said her name, the way it shivered out of him broken, split and separate.

"No!" She gave up on the useless bandage and gripped Az's hand tighter. He opened his lips as if he were going to say something more, and then he stilled. "Az, please," she whispered. "Please don't."

He stared up, eyes wide, unfocused. And then Eden felt herself, too, go still. *He's gone. He's dead.* She looked up at Gabe.

Two tears raced down to his jaw. With every blink his irises flashed redder, bloodshot and glowing.

They took him from me. From us.

Her chest ached. Her head throbbed with tears she wouldn't let herself cry. "If I had been a regular girl with a normal path, I wouldn't have been able to be with him. And Jarrod wouldn't have met Sullivan and . . . Gabe, we're all going to be mortal again and he wouldn't have been able to be on my path." She swallowed hard. "I wouldn't have left him. I wouldn't have!" she sobbed, falling against his shoulder.

"But," Gabriel said carefully, his voice breaking, "now you will. Because we're going to save the Siders."

She stood and took the first few steps backward, her eyes locked on Az, every fiber of her body screaming against leaving him.

I love you, she thought. And then she turned. "Come on. We're ending this."

The building was oddly quiet. No one fought anywhere that she could see. She and Gabriel took the stairs up a floor, had to climb over a body on the landing. A knife stuck out of the chest. Eden pulled the weapon free and took it with her.

He stopped them at the base of the stairwell. "Ready?" he asked, but she wasn't sure what she was supposed to be ready for.

She kept the knife at her side and followed him down the balcony. Another body blocked the way, and suddenly she realized Jarrod and Sullivan weren't with them, that she hadn't seen them since the brief glimpse over the balcony railing. "Gabe?" she called softly.

He raised a finger. Barely audible voices came from a room ahead.

As they got closer, she could hear muffled whacks. "Release her to us!" someone yelled.

"No!" The voice that answered was so full of venom, she almost didn't recognize it as Jarrod's. Gabriel's hand was on her shoulder, anticipating her reaction. *Hurry,* she thought at him desperately.

Gabriel burst across the threshold. "I demand cessation!"

His voice thundered through the room. Eden couldn't

see past him, but she heard the shuffle of feet, the rustle of fabric as the angels turned toward him.

"What have you done?" Gabriel demanded. Eden squeezed past him. Jarrod was the first thing she saw. Doubled over on his knees, he'd been stripped of his coat. A wide V of Bound spread out from him on either side, packed into the room. His white shirt was striped with dirt and grime. A few of the streaks were red at the edges where blood had soaked through. Even from the door, she could see the way he trembled. Under him, protected from the worst of the blows, was Sullivan.

The angel closest to him held a baseball bat–sized chunk of wood.

"Who allowed this cruelty?" Gabriel snarled. "Let them up! Now!"

"No one will do such a thing," a voice called out.

"Gabe." Eden held up a shaking hand when she spotted Michael. The angel swiveled to her, his gaze heavy and without pity. "He killed Az," she said.

Everyone's eyes were on her.

On the floor, Jarrod uncurled, his face contorted. Every movement was stiff, his shoulders pulled back in pain. He dropped his head again as if he couldn't take the effort, whispered something to Sullivan. To Eden's relief, she stirred.

Gabriel moved slowly toward Michael.

"It's true," Michael said simply. "Azazel offered me his life in a promise Upstairs. When that promise went unfulfilled, Azazel was ended by my hand with mercy in my heart."

Eden waited for some sort of reaction from the other angels, didn't understand when no one moved. "Why aren't they doing anything?" she cried.

Gabe kept his eyes on Michael. "Is that how he got out of the cell you all were keeping him in?"

Michael's crimson irises lightened, yellowed. "And now I fear our Gabriel has been tainted by these cursed creatures." His voice rose and sharpened. "Gabriel chose to surround himself with temptations. He has a history of giving in to sin. He failed a mission he never should have been trusted with!" he said, glaring down at Eden. "He is impure and unloyal. The Sider plague is being eradicated, and Gabriel consistently stands in our way."

Gabe's arm shot up, pointed at Michael. "I accuse you of having hands that shed innocent blood," he spat.

Michael gave a dramatic sigh. "Innocent blood! Azazel was not innocent."

"Not Az," Gabriel said. "Another." He trembled, but kept going. "At Kristen's, you found a girl on the back stairs. Do you remember her?"

"I do." Michael broke eye contact as a silent tear ran down Gabriel's cheek.

"Her name was Madeline," Gabriel said to the crowd, "and she's the one who helped me when I was Fallen. When every other abandoned me, she stood by my side. We learned so much about the Siders from her, and from Kristen and Eden and her friends, whom you've *beaten*." He paused. "Did you kill Madeline?"

A murmur passed through the crowd.

Eden felt a presence behind her just as Kristen's hand touched her shoulder, her sympathy silent.

Gabriel's voice boomed. "I accuse you, Michael. Do you deny it?"

Michael said nothing.

Luke gave a low whistle from beside Kristen. "Formal accusation? I haven't seen one of those since . . . mine."

"What is it?" Eden tightened her grip on the knife at her side.

Luke slid closer. She could smell the metallic tang of the blood drenching him, but couldn't look at him. He smelled the same as Az had. "Sins need to be spoken," Luke said. "Gabe accuses and then Michael must answer."

Michael sneered. "I was sent to exterminate the Siders."

"That wasn't an answer," Gabriel said. "Luckily, I wasn't finished." It was quiet enough to hear a pin drop. Gabriel's gaze was trained on Michael. "I accuse you of shedding innocent blood. Of savagely ripping Madeline, sinless and innocent, from a path she'd just started upon."

The words strained out. "And doing so knowingly. You knew she was mortal, did you not?"

Even from where she stood, Eden could see the betrayal sink in, Michael slowly shaking his head. "Gabriel, why?"

"You could Fall for that alone," Gabe said. "But I have more. How did the Siders start, Michael?"

The color drained from his face.

"You were always stubborn," Gabe said. "Jealous. But the last few years, you've become cruel and hateful. Sometimes you hide it well. Others . . ." He gestured to Jarrod, the bloodied dirty shirt he wore. "Not so much. I know how it felt to keep my sins inside for mere months before I Fell. I can't imagine what it feels like to keep them for years."

Raphael pushed his way through the crowd. "Gabriel, what's the meaning of this?"

Gabriel didn't waver. "The Siders aren't just some plague that happened into being. I met the first Sider today. A girl who told me about a chance meeting with Az."

The annoyance in Raphael's *tsk* wasn't reserved to him alone. Others grew restless. Eden shifted the knife.

"And again, Azazel had gotten involved when he shouldn't have. It does not bode well to speak ill of the dead, Gabriel," Raphael scolded as if Az hadn't been any more than an acquaintance to Gabe, instead of his best friend.

It took Gabe a second to recover. "You wanted a way to get rid of Az, make it so he didn't need me anymore. And so you stole away the path of a girl you thought was in love with him. You took her future. But that potential, that life force built in her still. You thought she was dead, so you left her body to rot, but she became a Sider. She spread Touch on to others until their own futures became so confused and crumbled that their paths, too, disintegrated. Michael, I accuse you of starting the Sider plague." He turned to Michael and uttered two words. "Deny it," Gabriel said, his face dark.

The room took a collective breath. Disbelief fluttered through the gathered angels when no denial came.

Michael glanced away for a split second before he struggled back, like looking at Gabe was a punishment he endured, a penance.

When Michael finally spoke, his voice was small, like that of a child. "I loved you, Gabriel. Always more. And *never* was I chosen."

Eden saw Gabe's cheeks flare red. "That's not true."

Heartbreak shone on Michael's face. "Azazel kept you away from me, don't you see that?" he said, reaching. Gabe shook his head, moved his hand behind his back. Michael grimaced, but went on. "He made you believe only you could save him from Falling. I tried to give him a girl who wouldn't leave, wouldn't die, because then you could come

Home. Then you could come back to me."

"The terrible part was, she didn't even know Az. You made a mistake, Michael. You stole her life," Gabe spat, shaking. "Just like you stole Madeline's. I accuse you of taking mortal life, Michael."

Michael closed his eyes for a beat. "Even dead you choose Az, and now I'm nothing." He turned to face the crowd, his head held high as his voice rang out, loud and clear. "I stole the path of a mortal girl. I did so for my own selfish gain. For love. And I took a mortal life. I am guilty." His voice fell. "Forgive me, Gabriel."

Eden watched as Gabe pressed his lips together.

"Forgive me. Please. Give me this one kindness." Michael clutched at him, but Gabe stepped back.

"No," Gabe whispered. "Your choices were your own."

In front of her, the dozen Bound angels all spoke at once. "He killed the girl? She was a mortal? He stole their lives. Then he's Damned. Damned."

Michael pushed through the crowd, past Eden, and broke into a run. Eden watched as he stumbled away, his shirt tearing apart as wings sprouted from his back. His scream curdled as the wings smashed against the metal railing and then shed their feathers. He writhed toward the stairs, his back a lacework of raised pink scars, the wings gone.

Kristen's words were a whisper: " ('When the rest of

Heaven was blue)/Of a demon in my view.'"

Eden stared in silence as he crawled. She wanted to feel vindication. Relief. Anything. She didn't realize she was collapsing until Kristen caught her, leaning her against her shoulder.

While she'd been watching Michael, Gabe had gone on speaking. "All they need is time," he was saying from the room. "We can help Rachel find the Siders, and she will cure them. They're no longer a risk to the mortal paths."

Sounds of agreement filled the air.

"Are you all right?" Kristen asked.

It's over, Eden thought. The Siders, the strange life she'd carved out for herself. Az. "I don't know," she managed.

CHAPTER 33

$\mathcal{A}$s the Bound wandered off, dazed, Kristen handed Eden to Gabe. Then she tugged Luke's hand. "We need to leave. Now."

He followed as she led him away from the others. Kristen only looked back once, to see Eden staring after her. She ducked into the stairwell with Luke, dragging him down two at a time.

Finally, four floors down, Luke stopped her. "I have weapons to retrieve."

"Make new ones!" Kristen spun on him. He raised an eyebrow. "Please, Luke. Let's just go."

"Why?" he asked.

The lump in her throat made it almost impossible to get the words out. "They're making Rachel turn us. They're going to have that girl change us back as quickly as they can to save their precious mortals." Luke didn't react. She shoved him with all her strength. "I don't want to be mortal," she yelled.

Her voice ricocheted through the stairwell, kept itself company in echoes. Voices on top of voices. The thought only made her more frantic. "What do I have to go back to? An expiration date and a mind . . ." She closed her eyes. "And a mind that *sours*."

"Kristen."

Luke's hand cupped the back of her neck. When she opened her eyes, she thought he was going in for a kiss, but his forehead met hers. "You avenged Sebastian and the others, yes?" he asked quietly.

She wasn't sure. Two of the Bound had died at her hand, but it hadn't changed anything. She felt no better. The empty hole where Sebastian belonged was still an open wound. No amount of death would fill it. "I guess so," she said.

He tilted his head back and locked eyes with her. "Then we've accomplished what we came here to do. I've sought an equal, who can stand beside me." His voice was filled with heat. "Mortals are *playthings*! You deserve so much more than that. It's beneath you."

"They'll come for me. The Bound won't let me stay a Sider."

"Let them try." Luke's irises swirled muddy and then blackened, bits of the Touch she'd passed him still working through his system.

"And what will our life be? Running, hiding?" she asked, misery in her voice.

"Kristen, Heaven runs from *me*, not the other way around. All the powers of Hell will protect you. As long as you stay by my side, this world is yours."

Silly, Lucifer, she thought. *I bet you never suspected someone would beat you at your own games.* She laced her arms around his neck and nuzzled against him to hide her victorious smile.

EPILOGUE

𝓔den snuggled in closer, the blanket around them both holding her to Gabe's shoulder. His shirt was cool against her cheek, wet with the tears she'd cried for Az. She felt safe here in her room, with Gabe. He hadn't left her side since last night.

"I guess I should go out. They're waiting for me," Eden said. When the Bound insisted Eden be turned mortal immediately, Gabe had refused them. Now, his arm tightened around her.

Gabe stroked her hair. "Let them wait," he said softly. "How's your ankle? I don't want them turning you until you're at one hundred percent."

Under the covers, she rotated her foot, expecting pain, surprised when it moved easily. "It's better," she said.

She shouldn't have been surprised. Healing her wounds had been able to burn up some of the Touch she'd taken in from Rachel. Siders had begun showing up just past midnight, and Rachel had started turning them mortal again. Even now, seemingly dead bodies filled Jarrod's room, laid out on the beds and the floor. It took three hours for them to reanimate, at which point they were told to spread the word and shown the door. Eden wondered what kind of lives they'd have. If they'd just end up starving on the street. She wondered what kind of life she would have.

"When Rachel makes me mortal, she'll be taking in any extra Touch left in me," Eden said. "And Sullivan's. All the other Siders coming here. It'll be too much for her."

"We're working on that," Gabe said. "Some of those at Kristen's did escape injured. They'll be dosed and given time to get well before they're made mortal. There are two other Siders, Annalise and Donavan, who I trust to spread it safely."

"And when there are no Siders left? What happens to her then?" Eden asked. Without taking in *some* Touch, Rachel would die. Slowly. In pain.

"You have my word, I'll figure out a way to make her mortal before time runs out. The Bound are no threat to her. Not anymore." Gabe held Eden close.

The blanket enveloped them like a cocoon. Fresh tears stung her eyes. She wanted to stay like this forever, not having to think. Not having to face Az's death and whatever the future held for her. When she tried to snuggle in closer, though, Gabe lifted her off his shoulder. His eyes were nearly as swollen as hers must have been. "You're going to be okay. You know that, right?" he said.

For a long time, she couldn't answer. She wanted a new start far from New York and all that had happened here. Teaming up with Jarrod and Sullivan, she knew it could work. She'd find a job. Maybe get her GED and go to college.

Grow up.

"I'm scared," she said finally, because it was the truth. Because in every plan she made, Az crept in. She pictured mornings and saw breakfast in bed with him. She thought about watching a movie on the couch and she pictured him cuddled up next to her. Saw them growing old together.

Except, now, that wasn't going to happen.

"Eden." Gabe stroked her hair. "That was never going to happen," he said gently.

He'd picked up on her thoughts. She hated him for saying it and hated more that he was right. "I wasn't finished," she said. "I'm scared, but I want to do this. He would want me to be mortal. He would want me to have a good life."

"Yes," Gabe said.

Eden sat up slowly, a smidgen of her stubborn self coming back. Even though the Bound had taken him, *she* was still alive. Well, at least she would be shortly. *I can do this,* she thought.

"Are Jarrod and Sullivan ready?" she asked.

"Sullivan is. Jarrod said he won't change until you're both mortal."

A ghost of a smile passed across Eden's lips. He was going to have a hard adjustment to being normal again. Eden turned to Gabe suddenly. "Kristen," she said. "Have they made her mortal yet? Is she here?"

"No," Gabe said, looking pained. "Luke took her." His face went bitter. "She's a smart girl, though, and his game's obvious this time. She'll come back."

"What do you mean?" Eden asked, confused.

Gabe waited, as if he wanted her to figure it out herself, but Eden was too tired to try. "Eden, Luke only needs one Sider to start this all over again."

A knock on the door interrupted before she could respond. Jarrod opened it. "Sorry," he said, looking from her to Gabe. "Raphael said to tell you it's time. They won't wait anymore."

Against her, Eden felt Gabe tense. "You tell him I said he can wait until she's—"

She laid a hand on his and gave it a squeeze, cutting him off. "No, it's okay," she said, braving a smile. *This is it. This is the start.*

She peeled back the blanket and dropped Gabe's hand as she stood. "I'm ready," Eden said.

ACKNOWLEDGMENTS

Thanks as always to Scott Tracey, Heather Aslaksen, and Courtney Moulton for dealing with the crazy. To Martha Mihalick and Eloise Flood for helping take this manuscript to the next level. To Ro Stimo for being in my corner. MANY thanks to Paul Zakris and Ali Smith for all three of the beautiful covers in this trilogy. To Princess Weekes for braving NYC alleys for me. And most of all, to you, the person reading this. Thank you for coming along on the journey with Eden and me.